Critical Acclaim for K. K. Beck

"Ms. Beck neatly brings everything together. The story is imaginative, the presentation light-hearted, the characters believable."
—Newgate Callendar, *New York Times* on *The Body in the Volvo*

"She knows how to combine mirth and murder in a slickly packaged, highly satisfying story."
—*San Diego Union Tribune* on *The Body in the Cornflakes*

"From the first few paragraphs of K. K. Beck's *We Interrupt This Broadcast* you know you're going to find the book smooth, easy, and a delight to read."
—*Houston Chronicle*

"You're likely to find yourself laughing out loud."
—*Seattle Times* on *We Interrupt This Broadcast*

"Beck's deft pacing keeps readers furiously turning pages."
—*Publishers Weekly* on *Bad Neighbors*

"Hitchcock would have loved K. K. Beck's new novel, *Fake*, a clever thriller that moves along at a terrific pace."
—*South China Morning Post*

"A finely tuned eye and ear and a benignly critical edge… Good work from Beck, whose unhackneyed stories get better all the time."
—*Kirkus* (starred review) on *The Body in the Volvo*

Tipping the Valet

MYSTERY FICTION BY K. K. BECK

Workplace Mysteries (with Lukowski & MacNab)
The Body in the Volvo
The Body in the Cornflakes
We Interrupt This Broadcast
Tipping the Valet

Iris Cooper Series
Death in a Deck Chair
Murder in a Mummy Case
Peril Under the Palms

Jane da Silva Series
A Hopeless Case
Amateur Night
Electric City
Cold Smoked

Other Mystery Fiction
Death of a Prom Queen
Young Mrs. Cavendish and the Kaiser's Men
Unwanted Attentions
Without a Trace
Bad Neighbors
The Revenge of Kali-Ra
The Tell-Tale Tattoo and Other Stories

For Younger Readers
Fake
Snitch

Nonfiction
Opal: A Life of Enchantment, Mystery and Madness

TIPPING THE VALET

a workplace mystery

///

K. K. Beck

2015 · Palo Alto / McKinleyville, California
Perseverance Press / John Daniel & Company

This is a work of fiction. Characters, places, and events are the product of the author's imagination or are used fictitiously. Any resemblance to real people, companies, institutions, organizations, or incidents is entirely coincidental.

The interior design and the cover design of this book are intended for and limited to the publisher's first print edition of the book and related marketing display purposes. All other use of those designs without the publisher's permission is prohibited.

A Perseverance Press Book
Published by John Daniel & Company
A division of Daniel & Daniel, Publishers, Inc.
Post Office Box 2790
McKinleyville, California 95519
www.danielpublishing.com/perseverance

Distributed by SCB Distributors (800) 729-6423

Book design by Eric Larson, Studio E Books, Santa Barbara, www.studio-e-books.com

Cover image: Stokato/iStock

10 9 8 7 6 5 4 3 2 1

LIBRARY OF CONGRESS CATALOGING-IN-PUBLICATION DATA
Beck, K. K.
Tipping the valet : a workplace mystery / by K.K. Beck.
    pages ; cm
ISBN 978-1-56474-563-7 (pbk. : alk. paper)
I. Title.
PS3552.E248T57 2015
813'.54—dc23
                        2015019065

Tipping the Valet

Chapter One

///

I HOPE THAT FELONY CONVICTION won't screw it up for you," said Jessica, Tyler's boss. "They're super-picky. I've told them we run a background check on everyone, so I hope they won't run one of their own."

Jessica was an energetic, no-nonsense blonde in her twenties, and her title was Seattle Account Manager for Elite Valet, a national company based in Pittsburgh. She was unloading orange traffic cones from the trunk of her car to replace a bunch that had been squashed by inattentive customers leaving the lot. Tyler Benson, whose title was Lead Service Associate, was stacking them up inside the valet booth in front of a casino in a suburb of Seattle. Tyler was about Jessica's age with sandy hair and blue eyes. He wore black pants, a white polo shirt, and a black nylon windbreaker with the hot pink ELITE VALET logo on the left side.

It was early evening and the lime-green neon sign that said DONNA'S over the entrance of the stucco Moorish-style building was flickering. Another valet, a wraith-like young man named Brian, sat in the booth scribbling in a notebook, which Tyler happened to know was his vampire screenplay. Brian lifted his feet so Tyler could stow the cones, and kept writing.

Tyler was excited. Jessica had just told him that Elite Valet's premium account, a chic downtown restaurant called Alba, needed some extra help tomorrow to accommodate a large private party. And the best news was that if they liked him, it could be permanent if another slot there opened up. He'd love never to have to work Donna's Casino again, even though he was lead valet. The tips at Alba would be fabulous.

"You got enough tickets, Tyler?" Jessica said.

"Yeah, we're good, thanks."

Jessica slammed down the trunk lid and drove off. Just then, out of the corner of his eye, Tyler caught sight of a large, square mass lurching toward the valet booth. It was a hefty man in a black suit, staggering from east to west as he approached in a purposeful but out-of-control manner.

"Geef me keys," yelled the man, lurching toward the booth and startling Brian, who looked up from his notebook with alarm.

He was one of the guys the valets referred to as "the Russians," a mysterious group of scary-looking Slavs who had taken over one corner of the cocktail lounge as their clubhouse. If Tyler had been Hughie, the manager of Donna's, he would seriously consider eighty-sixing the whole crowd. But Hughie, a kind of loudmouthed fool whom Tyler avoided as much as possible, probably appreciated their huge bar tabs. He was always hanging around their table, all friendly and joking around.

Tyler tried to intercept the Russian, tapping him on the shoulder. The man turned and gave him a massive bear hug and breathed a lot of booze into his face. He began to mutter into Tyler's ear in some Slavic language, and Tyler wasn't sure whether he was threatening him or being super-friendly. Probably the latter, because he now planted a sloppy kiss on Tyler's cheek.

Before he knew what had happened, the man had shoved him aside and pushed Brian aside as well. He now began pawing the keys hanging on rows of cup hooks on the board. Brian, perhaps terrified he would end up in a bear hug and also get a wet kiss, hastily grabbed the right keys off the board and handed them over. "Thank you for coming to Donna's Casino and Roadhouse," he simpered, part of the standard script Elite Valet required them to recite.

Before Tyler could do anything, the Slav was bounding toward the parking lot at an amazing speed for such a heavy, wasted guy. Logan and Carlos, two more valets, were ambling back from the parking lot toward him.

"Stop that guy," yelled Tyler. Carlos and Logan looked startled and stepped gracefully out of the man's way, turning to observe him as he barreled past.

"Maybe we should have called Security," said Brian. "Isn't he, like, really drunk?"

Tyler said, "Yeah, he was probably too drunk to find his keys, but that didn't matter because you were *so helpful*." In Brian's defense, however, it did occur to Tyler that no one could really have come between that guy and his car.

By this time Carlos and Logan had moseyed all the way back to the valet booth, and the drunken Russian, now behind the wheel, had driven past the booth, squealed to a halt, let out an earsplitting whistle, and opened the passenger door, while from the darkness another Russian, the skinny blond one with the scar, had dived in beside him.

They took off, the driver hunched over the wheel so that his red face was right next to it. Judging by his speed, his foot and all the substantial weight behind it had floored the accelerator. Tyler quickly grabbed his phone, called 9-1-1, and told the dispatcher that a very intoxicated individual had just peeled off northbound headed to Interstate 5 in a white 2010 two-door Honda Accord V-6 with custom chrome Acura rims. "God, Brian," yelled Tyler. "If he kills someone, their family can sue Donna's, because we handed over the keys."

"I think they'd sue Elite Valet, not Donna's," said Logan thoughtfully. "Or if they sued Donna's, Donna's would sue Elite Valet."

"Yeah, but either way, we're screwed," said Tyler.

"Not me," said Logan. "Sure, I work for Elite. But Donna is, like, my aunt."

"What!" Tyler was startled to hear himself shouting. "What do you mean Donna is your aunt? As far as I know, Donna is dead!" The green neon sign with her name on it flickering out over the old highway looked like something from the 1950s.

"No she isn't. She's just retired. Her kid runs it now. My cousin Hughie. She told him to tell Jessica to hire me," said Logan. "When they laid me off from my crap job at Subway. It's just temporary."

"Dude," said Brian. "As soon as I sell my screenplay, I'm outta here, too."

Hughie! That clown! Tyler had always thought he was just the incompetent manager! But apparently he was Donna's son. One of the things Tyler had learned soon after leaving his leafy liberal arts college back East was that morons seemed to be in charge of a lot of things.

VOLODYA Zelenko and Sergei Lagunov, the two men who had made a hasty departure from Donna's lot, were standing in the back of a body shop in Everett, Washington, an establishment that seemed to thrive, although the few body-and-fender-work customers who wandered in off the street were routinely chased away by surly staff members who said they were too busy to perform any body and fender work just now.

The big guy, Volodya, was in his mid-forties, heavy and jowly, with slicked-back iron gray hair and the face of a brutal commissar in a Cold War–era movie.

The skinny one, Sergei, was in his early thirties, and wore a dark suit, well tailored to his tall, thin frame. He had a blond, mullet-like hairdo and a thin scar running from one eye to the corner of his upper lip, pulling one side of his mouth downwards.

The two men were staring down at the body of Pavel Ivanovich Tarasov, a wiry-looking specimen with a lived-in face and strangely delicate hands suitable for reaching into dashboard crevices and tight spots around automotive frames. In life he had been a car thief and a specialist in setting back odometers and removing vehicle identification number plates from stolen cars and replacing them with VIN plates salvaged from junkyard hulks. He was known as Old Pasha, because a younger Pasha had once worked here, but he was long gone, leaving Old Pasha's nickname as the younger man's only legacy.

"Why the fuck did you do this here?" said Sergei.

"Because he was here and I was here when I found out he fucked us over. He was selling our parts out of here! Son of a bitch sold a couple of BMW airbags on Craigslist!" Volodya shook a cigarette out of a pack and poked it into his face. "You know what? I think Veek and Cheep are fucking us over, too. In fact, I know they are."

Sergei ignored this digression. "So you *shot* him? There are other ways to handle that kind of shit."

Volodya flapped his hand in a dismissive way. "It was self-defense. I confronted him with what I knew and he attacked me."

Sergei pointed to a cheap .22-caliber pistol that lay next to a wrench and some shop rags on a nearby cluttered workbench.

"You shot him with that?"

Volodya nodded, and absentmindedly picked the gun up, wiped it off with a greasy shop rag, and put it in his pocket.

"But couldn't you have taken him? He was pretty old and a lot smaller than you." Sergei managed to deliver this opinion in an admiring and respectful rather than a critical way.

"He came at me with that!" said Volodya. He pointed down at the corpse. Near its delicate right hand with the curved, tapered fingers that would never again perform their delicate work, lay a blowtorch.

"Was it lit?"

"Yes, it was. I turned it off after I shot him. He was working on that Civic when I confronted him. He sprang at me like a panther. Look!" Volodya lifted up his elbow. In the dim fluorescent light, there did appear to be a singed patch on the arm of his shiny suit.

Sergei reflected briefly on the poor judgment behind confronting a man with a blazing blowtorch in his hand, but saw no reason to bring this up. Instead he said, "Does Dmytro know about Old Pasha?"

"No. And don't tell him. He doesn't understand that we can't let people fuck us over. He is soft and weak."

"Yeah, but he's in charge, right?" said Sergei.

"Yeah, so don't tell him."

Volodya didn't seem to be following his drift. He was not a subtle man. Sergei tried to make the idea a little more clear. "I sometimes wonder why he's in charge and you're not."

Volodya shrugged. "I don't know. It's been like that since we were kids. Anyway, we need to get Old Pasha out of here. What should we do?"

"You want me to take care of this for you?"

Volodya remained silent but suddenly looked pathetically grateful.

"I can take him out in some woods somewhere or something," said Sergei. "I can do it tomorrow. I'll get a car no one can trace to us. Put him in the back. Drive up into the mountains. Then I'll burn the car up somewhere."

"Can you do it right away?" Volodya said. It now seemed to be dawning on him that this was a real problem.

"No, I can't. I got to go get the car to take him to the mountains. I'm not doing it in my own car."

Volodya nodded. "Okay, but we got to get him out of here. I don't want Dmytro to know about this. We got to park him somewhere while you get it together."

Sergei looked thoughtful. "You say Vic and Chip are fucking us over, too?"

"Veek and Cheep? Yeah. I got reason to believe they're operating on their own. Ungrateful bastards. We set them up, gave them a nice cut. No one has any honor or decency."

Sergei leaned over to Volodya, and said in a reassuring manner, "I got an idea. We take care of this problem," he gestured vaguely at the crumpled form of Old Pasha, "and we do it so later we can tell Vic and Chip they're kind of involved. This will give us some leverage with them."

Volodya looked confused, and Sergei said, "Leave it all to me. I'll take care of it. I'll get rid of that gun for you, too."

"Okay," said Volodya. "But I keep gun."

Chapter Two

///

THE NEXT DAY, TYLER STOOD in a small, austere-looking office just off the kitchen at Ristorante Alba waiting for Flavia Torcelli, the restaurant's hostess. He had been surprised to learn that she would interview him before he began his first shift.

In his experience, the hostess in an upscale restaurant like this generally had a job description that was limited to (one) answer phone, (two) squeal perkily into it and at arriving diners, (three) tap screen with manicured nails to find reservation and table, and (four) stalk with grace and authority on high heels through a sea of tables carrying giant menus under one arm.

The door to the kitchen opened, and for a moment, the hostess stood in the doorway. She wore a close-fitting curvy black suit with a short skirt from which emerged long legs ending in those hostess stilettos. She was framed by tendrils of steamy mist, presumably from boiling vats of pasta water.

Tyler thought that Flavia Torcelli was incredibly beautiful, but also that she looked like a high-priced escort. Her hair was all piled up on top of her head but with a few pieces artfully coming down in a tousled way, slightly curled by the steam. As she moved forward, he saw her face more clearly. Wide eyes, arched brows, pink-lipsticked mouth, smoky gray eye makeup.

Tyler had also realized she wasn't American as soon as he

saw her. It was something about the way she now stood, her arms crossed over her chest. And her unsmiling, businesslike face. An American girl would have been smiling. Apparently Flavia Torcelli was more than just the hostess, since she decided who got a shot at parking cars here and this seemed to be her own personal office. Maybe she was sleeping with the owner.

She nodded and sat down behind the small desk, cluttered with paperwork. Then she looked up at Tyler as if he were a peasant who'd been called into the manor house to audition for footman. "Okay," she said, her accent evident immediately. "I want to hear you say, 'Welcome to Ristorante Alba.'"

"Welcome to *Ristorante Alba*," Tyler said, using the perfect accent he'd picked up from that year he'd spent in Tuscany back in middle school. For good measure, he threw in an offhand *"Buona sera."*

"Okay, *grazie*," she said. "You can start tonight. We're going to be really busy. Go out and check in with Chip." She stood, then turned on her high heels and clicked back into the kitchen.

Chip, the lead valet at Alba, had to be somewhere in his late thirties. He had a kind of youthful-looking blond haircut, presumably bleached, but he also had crinkly lines around his blue eyes.

Tyler watched him open the passenger door of a 5 Series BMW with a flourish, and flash a winning smile at a middle-aged woman who looked smitten as she locked eyes with Chip, and smoothed her chiffon dress down nervously over her knees while getting out of the car. His canned greeting sounded totally sincere. "Good evening and welcome to Ristorante Alba."

Then he handed the husband his ticket and wished him a pleasant evening, without the same big smile, but with a kind of concerned guy-to-guy look. Chip had just the right mix of deference combined with a confidence that intimidated the customer into not wanting to seem cheap in such a nice place, thereby setting him up to tip well when he picked up the car later.

As soon as the couple left, Chip turned and blasted Tyler with the same charm he'd shown the customers. "Hey! Tyler! Great. Welcome to Alba. Let me show you around." He put a hand on Tyler's shoulder and introduced him to the other valet on duty, Vic.

Tyler remembered Vic, who had worked for Elite Valet at Donna's Casino, before Jessica had transferred him to Alba. Vic had high cheekbones, dark wavy hair, and brown eyes. He was a lot younger than Chip and looked kind of like a male model. Vic lifted his chin in an unsmiling greeting, then looked down at his phone and began texting.

"Hop in, and I'll show you where we park these fine vehicles," said Chip, getting behind the wheel of the BMW. As he drove, Chip explained that the slots directly behind the restaurant were reserved for especially valuable cars. "Like a Lamborghini or something, we'll stick it back here. And if it's a doctor on call who might have to tear out of here real fast, same thing. But we always make sure we let them know we're doing them a favor whenever we use this lot. Kind of 'I'm taking care of you so don't forget to take care of me.'" Chip indicated cars lined up here. "You got your exotics, your Maseratis, your top- of-the-line Mercedes, whatever," he said.

The main parking lot was further away, a sloping oblong of weedy gravel around the corner and down the hilly block, between an alley and a boarded-up old warehouse. It was surrounded by a chain-link fence with an open, yawning gate and there were a few Dumpsters in the adjoining alley. "Here's where we park most of the cars," said Chip. "We can really stack 'em in here. And it's pretty secure because we come in and out so often. This neighborhood looks really nice from the street, but these alleys and stuff back here, it's pretty bad. If the customers had to park back here themselves and walk back to the restaurant, half of them would never make it." He laughed, with the air of a street-wise operator. "Sometimes if things are slow we chase bums away from the Dumpsters." Tyler made a mental note to make sure any car he parked was completely locked.

Chip pulled deftly into a tight spot between two SUVs. They got out of the car and Chip said, "Dude, we have a shortcut to get back on foot if we aren't bringing another car back." Tyler followed him down the alley and onto the abandoned warehouse property. There was some scruffy grass growing there, and a haphazard footpath made of boards. The path led up an incline, into a loading dock area of what appeared to be an antiques store, and then past Alba's back kitchen entrance to the smaller parking lot with its expensive cars.

"So that's about it. Unless we really get slammed. Then we talk to our brother valets over at the Harborview Hotel. Elite has that account, too. They've got five floors and they let us have a few slots on the top." Chip, huffing and puffing a little now, said, "It's pretty sweet. You have to hustle, sure, but the tips are really good.

"In fact," he chuckled a little in what Tyler thought was a slightly phony way, "I have some other business interests. But the money here is so good I just can't resist. It makes a big difference in my quality of life. Last month I took a week off, and I went to Paris, like, just on a whim." Chip snapped his fingers to indicate the spontaneous nature of the trip. "I met this chick and just asked her to come to Paris for a week." Chip tossed off a smug little laugh, popped up the collar of his white uniform polo shirt, and kind of adjusted his shoulders back and forth as if he were flexing the muscles there. "That got her attention."

"That's cool," said Tyler in a noncommittal way, gazing away from Chip. He hoped they'd be really busy so he wouldn't have to hear more stories about Chip's bank account or his success with women.

"Anyway," said Chip. "It's a great gig." He now assumed a thoughtful air. "You know, there's a service-industry vibe about the valet thing that I like a lot. It's almost like show business in a way. Like you're part of the nightlife in this town. And, yeah, maybe it gets kinda crazy now and then, but I kind of like that challenge."

"Right," said Tyler, thinking that if he ever thought doing the valet thing at Chip's age was glamorous that he'd kill himself. Business interests? Maybe Chip was skimming. Tyler decided to keep a close eye on him. If he could catch him not handing out claim checks, he could go to Jessica and suggest she should send out a secret shopper to try and nail him pocketing wads of cash. She was always under a lot of bottom-line pressure from management, and Tyler would be glad to help her out.

By now, they had arrived back at the front of the restaurant. Vic, still texting, took advantage of their presence to slide behind the wheel of a waiting Audi sedan and drove off at top speed.

"Okay, now listen up," said Chip, lowering his voice conspiratorially. "Scott Duckworth's people called. He's on his way. He's part of this special private event for some of the classier people in town for the food convention. And he has very specific requirements. So when a silver SL65 V12 Biturbo Anniversary Edition pulls up, that's him."

"Okay," said Tyler.

Chip looked irked that Tyler wasn't impressed and said, "You do know who Scott Duckworth *is*, don't you?"

"Oh sure," said Tyler. "My dad used to work for him back in the day."

"No shit," said Chip. "Well I guess *he* didn't get one of those gazillion-dollar payouts back when DuckSoft went public, or you wouldn't be parking cars." He laughed.

BEHIND the wheel of the Audi sedan, Vic Gelashvili paused at the gate to the main lot. There, standing in shadow, stood Volodya Zelenko. It was weird seeing him here instead of at Donna's.

Leaning out the car window, Vic said, "Okay, I got your text. What's up? Is there a problem?" What the hell was Volodya doing here?

"No problem. Not if you help me out," said Volodya. He smiled widely, revealing gold dental work and large teeth.

Vic managed a nervous smile back. "Um, okay. What do you need?"

"I just need somewhere to put this." He stepped aside and revealed a large black wheeled suitcase. Volodya touched the handle lightly. "Someone's going to pick it up in about twenty minutes."

"Well, can't you just wait for them here with it?"

"It's complicated," said Volodya. "We mustn't be seen together. The other guy and me. For our mutual protection."

"What's in there?" Vic asked.

"You don't want to know nothing about it," said Volodya in a firm but kindly way.

Vic didn't like this. "But where do you want me to keep it?" he asked. Where was he supposed to put the damn thing? In the valet booth?

"Don't worry about that," said Volodya. "You're not even going to touch it. We'll just put it in the trunk of this Audi. Those folks just showed up for dinner, right? We're good for at least an hour, maybe two."

"But I'm not sure—"

"Shut up and pop trunk," said Volodya sharply. He vanished toward the back of the car, dragging the suitcase behind him through the gravel.

Vic popped the trunk lever and heard the click and slight hydraulic puff that meant the trunk was open. Vic protested, "But how will he know which car it's in?" He turned around in the driver's seat and faced the rear window.

"I'll give him the license plate number, for God's sake," said Volodya. "Park it as close as you can to the entrance from the street. I'll watch where you park it." The trunk lid now obscured the rear window.

"But if one of the other valets is around when this guy comes to pick it up—"

"No worries," said Volodya. "No worries at all. This guy will be in and out so fast, no one will ever know. We'll leave the trunk unlocked. Closed but not totally."

"But—"

"Just fucking do it!" said Volodya, who by now was speaking in a breathless way that indicated physical exertion. Vic heard a thump and felt the car shudder a little, and then heard Volodya let out a relieved sigh. Whatever was in there, thought Vic, was pretty heavy.

Chapter Three

//

ROGER BENSON WAS HAVING a lot of trouble with his website. The fonts kept morphing into other weird fonts. And there was something he was supposed to do to attract more hits. Tag the thing so searches would take people there. He sighed. It was pathetic, his having to build his own site like this.

Roger was a fit and tanned fifty-seven-year-old with thinning silver hair and a small matching goatee. He wore a diamond stud in one ear.

He sipped his white wine and stared in frustration at the screen. Then he jabbed at a few function keys on the top of the keyboard. He remembered the old days before the invention of the mouse. Everything was probably still programmed into function keys. An ominous error message appeared with a big red X on it. He didn't have his reading glasses on, so he couldn't read the tiny letters and he didn't want to anyway. This sucked.

Roger would simply have to appeal to his son. Surely Tyler could help him get this site launched. The whole family should be pulling together at a time like this.

TYLER was driving down to the parking lot when his phone rang. Damn. It was his dad. Tyler had refrained from picking up a call from his dad for about the last five times, so he supposed he may as well face the music. He had a moment.

"Hi Dad. What's up?"

"Not too much, not too much. You know how it goes. Working on my site. How are you?"

"I'm okay. I got put on at Alba for tonight." Tyler headed the car toward the parking lot around the corner and down the hill.

"Alba. Wow. That's great," said Roger. "I've been meaning to go down there. It's cuisine from the Piedmont region. That's very cool."

"That's right," said Tyler. "Alba is a town in Piedmont." He looked over his shoulder as he backed the Civic into position for a fast exit.

"I read about that super-hot chef who owns it." His father's voice grew solemn. "Seattle is really a great food town. We're so fortunate."

"Yeah," said Tyler, yanking the parking brake. "They're having some big foodie event here tonight, so I'm kinda busy, Dad."

"Really? I suppose you can't get me in there on a courtesy basis? Like I'm going to write about it or something. You know. As a food marketing professional?"

"No!" said Tyler, trying not to shout. "If you can't afford to eat here, then stay home. Make yourself a sandwich." Typical! Now he was trying to scam free meals. "Got to go, Dad."

"Wait, wait!" said his father. "How about if I come down there tonight just as a customer? Maybe meet and mingle a little. Do a little networking with the food community."

"Forget it, Dad," said Tyler. That's all he needed. His dad lurking around on his first day on the job. "It's a private gig," said Tyler. "In a private dining room. Scott Duckworth is going to be there," he added cruelly, letting Roger know the gathering was out of his league.

"Scott! No kidding?" Now Roger was really interested. "I wouldn't mind seeing him again. I understand he's very loyal to the folks he started with."

"Do. Not. Show. Up. Here. Tonight. Please," said Tyler. "Gotta go. Text me." Tyler crammed the phone into his pocket, secure in the knowledge his dad had never bothered to learn how to text.

Tyler got out and noticed that he had parked the Civic next to a gray Audi that looked strangely familiar. He glanced in the window and noted some matted-looking dog hair on the backseat. Walking past it, he recognized a slightly rusted-out tailpipe, and a bumper sticker that said My daughter is an honor student at McClure Middle School.

Tyler also noticed that the trunk wasn't completely shut. Maybe the latch was broken. He lifted the trunk lid slightly, and the tiny light popped on, revealing a large black suitcase. This was a bad idea in this poorly secured lot. Tyler examined both halves of the latch carefully to see if something was obstructing the opposing part or if the latch was misaligned somehow. Everything seemed normal. He placed both hands on the trunk lid, banged it firmly into place, and was relieved to hear the sound of the latch engaging, and then tested it just to make sure it was closed.

The car wasn't waxed and polished. Whoever owned it apparently wasn't one of those finicky customers. Tyler figured no one would care if there were a bunch of fingerprints on the trunk.

ROGER Benson went into the kitchen and refilled his wineglass from the box of Chardonnay in the fridge. It all made such sense. If anyone could get his dream back on track, it was Scott Duckworth.

Roger fiddled impatiently with the plastic spigot of the wine box. Costco wine! It was so damn pathetic. Why had Tyler been so negative? Why shouldn't he go down there to Alba and casually run into Scott? And remind him of the old days. Scott had hired him right out of the staff of the University of Washington *Daily*, in Scott's old hangout, the Last Exit. It had been one of the first places in Seattle to get espresso. Roger had loved going there for cappuccino after class.

Of course *now* he knew that Italians only drank cappuccino at *breakfast time*. He should have been ordering *shots* of espresso. In fact, he'd even called it "expresso" back then, with an *x*. But, Roger reflected, unschooled as he had been in the ways of Italian culture, even as a raw youth he'd been interested in the finer aspects of life. Scott had been there at the Last Exit for the chess, of course. But maybe now he'd be receptive to a DIY artisanal food enterprise, something with terrific franchise opportunities.

Roger knocked back half of the wine standing in front of the fridge, and refilled the glass to the brim, saddened again by the humiliating plastic spigot.

He returned to his office, and to the website for Scott's foundation that he'd just discovered. He reread the bio that described Scott as "a world-class philanthropist whose vision is poised to lead the initiatives of the twenty-first century and shape a better world, and an innovative, cutting-edge investor with a forward-looking approach to identifying solutions that will benefit global citizens everywhere."

Roger was sure Carla had approved that clunky sentence. Carla hadn't had much to contribute back when the business was struggling. It was always Helene, the office manager, who held everything together during the heady youth of DuckSoft. Helene was always so pretty and cheerful and feminine, while Carla, Scott's bossy big sister, was just a bitch on wheels.

He remembered how Helene had tried to comfort him when Carla rewrote his copy. It was Helene who tried to hint to him that Carla might have it in for him. He remembered that drunken lunch where he'd poured out all his professional fears. He remembered Helene's hand on his at the table, and later her soothing low tones after he'd been fired.

"WHAT! Why the hell did you put him there? Are you crazy?" demanded Sergei Lagunov. He was sitting next to Volodya Zelenko in the bar at Donna's.

Volodya waved a chubby hand in the air. "I have reasons."

"But there are people coming in and out of there all the time," said Sergei.

"That's right. Veek and Cheep are coming in and out of there all the time." Volodya caught the barmaid's eye and moved his index finger up and down like an oil derrick over the rim of his empty vodka-rocks glass.

"I don't get it," said Sergei.

Volodya turned to him and looked hurt. "It was your idea.

You're the one who said we should put squeeze on them by letting them know they are somehow involved. So I involve them. Veek was guy who parked car. Maybe we tell him he's involved."

Sergei had mentioned something like this, it was true. His idea had been to maybe threaten them with a false accusation if the cops came around wondering what happened to Old Pasha. Maybe threaten to plant the gun on them or something.

"I don't want you to tell Vic and Chip anything," said Sergei now.

"Anyway," said Volodya, sipping his fresh drink, "you better get over there right away. The car was parked twenty minutes ago, and the owners are probably halfway through the first course." He handed Sergei a Donna's matchbook. Donna's was one of the last places in town that provided its customers with matchbooks. "The license number is inside. Gray Audi. Right by gate."

Sergei grabbed the matchbook and took off. If there was any traffic on I-5, the car's owner might leave the restaurant before he got there. Sergei Lagunov was losing his patience with Volodya. It was time to move on up to Dmytro and deal with him.

A red SL55 AMG Mercedes sports sedan with the top down pulled up to the Alba entrance. "Nice!" Chip said, leaping into position to open the door for the wiry ginger-haired male driver, while Tyler opened the passenger door to let out his plump female companion. Chip eased himself behind the wheel and caressed the gear shift. "You know how much this car would set you back?" he asked. Tyler assumed it was a rhetorical question, but Chip went ahead and answered it. "At least a hundred grand."

Tyler kind of hoped Chip would take him along to demonstrate how the retractable convertible roof worked. He'd never parked one of these, and if Chip had been a good shift lead, he would have realized that and trained him on it so if another one like that came in, Tyler wouldn't look like an idiot.

But just then, a customer Tyler knew he'd seen before, accompanied by a thin, dark woman who was presumably his wife, came bursting out of the restaurant. She was on the phone. "I'm *really* sorry, sweetie," she said in a trembling voice.

After more than a year as a valet, connecting a person with a car was hard-wired into Tyler's brain. This guy was a regular at Donna's. And now he realized that the gray Audi with the popped trunk that had looked familiar to him was this guy's car.

Tyler stepped forward, took their ticket, and recited his scripted "I hope you enjoyed your dining experience."

The gray Audi guy said angrily, "What dining experience? We didn't get to eat anything but our appetizer!"

"We have an emergency at home," the woman said, sounding distraught.

The gray Audi guy, usually mild-mannered at Donna's, snapped, "An emergency! Give me a break! My parents never did my homework for me!"

"But it's a special project! There's a diorama *and* a Power-Point!" she said in an anguished voice.

"I'll get it right away," said Tyler. He took the keys off the board. "I know exactly where the car is." The gray Audi guy looked at Tyler sharply. He seemed to be wondering where he knew him from.

Tyler took off loping. When he passed through the back lot where the better cars were parked, he was startled to see Chip rise from behind the red Mercedes. Tyler wondered what he had been doing crouched behind it. Maybe he was checking to see if he'd scratched it. He was probably so excited about Scott Duckworth's arrival he was off his game.

By the time Tyler returned with the car, Mrs. Gray Audi was standing with her arms across her chest in a defensive position, and her husband was scowling. Tyler had thought of mentioning he'd closed the trunk—it might be worth a better tip. As Tyler handed over the keys, the gray Audi guy said to his wife, "God damn it, Caroline, can't the little brat make her own goddamn diorama?" The wife's eyes filled with tears. Tyler decided to forget about mentioning the trunk. He figured he was lucky to get the buck the gray Audi guy jammed into his hand.

Chapter Four

///

INSIDE ALBA, IN THE BANQUET ROOM off the regular dining room, Flavia Torcelli was mingling with the specially invited guests from the food convention. "I think," she was saying carefully to a woman in a muumuu and a necklace that seemed to be made of beach rocks, "that although Piedmont may be a very traditional area, it is important to realize that today, in such a global environment, we can also build on these traditions in a progressive, um, innovative way." The woman brandished a notebook and pencil and wore a convention bag with a crossed-knife-and-fork logo that said PRESS on it.

Flavia led her companion toward a long table, where foodies with small plates and glasses of Barolo and Barbaresco were hovering. Some were sampling in consultation with others. Moving food around in their mouths, their eyes unfocused, they described the textures and flavors of what they were eating in turn. Others were working solo, aggressively replenishing their plates, their hands scuttling eagerly over the table's offerings like fleshy crabs.

"Come and see what we've done with traditional elements such as asparagus and hazelnuts, and of course truffle oil. But in a new way, with the addition of quinoa. I will be so interested in your opinion," said Flavia.

"So," said the other woman, as they approached the table, "I heard a rumor Scott Duckworth will be here. I had no idea he was a foodie!"

Flavia tilted her head to one side. "He is a man of many interests," she said with a mysterious smile.

"Does he eat here? I heard he was a total recluse."

"I can't discuss anything about Mr. Duckworth," said Flavia. "Other than to say we will be very happy to have him here tonight if he can come." She looked a little nervously at the door, where a waiter was now signaling. "Excuse me," she said. "I must go." Smoothing down some strands from her chignon, she tripped toward the door, her lips parted in an eager expression.

"He's on his way," the waiter said.

Flavia Torcelli put one well-manicured hand on her heart and smiled broadly.

TO Tyler's horror, a familiar bottle green PT Cruiser pulled up to the valet booth. Tyler couldn't believe it. Roger was at the wheel in one of his tropical Margaritaville shirts. This one had sailboats and big palm fronds all over it.

Tyler wrenched open the driver's door. His dad smiled at him in a lopsided way, swiveled awkwardly in his seat, and managed to get his feet down on the ground. Tyler was horrified to note he was wearing the Australian sheepskin bedroom slippers Mom had given him for Christmas. He'd left the house in his slippers! Thank God he wasn't also wearing his bathrobe!

With a determined look, Roger now grabbed the sides of the door opening and prepared to haul himself out of the car. Tyler placed his knee in his father's chest and pushed him back into the car. Now that his face was within a few inches of his dad's, Tyler smelled the wine. His hair looked all messed up and there were two bright red spots on his cheeks. It was bad enough he was here trying to crash the reception. *And* on Tyler's first shift at Alba! But the idea of him staggering around hammered in his bedroom slippers was even more frightening.

Vic was nearby but was now preoccupied with a stretch limo that was disgorging a whole bunch of portly people with convention badges on. No valet money in that operation, but Vic was greeting them all as they emerged in clown-car fashion.

Tyler felt a big push to his chest, and realized Roger was once again preparing to eject himself from the car.

"Dad, you are really drunk," said Tyler. He managed to open the rear door, then pull his father out from behind the wheel and throw him in the backseat, slamming the door after him. Then Tyler jumped into the driver's seat, threw the car in reverse, went back a few feet, and then jammed into drive and made a wide loop around the limo. In no time at all, he was on the street, frantically calling his mother.

She answered on the first ring. "Mom, you have to come get Dad. He's really drunk!"

"Maybe, but he's here in his office," she said.

"Listen, Mom," said Tyler. "Drive to the valet stand at the Harborview Hotel."

"It's okay," said his dad from the backseat, sounding as if the whole episode were no big deal. "I can get a cab. Don't bother Mom."

Tyler drove the three blocks to the hotel, and got his mother's solemn promise to collect Dad and his car. His sister, Samantha, would drive Mom's car back. At the valet stand another guy in a black windbreaker with the pink ELITE logo named Kyle was standing there.

"Hey," Kyle said. "I heard you guys might have some overflow from that event at Alba."

"Not really," said Tyler. "Listen, I got a guy in here and he's drunk. His wife is coming to get him." He reached into his tip pocket and peeled off thirty bucks' worth of fives and ones. "Family wants us to park him up on top. Making it worth our while. They don't want him to wander off."

"No problem," said Kyle, deftly pocketing the roll. "Take him up to the roof. We can even lock off the elevator." He peered in at Tyler's dad. "The old guy looks easy enough to handle," he commented.

WHEN Volodya Zelenko had noted that the incoming call was from Sergei, he thought it might be a good idea to carry the phone out of Donna's bar for privacy, considering the delicate errand Sergei was on. He was now standing outside across from the Elite Valet booth where a pale, goofy-looking valet kid seemed to be scribbling in a notebook and paying no attention to Volodya.

"What do you mean *gone*?" demanded Volodya.

"The car was not where you said it would be," said Sergei. "Do you know where it is?"

"But the guy should still be in there eating dinner," said Volodya.

"Maybe he didn't like the food," said Sergei.

"Go ask Veek or Cheep where the gray Audi is," suggested Volodya.

Just then, Volodya was startled to see an unfamiliar car pull up with Sergei in person at the wheel. Sergei leaned out the window. "I didn't stick around," he said. And in Russian, he added, "I don't think it's so smart to ask someone if they happened to know where your dead body went."

Volodya stared at the phone in his own left hand and ended the call, then looked down at the vodka-rocks in his right hand and knocked it back. "Goddamn Veek and Cheep," he said. "Are they fucking with me on purpose?"

WHEN Tyler arrived back at Alba, panting from his run from the Harborview Hotel, a silver Mercedes fitting the description of Scott Duckworth's car had just pulled up. The windows were tinted. There was no one else around, so Tyler began to reach for the handle of the front passenger door. Two large men in dark suits burst out of the car, one from the front and one from the backseat. One of them, a short, red-haired man with a pug nose, wrestled the front passenger door away from Tyler.

"Welcome to Ristorante Alba," Tyler said as he was being shoved out of the way by the other guy, who looked like a retired halfback gone to seed. The two men scanned their surroundings with grim expressions.

Now, the seedy halfback opened the rear driver's-side door and a third man, presumably Scott Duckworth, emerged—tubby, fiftyish, with a mild expression, a gray beard, and thinning hair. He wore a pair of rumpled khakis and a plaid shirt.

The halfback and the red-haired man hustled Duckworth toward the restaurant like the Secret Service shoving a bemused president around, and Tyler, feeling slightly dazed, went over to the driver's side.

He tried to open the door but it was locked. The unsmiling driver, a heavily muscled Asian man with a shaved head, lowered the window and stared at Tyler.

"I can park this in a special lot we have just behind the restaurant," Tyler said. "I think it's better for security."

"No one but *me* drives Mr. Duckworth's car," said the driver. "Hop in and tell me where to park it." Tyler heard the doors unlock.

Tyler looked over the guy's shoulder and checked out the car's interior. There was a custom computer screen in the dash and some other electronic items Tyler had never seen before. A female voice said, "You have arrived at your destination," and then repeated it, which seemed to rattle the driver, who looked at the dashboard gadgetry in a panicky way.

"If you turn off the engine, she'll stop talking," said Tyler.

The guy gave him a dirty look, and then Chip appeared, coming around the corner of the restaurant.

Chip rushed to where Tyler was still standing at the driver's open door. "Welcome to Ristorante Alba, sir," Chip said to the driver. The female voice said, "The door is open."

Tyler, relieved that Chip would handle all this, stepped back and turned away to look at the entrance of the restaurant.

Duckworth, flanked by his two minders, had waddled up to Flavia Torcelli, who was just coming out of the entrance. She was standing there looking up at the rumpled billionaire with a dazzling smile, one leg stretched out sideways in a kind of fashion model pose. Tyler had no doubt at all that she knew she had great legs and had choreographed that stance to show them off. ‑

Now she greeted Scott Duckworth, and extended her hand for him to shake. She was turning on all the charm she hadn't bothered to use on the help when he'd met her earlier. Duckworth was beaming at her, and his two bodyguards hovered behind him.

Everyone in Seattle knew that Scott Duckworth, Dad's old boss, had never gotten around to finding a Mrs. Duckworth. Flavia Torcelli seemed to be auditioning for the part.

"Get in," said the man in the Mercedes to Chip. "Show me where to park it. I'll stay with the car until he's ready to go home."

"I know," said Chip. "He's been here before. I know the process."

Tyler glanced back over at the tableau by the entrance. The pug-nosed guy, whose red hair Tyler now saw was arranged in a bad comb-over, and who seemed to be in charge, put his hand on Duckworth's shoulder as if to guide him into the restaurant, but Duckworth just stood there, staring into the eyes of the hostess, and holding her hand in what had ceased to be a handshake.

Suddenly, a black Camaro came full-speed at the valet booth, as if the driver had had a heart attack and collapsed with a leaden foot on the gas.

And then, Tyler heard the popping noises, like tiny firecrackers.

At the entrance to the restaurant, the two minders pushed Duckworth toward the restaurant doors and seemed to be clambering on top of him. He tumbled onto the hostess. Tyler heard a muffled female scream.

The Camaro had now maneuvered away from the booth and it stopped alongside Scott Duckworth's Mercedes with a huge lurch. From the window, Tyler saw the outline of an arm with a gun at the end of it and heard more popping sounds.

He ducked down in front of the Mercedes, facing the headlights, and heard the ping of what he suddenly decided was a bullet hitting the car.

Should he get under Scott Duckworth's car? But what if the car took off and ran him over? Maybe the best thing to do would be to lie flat on the ground and centered between the tires, so if the car took off it wouldn't run over him. He heard another pop and decided crouching beside the passenger side behind the engine block was definitely the way to go. There was more mass there to stop a bullet.

But before he had a chance to make his move, the Mercedes moved forward and he found himself clambering onto the car's hood, grabbing the Mercedes three-pointed-star ornament to pull himself up and staring at the startled bald Asian guy through the windshield. The car kept moving and Tyler tried to roll off to the side before it picked up speed. But before he could execute this maneuver, he fell off all by himself. Now he was flat on the ground on his stomach on the passenger side

There were more pops and another strange ping came from the Mercedes. He tried flattening himself even further, and smashed his face against the asphalt.

He squeezed his eyes shut, then he heard the sound a valet never wants to hear, the crunch of car hitting car. "You are experiencing a collision," the disembodied female voice said. "Airbags will deploy."

After that he was aware of the sound of a car taking off very fast and hurtling away, and he was afraid it was the Mercedes, which would leave him exposed. But when he turned his head to look to his side, he saw the Mercedes was still there. Presumably, the airbag had given the driver of the Mercedes pause. So it must have been the Camaro that sped off.

He peered beneath the undercarriage of the Mercedes and the Camaro didn't seem to be there anymore. But Chip was lying on the ground, facing away from Tyler. Chip was very still and there was a pool of blood forming around his head.

Chapter Five

TYLER PULLED HIS CELL PHONE out of his pocket and punched in 9-1-1. Why hadn't he done that before? But he guessed it had only been seconds.

"There's been a shooting," he yelled into the phone. "At Alba. A restaurant. I don't know the address. Down on Second Avenue. Near Marion. There's a guy bleeding. There were tons of shots."

"We're on the way," said the dispatcher in a voice not unlike the voice coming out of Scott Duckworth's dashboard. "Are shots still being fired?"

"No," said Tyler, although it took him some time to realize this. "No. The car that did it is gone. I gotta see if the guy's okay."

"Don't do that, sir. Remain safe," said the dispatcher. "Can you describe the vehicle?"

"A black Camaro. It's gone now."

Tyler got up, jammed the phone back into his pocket, and went over to take a look at Chip who was lying prone with his head to one side.

The guy in the Mercedes was batting away at the marshmallow of white vinyl airbag. "It's okay, they're gone," yelled Tyler to the driver, and knelt down next to Chip.

Chip's eyes were wide open. His mouth was open, too, and there was a trickle of blood at the corner. The pool of blood around his head seemed to be growing.

IN the restaurant's kitchen, Flavia Torcelli gave one of Scott Duckworth's bodyguards, the one Tyler had thought looked like a halfback, and who was now blocking the door from the kitchen to her office, a frantic little push to his chest. "You have to let me out of here," she said. "I need to make sure everything is all right in the restaurant."

"It's for your safety," he said. "No one leaves until Mr. Ott gets back. He's securing the area."

Nearby, the kitchen staff and the chef in starched uniform and toque, a man in his early thirties, watched her efforts with a sad expression. She turned to him and let out a stream of Italian, and he shrugged. Then she turned back to the man blocking the door. "Securing the area? It's my area, and I didn't ask him to secure it. I want to make sure the customers and the staff are all right." She turned to Scott Duckworth. "He works for you, right? Tell him to let me out of my kitchen!"

"Do you think that's a good idea? I don't know if it's safe." Duckworth blinked a few times, and looked pained. He addressed the man blocking the door. "Can we go, Doug?"

"No!" The man named Doug turned to Flavia. "Ma'am," he said, "Red, uh, Mr. Ott, is Mr. Duckworth's chief security operative. He's calling the shots here."

Just then the door Flavia had been trying to reach began to open and hit Doug in the back. He whirled around and held the door shut.

"Let me in, it's me, Red," said an angry voice from the other side of the door.

Doug stood back and Red Ott, the pug-nosed man with the reddish comb-over, burst into the room. Flavia darted out behind him and through the door.

"We're getting Scott back home," said Ott. "Right away." He flapped open an old-fashioned phone and jabbed at it. "Kimo! You're okay! Great. Come around to the back and we'll load him into the car from the kitchen exit." He paused, listening.

"Damn," said Ott. Addressing Doug, he said, "The assailant

is gone. Kimo's talking to the cops." He walked over to a sink and glanced up at the sign above it that said Wash Your Hands in English and Spanish.

Flavia burst back into the kitchen and had another spirited discussion in Italian with the chef, then turned to Scott Duckworth. "You can come out now. The police are here. Let me show you to the private dining room. All the food people are there." She glanced over at Ott, who now seemed to be doing what the sign told him to and was washing his hands with the disinfectant soap from the dispenser. "We'll be safe there."

Ott turned around, still lathering, and said, "Scott, you're leaving. Period. Someone tried to kill you."

"People are shooting guns in America all the time, right?" said Flavia with a nervous laugh. She turned to Scott. "At least you can stay for some appetizers and a glass of wine." She smiled at him and took his arm. "It will calm you down. The police will want to talk to everyone. No reason you should be stuck in the kitchen. Come with me." Duckworth turned pale pink and beamed down at her. "Okay, Flavia," he said.

"Doug, you go with them," said Ott, now drying his hands on a paper towel. "I'm checking out the rear exit so we can get Kimo to pull up behind here when he's finished being interviewed."

Ott went outside onto the loading dock, opened his jacket, removed a gun from an armpit holster, wiped it off with the paper towel he had just used, and tossed it into a garbage can. Then he covered the gun with some coffee grounds and wilted lettuce.

IN front of the restaurant, Tyler watched the medics strap Chip onto a gurney, load him into their ambulance, and peel away with screaming sirens. He guessed that Chip wasn't dead because they didn't put him in a body bag or anything. But he'd also heard that medics always put dead people into ambulances, and rushed off with their sirens on so they didn't have to deal with upset people or look like they weren't trying.

Now the police were stringing a bunch of yellow crime scene tape around the entrance drive. A uniformed officer came up to him and said that detectives wanted to talk to anyone who had witnessed the event.

When the detectives arrived, one of them, a motherly-looking lady with curly light brown hair, asked him what he had seen and he realized he couldn't describe the man in the car at all. It was just a blur. "But I remember the car. It was a black Camaro Z28 IROC. Kind of a bad paint job and dirty, but it sounded mean."

"Mean?" repeated the motherly-looking detective.

"A powerful, well-tuned engine. And it didn't have stock IROC rims. They come with alloy rims." While he was talking, he noticed another woman pointing a camera down at the ground.

"Very good description," the detective said encouragingly. "But you have no idea what the guy *in* the car looked like?"

"No," said Tyler. "I'm used to memorizing cars. I only memorize the person that goes with the car when they get out and I hand them the ticket."

He followed the direction of the camera down to the ground to see what the photographer was taking a picture of. The detective followed his gaze.

The woman with the camera looked up. "It's a funny place for a slipper," she said.

Tyler said, "Oh shit!"

The detective turned to Tyler. "Know why there's a slipper there?"

"Not really," said Tyler. He paused. "Maybe it fell out of a car. We find a lot of weird stuff in people's cars." The photographer now stood back while a man wearing latex gloves picked up the sheepskin slipper Mom had given Dad for Christmas and put it into a Ziploc bag.

THE next morning, thirteen-year-old Kaitlin Smethurst stood next to her parents' gray Audi in the circular driveway in front of her house and said, "God, Mom, you're making me late." She was a thin child, and only stood about four foot eight, but she bristled with angry power. Her jaw was as tightly clenched as it could be considering her massive orthodontia.

A large backpack was strapped to her slight frame, and she was struggling with an awkward cardboard object, a diorama of the life cycle of the Pacific salmon. The cardboard triptych took its subject from its early life as an egg in a freshwater creek; through its heroic swim out to the open sea, its struggle back to spawn, facing such challenges as predators, loss of habitat, and chemical pollutants; and finally, its successful mating before dying, having sacrificed all for its ungrateful offspring.

"If you hadn't changed outfits three times, we wouldn't be late," said her mother. In her hand was a leash and at the end of it was a Springer Spaniel.

"Yeah, but *you* totally messed up the PowerPoint," replied Kaitlin. "God, Mom. You're supposed to be supportive. But you and Dad went *out!*"

"I'm sorry," she said, sighing. "It was our anniversary."

"God, Mom," continued Kaitlin. "Parental involvement is *key.*"

The dog jumped up on Kaitlin.

"Mom!" she screamed. "Patches is messing up my diorama. Make him stop. And put my diorama in the trunk!"

Caroline Smethurst wrenched the diorama from her daughter's hands and went around to the back of the car, waving her key at its lock.

Caroline was shocked to see a large suitcase in the trunk. It didn't look like any suitcase they owned. Was this somehow connected to her husband's weird excuses about working late? She'd been worried he was gambling again, but maybe there was another woman! Was there another woman? Was he all packed up and ready to move out? A black zipper ran around the perimeter of the suitcase. Caroline leaned over and tugged at it, then unzipped it fiercely and threw back the flap.

Inside the suitcase was a very pale man gazing up at her with milky blue eyes. His chin rested on his drawn-up knees. He looked about sixty, with a short, iron gray haircut. His arms and legs seemed to be folded up in an unnatural position, and he didn't move. Patches began barking furiously, and leapt up at the trunk, putting his paws on the bumper, but the man remained still.

Chapter Six

THAT EVENING, IN A SUBURB north of Seattle, Tyler's fellow valet from Alba, Vic Gelashvili, sat on a black leather sofa drinking vodka with Volodya Zelenko's cousin Dmytro, a short, stocky man in his forties who wore an Adidas track suit— navy with white stripes. The top was unzipped about six inches, revealing a heavy gold chain resting against gray chest hairs.

A pair of Rottweilers snoozed in front of a huge marble fireplace.

"So enjoy your drink, then get out. You got a lot of nerve just showing up here. Did I ask you to come here?" Dmytro said belligerently in an accent that was less thick than his cousin Volodya's.

"I'm sorry, Dmytro," said Vic, gnawing on a cuticle. "I didn't want to use the phone. You know. Because of what happened at Alba." Maybe it had been stupid to come here. But after that stuff with Volodya and the suitcase, Vic was scared to go to him. And besides, he had a message to deliver. A message that would buy him the time he needed.

"So what the fuck did happen? You were there last night, right? And I'm curious about that. That's the only reason you're sitting on my couch drinking my booze. Tell me what happened."

"I was there but I was parking a car when it all went down. A guy drove in there and started shooting and shot Chip," said Vic. "Then he drove away."

"I saw all that on the news," said Dmytro, waving a pudgy hand with a large diamond pinkie ring. "Someone tried to take out that computer guy—Duck something. What's the big deal? People like that get shot at all the time. Who knows what kind of business that computer guy is involved in. You can't get rich like that without making enemies. Maybe he made someone mad at him. And Chip just got in the way. Anyway, it says in the news he's gonna pull through."

"Yeah, okay," said Vic. "But what if that drive-by had something to do with us? Do *we* have any enemies?"

"No way," said Dmytro. He paused thoughtfully. "But meanwhile, we should take it easy. For a week or two. The cops will be all over the place. But not like they would have if they got the computer guy. So the valet gets shot. Big deal." Dmytro took another sip. "Listen, the police will be asking you some questions maybe." He leaned back and closed his eyes in concentration. "About Chip. You don't know nothing about any cars or what you guys were doing."

"Naturally," said Vic. "What do you think? That I'm a snitch? That's not the way we do things."

"How *we* do things." Dmytro's eyes flew open. "We? Please. We have an arrangement. We are doing business. But you aren't one of us. Don't think talking to the cops about us is ever gonna help you. And if we find out you did talk to them, we'll have to take care of it."

Vic now drew himself up, stared directly at Dmytro and switched to Russian. "But I am a part of this life."

"Speak English," said Dmytro. "For chrissakes. I'm not a Russian anyway. I'm a Ukrainian. And you're not a Russian either. You're a fucking Georgian. I can tell by your name and the way you look. Georgians are always trouble. Crazy, wild people. Now please, get the hell out of here. You wanna talk to someone if you're worried, if you've got a problem, talk to Volodya. If it's important, he talks to me about it. Not you. Never come here again."

Vic gazed directly at Dmytro and said in English and very

purposefully and with a little toss of his head, "This life. It's in my blood."

"Huh?" said Dmytro. "What the fuck are you talking about?"

"I've never mentioned to you my uncle Ivan in Tbilisi. Or his son Gleb."

Dmytro's eyes narrowed. That had got his attention! Vic decided to drive his point home in a simple, dignified manner. "I was born here, but my parents are from the old country. And my father's brother, my uncle in Tbilisi—he is a *vor*, a part of a brotherhood that goes back to the time of the czars. The *vory v zakone* have a long history of honor. This is what I meant when I say this is not how *we* are."

"Really? I had no idea! Why haven't you told me this before?" said Dmytro expansively, and in a way that made him seem unthreatened—simply impressed with such an interesting genealogical nugget.

Vic shrugged. "We don't talk about it here in America. But my uncle and I are very close."

"And that is a good thing," said Dmytro respectfully. After a pause, Dmytro laughed and said in a teasing tone, "Now get the fuck out of here before I get mad and fuck you up." His voice rose and one of the dogs opened its eyes, lifted his head, then went back to sleep. He smiled and chuckled. "Just joking. You know I'm just joking."

"Right. I'm going," said Vic. He rose from the sofa.

"I'm glad you came by," Dmytro added. "And please, give my respects to your uncle. And your cousin, too."

"For sure," said Vic.

Dmytro saw Vic out into the foyer. Vic smirked as he took in the zebra print carpeting, the gilded plaster statue of a naked woman holding a torch, and the red lacquered table with a smoky mirror veined with gold hanging above it. He let himself out the massive double doors, and walked confidently out onto the circular driveway. As he walked toward his car, parked behind Dmytro's gold El Dorado, Vic smiled.

As soon as Vic had left, Dmytro fired up a cigarette and sighed.

Then he picked up his phone and called his cousin, Volodya. From the bar noises in the background, he imagined Volodya was hanging out at Donna's as usual.

"Volodya!" he shouted, as if to overcome the din. "Stay where you are. That little Georgian was here. I'm coming to talk to you about it."

"Does he know we know that he's stealing from us?" asked Volodya.

"I hope not," said Dmytro.

THE day after the shooting at Alba, Tyler was working a shift there. Jessica had asked him to fill in for Chip until he could come back to work. Apparently he was doing well and had said he was game to return to work right away.

Tyler was looking forward to 2:00 A.M. when he could close up and go home. Every time a black car came in, he tensed up. The other two guys he was working with hadn't been working the night of the shooting, but they seemed skittish, too. Tyler kept telling himself that some crazy person had it in for Scott Duckworth, so if Scott wasn't around, there was nothing to worry about.

Surprisingly, business hadn't been that bad. There'd even been a little rush at seven, when a bunch of food conventioneers who were still in town came by. But now there was just one vehicle in line, a big burgundy Yukon. Tyler rushed over to the door, and felt a sudden disconnect. The face didn't match the car. Oh, this was the gray Audi guy. The guy he'd seen at Alba last night—the night of the shooting—who'd been bickering with his wife about their kid's homework. He'd never come to Donna's in this vehicle.

"Good evening, sir," said Tyler. "Welcome to Ristorante Alba."

"I don't need to park the car tonight," said the gray Audi guy nervously. "I just wanted…" He stopped and looked clearly terrified. "I've seen you before, right?"

"Yes, I believe I got your car for you the other night. You had to leave early."

The man nodded. "But before that…"

"I remember you from Donna's," said Tyler. "You've been a customer there, too."

"Listen," said the Audi guy, "I'll be honest. My wife doesn't know I come by Donna's to unwind after work, okay?" He smiled nervously. "My wife thinks I work late every night. She'd be pissed I wasn't home helping with homework or whatever."

"Okay," said Tyler. What did this guy want? All Tyler wanted to do was make enough money to pay off his student loan, and get his engineering degree before he turned forty. Couldn't the customers get on with their lives and just let him park the damn cars?

The Audi guy cleared his throat. "Well, if anyone asks, like a detective or something, I'd appreciate it if you don't mention that I come by Donna's sometimes. I don't want any misunderstandings with my wife, you know what I mean?"

Before Tyler knew what had happened, he felt a stack of bills being folded into his palm. Instinctively, he pocketed it. A true professional, he didn't break eye contact to look at the denomination of the bills.

In what he hoped was a reassuring manner, he said, "We would never discuss our customers with anyone." Wow! The guy's wife must have hired private detectives to check up on him! It was like something out of an old movie. Tyler was kind of glad to be distracted by this little drama.

AFTER his visit to Dmytro, Vic felt good. He felt so good in fact, that he decided now might be a good time to collect one more car, even if Chip was out of commission for at least a week. Maybe he could make it into a one-man job.

Vic pulled into a convenience store parking lot and gazed down at his smartphone. There, he moved his finger along a Google map of Seattle and took a quick look at the red teardrop shapes that showed the whereabouts of his current fleet, seeking just the right target. Wow! This was a great omen. That red SL55 AMG Mercedes sports sedan Chip had tagged the night he got shot was apparently sitting all by itself on a quiet street in an industrial area that didn't even have sidewalks! A nice secluded spot!

For a second, Vic thought maybe it was a little weird, this Mercedes sitting, presumably, all by itself in such a remote area at night. And then he thought, what the hell, it wouldn't hurt to just take a look.

DMYTRO pulled up to Donna's and waited impatiently while the pale valet there, who seemed to be writing something feverishly in a notebook, finally noticed him, then put down his pad and pen and ambled slowly over to the car.

"Good evening, sir, and welcome to Donna's," he said.

Dmytro didn't bother to reply and tossed the keys at the kid's chest, where they bounced once before landing on the ground with a jangling sound. Then, as the kid bent down to retrieve them, Dmytro shoved him aside and strode into the casino.

Volodya was sitting in his regular corner with a bunch of his cronies, all laughing loudly, drinking heavily, and speaking a mixture of bad Russian and bad English.

Dmytro paused at the entrance to the bar, then gave his cousin an unsmiling combination greeting and summons by lifting up his chin about an inch, then strolled over to the bar. He didn't greet the others. But he gave Sergei Lagunov a nod. He was the only real professional in the bunch. And he might be helpful.

Volodya came over a little unsteadily, sloshing his drink, and joined his cousin there, leering at a large middle-aged barmaid with bleached hair. "Your hair is as golden as the wheat fields of my country," he said. She avoided eye contact, turned her back on him, and began cutting up limes. "I am from Ukraine," he continued, addressing her ample back. "People think I am Russian but it is not same thing."

"We need to talk about what happened at that snotty Italian restaurant," said Dmytro in Ukrainian.

Volodya continued addressing the waitress's back. "You see on the news Russians and Ukrainians are fighting back there, but we leave these problems in the old country."

Volodya shrugged and turned to his cousin. "Someone took a shot at that millionaire," he said. "So what?"

"It doesn't have anything to do with us?"

"No, of course not."

"The Georgian was parking cars when it happened. I don't want them to find out what he's been up to."

"Stealing from us!" said Volodya in a low menacing voice. "With his little buddy Cheep. That's what the little fuck has been up to." Volodya slammed his fist on the bar. "Dmytro, why do you take this from those two guys! Even if we let them do business outta there, we deserve a percentage."

Dmytro switched to English to order a beer, then turned back to his cousin and switched back to Ukrainian. "You are right, of course. We can't allow this insolence."

Volodya gave a kind of snort that seemed to indicate simultaneous indignation and agreement.

Dmytro sighed. Sometimes, he wondered if it wouldn't be better just to scale back on his lifestyle. Relax a little, and go back to regular body and fender work.

Volodya knocked back the rest of his drink and lurched slightly to one side. "You need to think bigger, Dmytro. You can't go soft."

Dmytro didn't answer. He decided he had to tell his cousin about Vic's uncle in Tbilisi. "For God's sake, Volodya, don't talk about any of this with your pals over there." He indicated the Slavic posse in the corner of the bar with a lateral movement of his eyes. "That Vic came over to my house. And he told me his uncle and his cousin are big players back in the old country. *Vory.*"

Volodya looked flabbergasted. "Really?"

"So we can't mess with him until we know for sure. First, we're gonna find out if it's true. Put Sergei on it. The Georgian used to hang with him right in this very bar. Hell, that's how we got mixed up with him in the first place. Sergei recruited him. Tell Sergei I want to talk to him. Bring him by the house. In a couple of hours."

Dmytro rose to go, but Volodya grabbed his cousin's plump hand as it rested on the bar. "I swear to Almighty God, Dmytro, whoever this kid's relatives are, we gotta do something. If you don't take care of this, I will."

In the corner of the room, Sergei Lagunov watched the Zelen-ko cousins huddled at the bar, their large heads down close together in a conspiratorial way. Something big was up. And he could tell from their body language that there was clearly tension between them.

Dmytro looked at his cousin's scowling face. "Just relax," he said. "I've got it covered. And don't do anything without consulting me." He held up his hand like a cop stopping traffic. Volodya turned away from him with a disgusted look.

Sergei smiled, a maneuver that tilted his scar in a quirky way. This was all very promising.

CHAPTER SEVEN

///

VIC KILLED HIS LIGHTS AND slowly patrolled the area. This was perfect. He was in Ballard, a Seattle neighborhood that a hundred years ago had been a Scandinavian town of shingle mills and fishing boats, and that now sported masses of high-rise condos and chic little clubs, restaurants, and shops.

But the old Ballard lingered along the edge of Salmon Bay, and at this time of night this little remaining slice of working waterfront was pretty much deserted and poorly lit.

Vic found the Mercedes, a shiny red presence sitting in solitary splendor as if it had been Photoshopped into its surroundings, in a gravel parking lot near the waterfront on the other side of the old Burlington Northern railroad track, tucked behind a cinderblock building that housed a marine electrical company and next to a little creosoted wharf where an Alaska crabber was moored.

Okay, so maybe alone he couldn't get it stored safely away, but he could sure as hell move it somewhere else and pick it up later at his convenience when Chip was available or whatever. If he had to, he could even take the bus back from the storage unit. This was a very sweet car.

With his lights back on, Vic drove his own car back to Ballard Avenue, a busy venue at this time of night, and angle-parked on a quaint street outside a French restaurant. He set out on foot to the Mercedes.

Vic was feeling pretty good. He'd been depressed, thinking Chip's hospital stay would really slow things down and mess up their deadline, but now Vic congratulated himself on his resourcefulness. Compared to those thuggy chop-shop losers in their stupid track suits, he was a smooth criminal genius.

He walked carefully over to the car, rolling along on the balls of his feet to keep the sound of the gravel down, and then walked up to the passenger door with his duplicate key. Right before he did, he noticed the windows seemed all steamed up, and right after he actually opened the door and prepared to slide behind the wheel, he noticed the soles of a pair of female naked feet about a foot and a half apart, that were firmly pressed against the rear passenger-side window.

Then he heard a woman's frightened voice whimpering, "Oh my God!" and a man's angry voice snarling, "What the hell!"

Vic stood there for a second. Standing there was a stupid thing to do, he later realized, but he was in a state of shock. Time seemed to stand still as he watched the man pull himself off the woman, and fumble with a belt. Behind him, Vic got a vague impression of a chubby woman with a partially buttoned blouse and a lacy bra around her neck covering her face with her hands. He also found himself thinking that he should have thought longer and harder about why a car would be parked here all by itself at night away from any possible place its owner would want to be at.

By the time Vic had taken all this in, the guy was out of the car. He seemed to roll and eject himself out of the rear passenger door like a trained paratrooper. Vic came to his senses, turned and ran. The man in the car, short and muscular, was in pursuit, tugging on his zipper.

Some time later, after Vic had been tackled; after he had felt himself being flipped over on his back; after he had received a punch to the face; after he had been relieved to hear the woman say, "Justin, stop it. We have to get out of here"; after he had denied vehemently between blows that he was a private detective, while she continued whimpering, "Oh my God," over and over again; and after he had been kicked a few times in the kidneys and left to lie in the fetal position in the gravel as the car took off, Vic reflected that he was pretty damn lucky. They hadn't stopped to ask him how come he had a key to their car.

ROGER Benson was eating a ham sandwich in front of his computer when his wife, Ingrid, came into his office. Tyler's mother was a tall, blond, well-groomed woman with a solid jaw and piercing blue eyes. "What are you doing?" she asked.

Ingrid had been so down on him since last night at Alba, he'd been kind of hiding out in his office whenever she was home.

"Oh, I'm working on my website," he said, twirling around in his office chair.

Ingrid executed the eye roll that was becoming a bad habit. "Whatever. Did you tell Samantha she could have the credit card back?"

"I told her to ask you."

"The correct answer was no," said Ingrid. "We cannot *use* the credit card," said Ingrid. "We have to try and *pay off* that credit card. The only money we can *use* is my salary. Or what's left of it after we make payments on the credit card."

"It's going to be okay," said Roger. He rose and walked toward her, and gave her a warm smile. "I'm putting together a pitch for Scott Duckworth." He put his arms around her.

In an extremely deft maneuver that Ingrid had never performed before, shimmying her shoulders and doing something with her elbows, she managed to unwrap his arms smartly from her torso. He found them dangling limply at his sides.

"Don't touch me," she said, wheeling away and leaving the room.

Roger sighed. Fate had sent Tyler to Alba to cross paths with Scott. It was even an *Italian* restaurant. How significant was that! But it had all gone so badly. First Tyler had manhandled him out of there. His own son! Just for wearing slippers! And then someone had tried to assassinate Scott that same night! You'd think that would make Scott realize the only people he could trust were his old associates.

It could still work out. Roger went to his laptop's Sent file to refresh his memory about the message he'd sent to the Scott and Carla Duckworth Foundation's "Contact Us" link before he'd decided to go casually run into Scott at Alba. Things had been kind of a blur that evening.

"Hey Scott," it read.

> Remember me? Roger Benson? I understand you'll be at Alba tonight. What a coincidence! So will I. I'm really excited about seeing you again after all these years. In fact, I've been waiting a long time for our paths to cross again. I'll never forget my experience at DuckSoft and I'd love to talk to you about how my life worked out. You were a key part of it all. And there's also something really important I'd like to communicate to you about how we could be intertwined again and your possible future. Here's a hint: think "taking out."
>
> Say, does Helene Applegate still work for you? She was a great gal! So loyal and kind. And such a sweet face. I must admit—I had a HUGE crush on her. Whoever snagged her is one lucky guy. What a woman! If you know where she is these days, could you send me her contact details?
>
> Well Scott, I'm off to meet you now. Think of it as a rendezvous with destiny.
>
> Best Regards, Roger Benson

Roger was somewhat taken aback. He'd forgotten he'd put that stuff in there about Helene. Thank God there weren't a bunch of typos. He must have been sober enough to spell-check. But that "think 'taking out'" line was really a kind of clunky teaser for a pitch to get help launching the Ricotteria concept. He hoped he'd hear from Scott soon. It was natural he hadn't had time to reply. After all, someone had just tried to kill him. He was probably pretty distracted right now. He'd probably get in touch soon. And maybe he'd even tell him where to find Helene.

VOLODYA Zelenko and Sergei Lagunov were headed north along a curving wooded stretch of old Highway 99 at about eighty miles an hour, on their way to Dmytro's house as he had requested, when Sergei heard the sirens. Volodya presumably couldn't hear them because he was singing at the top of his lungs.

Sergei, noticing back at Donna's that Volodya was fairly drunk, had suggested they take some side roads to approach Dmytro's house for their meeting, but Volodya had taken no notice.

Now, Sergei punched Volodya's arm. "Cops!" he shouted. "Listen! You should have taken those side roads like I said."

Volodya stopped singing, said, "No problem," and steered off the highway onto a side road with squealing brakes.

"If they pull you over, they might search us," said Sergei. "You still have that gun?"

"I have to keep driving. I can't get another DUI," said Volodya. "My cousin will kill me."

"The gun you killed Old Pasha with?" continued Sergei. The sirens were getting closer. Sergei was thinking quickly. He wasn't the driver. They couldn't do anything to him. But they still might search him.

Sergei had two objectives in mind. Get out of here before the cops came and wondered who he was. And make it to that appointment with Volodya's cousin Dmytro. He'd been waiting to have a talk with him for some time. It would be better without Volodya.

"Give me that gun," he said. "Let me run for it. They can only get you for being drunk. You don't want to be found with that gun!"

Volodya, crinkling his eyes and trying to navigate in the dark, seemed not to hear him. They turned a corner. It was now clear that the sirens were behind them on this side road.

Sergei yelled, "I don't want you to get busted. I'm younger and fitter. If you don't give me the gun, they'll arrest you and put you in jail. Me, they might just deport. No big deal."

Before Volodya had a chance to mull this over, Sergei shoved Volodya and cranked the steering wheel off the road, pointing the car into a ditch. The car landed nose down, the windows surrounded by dense branches of alder trees. Volodya's head hit the windshield and the horn started to sound.

Sergei reached over into Volodya's jacket and pulled out the .22. Then he leapt out of the car and thrashed through some shrubbery. He had expected to end up in some forested area, but was astonished to see himself standing in what appeared to be a large, scrubby yard of poorly tended lawn with a plastic children's wading pool, a rusted lawnmower, and some tricycles strewn around. Across the lawn he saw a ranch style house with a satellite dish on the roof, a carport with a green Ford pickup truck, a collection of junker cars, and a listing shed. He was also disconcerted to see a large dog dish.

From the other side of the shrubbery he'd just blasted through, Sergei now heard the siren give its last scream, and the crackle of a police radio. A light went on the house. Sergei now took off across the lawn and neatly vaulted a chain-link fence, landing in a neighboring yard. There was an unlocked older Toyota pickup truck sitting right there in the driveway. He was in luck. These were a lot easier to hotwire than old Fords. Sergei got behind the wheel, spent about forty seconds fiddling around under the dash, and was soon back on the road.

Chapter Eight

"PRETTY STRAIGHTFORWARD," said Lukowski. "He was shot in the head at very close range. Cheap .22 pistol." That morning, Lukowski and his partner MacNab, both Seattle homicide detectives, had gone to the Smethursts' soon after the body had been discovered. Caroline Smethurst had been, naturally, pretty hysterical, and there was a big dog jumping up on everyone, and a spoiled-brat kid, and eventually the husband Gary arrived from work. The Smethursts explained that the last time the car had not been in their garage and was unattended had been the night before, when the couple had been at Alba, having an aborted anniversary dinner.

Now, the two detectives were on night shift in their joint cubicle eating a quick takeout teriyaki chicken, and Lukowski was bringing MacNab, who had spent the afternoon in court on the witness stand, up to speed on the coroner's report.

Lukowski, tall and thin, with prematurely gray hair, and wearing a dark suit, picked carefully through the meal with wooden chopsticks, avoiding the rice. He had gained five pounds this month, and he was trying to cut down on carbs. MacNab, shorter, rounder, and older, with thinning hair and an orange-looking sports jacket, had stirred his portion together with his plastic fork and was leaning over the little cardboard serving dish and shoveling it in in a workmanlike manner. "What can they tell us about him before he got shot?" asked MacNab.

"Well-nourished Caucasian male. About sixty-five. A lot of gold dental work. They think it might not have been done in this country. A couple of nasty scars on the torso. Look like they might have been made with a knife. A while ago. Smoker. Clogged arteries. And he'd packed away a lot of booze by the time he got killed. His liver looked like Swiss cheese."

"Doesn't fit any of the missing persons we checked out," said MacNab. Recently disappeared local white males had included an elderly man who had wandered away from a nursing home, a vegan college student who had told friends he intended to go into the wilderness and live off the land, and a thirty-seven-year-old self-employed housepainter who was getting leaned on for ten thousand dollars' worth of back child support payments. "It might be hard to ID him."

Lukowski handed over some glossy color photos. "Maybe it won't," he said. "The guy was covered in tattoos. But we'll start with releasing an artist's sketch to the media."

MacNab took a look at the shots. "That's some pretty ugly ink," he commented. Indeed, the blue tattoos looked smudgy. "Look at this. A couple of kitty-cats and a rose. And a couple of stars on his knees."

"Keep going," said Lukowski.

MacNab riffled through the shots. A couple of menacing floating eyes, barbed wire, a dagger.

"I don't care how many guys have tattoos these days," said MacNab. "It just doesn't seem like a manly thing to do—decorate yourself like that." He frowned and reexamined the floating eyes. "This looks kinda familiar." MacNab started tapping away at his computer.

"Hey," he said. "I was right. Those are classic Russian mafia tattoos. It says so right here on Wikipedia."

"Maybe Auto Theft knows who this guy is," said Lukowski. "Russians love to steal cars. Maybe they end up shooting each other, too."

"Try the auto guys up in Everett, too," said MacNab. "They got a ton of Russian chop-shops up there."

Lukowski looked down at the valet tag on his desk, the one that had been placed on Smethurst's key chain at Alba. "But let's make sure Smethurst is totally cleared. I can't imagine for a minute he's got anything to do with this, but let's cross him off the list right away."

"Any word yet if the bullet in tattoo guy's forehead matches the ones that shot up Duckworth's car?" asked MacNab. "It's pretty weird—a body and a shooting the same night in the same place."

"I talked to Debbie Myers in Crimes Against Persons. She's working that Duckworth case. They got the bullet out of the valet who took it for Duckworth. She says they're still digging bullets out of the vehicle."

MacNab nodded. "Anything on the suitcase?"

"No tags or airline baggage-handling barcodes or anything. The suitcase is a pretty ordinary Samsonite suitcase. Black nylon. Macy's sells about a jillion of them."

"How come luggage always seems to be on sale at Macy's?" said MacNab. "It's never not on sale."

Lukowski shrugged. "Beats me. Anyway, it also seems that the gray Audi is covered in prints. So maybe we can get a break from that. There are some really clear ones around the trunk area."

AFTER alighting from the truck a few blocks from Dmytro Zelenko's circular driveway, Sergei Lagunov tucked his black shirt into his trousers and brushed off the shoulders, lapels, and knees of his suit, then ran a hand over his hair. He hoped there weren't any leaves or twigs sticking to him.

On the ride over, he had thought about what he would tell Dmytro about his cousin when they met, and what he would omit. One thing he would certainly omit for now was what had happened to Old Pasha. That little episode had given him a keen insight into Volodya's character. Whatever other shortcomings he may have had, he wasn't afraid to kill.

Dmytro answered the door with one hand on the collar of a

frisky-looking Rottweiler. Sergei hoped the old guy could control this animal better than he controlled his cousin.

"You wanted to see me?" said Sergei.

"Yes. Please come in. But where's Volodya?"

"I think maybe he's in jail," said Sergei, managing to give the impression he was sorry to pass along news of this development but felt it his duty to do so. "He was drunk and the police pulled us over in his car. I wanted to protect him from any serious trouble. He had a gun on him and I took it away with me, and escaped."

Dmytro nodded. "I see. Where's the gun now?" he asked.

Sergei smiled. "I got rid of it during my escape. In case I was caught and it was traced to Volodya. I doubt he's allowed to carry a gun. Didn't he do some time?"

Dmytro pushed the door closed and locked it.

An elderly female voice called out from somewhere in the house. "Dmytro? Is my ride here?"

Outside, Sergei heard a car pull up.

A pale old woman with her hair arranged in a wispy bun appeared in the foyer. She wore a drab floral-print housedress, and carried a cracked plastic handbag in one hand and a huge Bible with Post-it notes sticking out of it in the other. She wasn't fresh off the boat, thought Sergei, because she wasn't wearing a scarf on her head, but that's about all that had changed. He acknowledged her with a polite nod.

Dmytro spoke briefly to her in Ukrainian, then turned to Sergei. "Go on into the living room and sit down. My mother is going out. Her ride seems to have just arrived. I'll see her out."

Sergei looked down at the Rottweiler, and held out his hand. The dog licked it and padded away. Sergei followed it into the living room where another one lay in front of the fireplace. The second animal stared at Sergei with a bored expression, then put its head down on the carpet.

Dmytro bustled back into the room, self-possessed once again. "You want a drink?" He strode over to a well-stocked bar.

"Sure. You got any cognac?"

Dmytro poured himself a shot of vodka and handed a cognac

to Sergei in a balloon-shaped glass. "I appreciate your helping out. You're sure that gun is lost?"

"Absolutely," said Sergei. "I threw it off a bridge."

Dmytro pulled out his wallet and handed five hundred-dollar bills to Sergei. "I appreciate it. Quick thinking. Now I want you to do another little job for me. I'm interested in Victor Gelashvili. Tell me everything you know about him."

Sergei slipped the bills into his pocket right next to Volodya's pistol. "He used to spend a lot of time in the bar at Donna's," said Sergei. "He talked to us a lot. He parked cars there. Then he parked cars at that Italian restaurant, but he still came and hung out with us at Donna's. His parents are Russian, and he speaks it pretty well. He told us about the kind of cars he was parking there, and I asked him if he'd like to make some money and hooked him up with Volodya. So now he works for Volodya. Like me. His buddy Chip helps him out. They scout cars for us, slap a device on them so we can find them, get the manufacturers' key codes if they can so we can get dupes made, and we give them a commission on every one that works out."

"But what do you know about him personally?"

"Hardly anything," said Sergei. "What do you want to know?" Presumably, Dmytro wanted to know if, as Volodya believed, Vic was helping himself to what belonged to the Zelenko cousins.

"He says he has uncle in Tbilisi. A *vor*. Do you believe this?"

Sergei shrugged. He wasn't expecting this. "There are a lot of them in Georgia. Hard men."

Dmytro nodded. "I know before you came here, you lived in Brighton Beach."

Actually, Sergei had lived in Long Beach, California, but that wasn't the story he'd told Volodya. He'd also hinted to Volodya that he was part of a witness protection program, but not because he'd ratted out anyone from his own organization. He had, he explained, sent some Italian mafiosi to prison for messing with the Russians.

"That's right. But I don't want that to get around. It's a delicate situation."

"Yes, I understand completely," said Dmytro. "I was wondering if you were able to find out some way, or if perhaps you had heard something. He said it was his father's brother, so the man's name would be Gelashvili. And his first name was Ivan. His son Gleb is also involved."

Sergei looked doubtful. "I can maybe find out for you. But there are quite a few Gelashvilis in Georgia. You said from Tbilisi?"

Just then, Dmytro's cell phone rang. He pulled it out of his pocket and looked down. "Bah!" he said. "The county jail!" A second later, he began shouting in Ukrainian. As a Russian speaker, Sergei understood enough to get the gist. Dmytro cursed Volodya out, said he should never have called, and refused to make bail for him. "My stupid fucking cousin," said Dmytro with an exasperated look.

"You must be worried about him," said Sergei.

IT was quarter to two in the real world, but in the bar at Alba the clock already said two to give the staff time to clear out everyone by legal closing time. The foodie conventioneers were apparently closing the bar, judging by the cluster of Hertz, Budget, Alamo, and Avis key chains on the board, so Tyler expected them all to come out at the same time, any minute now.

Sure enough, they swarmed out together a few minutes later, all chatty and bouncy after hours of eating and drinking.

"I hope you enjoyed your evening here at Ristorante Alba," said Tyler with as much conviction as he could muster. He sure as hell hadn't enjoyed his evening here, wondering the whole time if the valet area would get shot up again. And the tips weren't that great. Foodies saved their generosity for inside the restaurant so they could suck up to the wait staff. And they usually weren't out on dates trying to impress women.

"Oh my God, we sure did!" said one effusive female foodie with a New York accent. "We got to meet Chef Torcelli and everything! We got a tour of the kitchen!"

Chef Torcelli? Tyler was startled. That was Flavia's name.

She must be married to the owner. That explained why she seemed to be running the place. So maybe she didn't want to be Mrs. Duckworth after all. Or maybe she did. Maybe the chef was just a first husband.

"Everyone knows Piedmont is the new Tuscany," said her companion, a lady with a purple hat. "But what's so exciting is how they're taking it to a whole new level here." She was digging in her purse looking in vain for her ticket. "I know it's in here somewhere." She paused her search briefly to describe to Tyler what she had eaten. "We started with a really simple carpaccio—"

Tyler cut her off. "I'm glad you had a great time," he said, resisting the temptation to tell her about the excellent chicken burrito from the food truck down the street he'd had earlier.

"And Flavia is so *sweet!*" said the first woman. "And so brave! Opening up right away after that terrible tragedy. We wanted to come and show our support and they really appreciated it."

"That's great," said Tyler. "Why don't you step to the side and find that ticket, while I help someone else." Flavia hardly struck him as sweet. And how brave did you have to be *inside* the restaurant. He was the one in the line of fire.

He turned to the large bearded man who was next in line. "Ford Escape SUV, right?" he said, taking his ticket and handing it to another valet. This guy had come in with about a half dozen people, so as soon as he got them packed into their vehicle and on the road he'd have cleared out half of them.

After the last car left, he organized his tips, putting all the bills face up with the heads in the same direction and sorting them by denomination. Tyler was astonished to find a roll of six fifties in there. Apparently, the gray Audi guy who'd come in earlier to ask him not to rat him out to his wife had slipped him three hundred bucks.

Chapter Nine

BEFORE HE WENT INTO Jessica's office, to pick up his last check from Donna's, Tyler had told himself not to tell her about the way things had gone wrong at Donna's during one of his last shifts there. But he couldn't stop himself.

It had been a nightmare. Logan had used a customer's car to go out and get something to eat. The customer was an old guy with a beloved 1988 Oldsmobile he'd bought new. The guy had stood there at the valet booth for twenty minutes, saying, "Where the hell is my car?"

"When the car finally came back, it smelled of burgers and fries, but thank God the old guy hadn't noticed! You should get rid of him!" said Tyler.

"I can't get rid of him," said Jessica. "Donna's his aunt. Logan's cousin Hughie won't let us. And we owe Hughie big time. It goes beyond Donna's."

"What do you mean?"

"Hughie got us the Alba account. Don't ask me how."

"You're kidding."

"It was amazing. He just told me to go down there and it would be a done deal. I talked to that Italian gal for ten minutes and she didn't say anything or ask any questions about us. She just fired the old valet company and hired us, like Hughie said she would. And it's a prime account."

Tyler mulled this over. It seemed unlikely that Hughie would have any influence over Flavia Torcelli.

"So you're on full time at Alba for now," said Jessica. "A couple of guys quit after the shooting. And Vic will be Shift Lead until Chip gets back."

Just then, two men walked into the tiny office.

"Oh," said Jessica, looking animated. "You're those detectives." Tyler assumed they had something to do with the shooting. This could be interesting.

"That's right," said the younger one with the gray hair. He handed over a business card, which Jessica examined carefully. "I just want to double check," he said. He held out a valet tag, the kind Tyler attached to bunches of keys every night. Green cardboard. A printed number in black. The Elite logo in pink.

"Yeah, that's ours," said Jessica.

Lukowski nodded. "So we're talking about a gray Audi, two nights ago at Alba. The party had to leave early. You wouldn't keep any record of that, would you?"

"No, not really," said Jessica. "The tag is only there to match the keys to the right car. It's not any kind of permanent record. Maybe the valet might remember."

Gray Audi? Suddenly Tyler realized that these guys weren't investigating the shooting. They must be private detectives after the poor jerk who tipped him three hundred bucks last night to hide the fact that he hung out at Donna's Casino after work. Maybe the guy's wife had found this tag and had hired these guys to track his movements. He wasn't sure why Jessica would be so cooperative with a couple of private detectives. It seemed to him that they shouldn't be discussing people whose cars they parked.

But how had they known the tag came from Alba? They were all the same. Maybe the wife had found it and the husband had sworn it was from Alba. Which it actually could have been, seeing as they had both been there two nights ago.

"We'll check," said the second man. "Just wanted to confirm that was your tag."

"Oh sure," said Jessica.

"Thanks for your time," said the shorter, older guy in the orange-looking sports jacket. He turned around and nodded at Tyler also. Their eyes locked, and Tyler suddenly felt a little sleazy, remembering that three hundred dollars. He cast his gaze away.

AS MacNab and Lukowski got back into their car, Lukowski said, "Did I tell you I got an update from Debbie Myers in Crimes Against Persons? The Duckworth car is *still* at the lab. You know how long Ballistics takes. I'm going to try and get them to check out the bullet we took out of tattoo guy with the valet's at the same time. I figure we can get some answers faster if we piggyback on her case."

"Good idea," said MacNab. "Scott Duckworth has got to be more important than our dead guy. As far as I know, our guy isn't a pal of the mayor's. What else did Debbie say?"

"She said it seemed like a semi-pro drive-by. Powerful Camaro, the kind of thing you'd steal for a job like that. Only weird thing they haven't figured out yet is a bedroom slipper they found at the scene. They're not sure if it's related, but no one could account for it."

Lukowski looked thoughtful. "Could be some kind of gang calling card."

"Yeah," said MacNab. "Like that restaurant union guy back in the eighties who had parmesan sprinkled all over him."

"You're kidding," said Lukowski.

"Before your time," said MacNab. "They found him dead in his own bathtub. Not your typical Seattle killing, that's for sure."

"Let's go over there and check the place out. Where the car was parked and all that," said Lukowski. "While we're there we can see if the valet remembers Smethurst and his wife. That gal was a little vague about where that tag came from."

"I didn't like the look of that kid in there with her," commented MacNab. "He's good for something. He had a guilty, weasely kind of look. Wonder what *he's* got to hide."

"Probably lifting meter money from the beverage holders in the cars he parks, one quarter at a time," said Lukowski.

RED Ott hadn't wanted to climb into the Dumpster, but he figured he had to. If only he'd been able to get back sooner and retrieve his weapon from the garbage can outside the restaurant door. But he'd been tied up in meetings and eventually he'd had to escort Scott Duckworth to the airport where he had flown off in his business jet to a comics convention in San Diego.

He had staked the place out and discovered that the garbage can outside the restaurant got emptied into this Dumpster. Fortunately it was out of the line of sight from the restaurant's back door, halfway down a hill by what was apparently the restaurant's rear and hidden parking lot.

He had chosen three in the afternoon for this retrieval operation. He figured there wouldn't be any action here now. The lunch trade would be over and dinner wouldn't have started yet.

Sighing, Red removed his light tweed jacket, folded it neatly, and laid it down on the asphalt next to the Dumpster. Then he pulled himself up to the metal lip a few feet from the ground and grabbed the top, doubting that he actually could pull himself up and over the edge, but knowing he had to. The Dumpster had two sections to its lid. He'd be able to look down into it from the top of the closed part. After a few attempts, he managed to scramble up onto the top.

Lukowski and MacNab were now walking down the path of boards over damp grass, following Flavia Torcelli, who managed to pick her way rather neatly across the hardscrabble terrain, even in her heels. "You'll need to talk to the valets themselves," she said, "but this is where the cars go."

Ott, splayed out on the Dumpster, looked over his shoulder and decided he really didn't want the babe from Alba to know he was diving into her Dumpster. How could he explain that? He had a vague impression that she was accompanied by two men, but he didn't stop to scrutinize them, he just slid into the Dumpster, feet first, and hoped he'd land on something stable.

To his horror, he landed on another human being, who was

moving in an agitated manner and yelling in fear. He then took a header into something damp and clingy and scrambled to get himself vertical again. Now he was staring into the gnarled face of a grizzled old bum with a bushy beard and the stench of stale booze mixed with urine.

Red Ott screamed.

Before he knew what was happening, two male faces appeared above him looking into the Dumpster.

"What are you guys up to?" demanded MacNab. "Get the hell out of there."

It took Red Ott and the bum a while to clamber out.

MacNab picked up the tweed jacket Ott had carefully folded and laid down. "Which of you gentlemen owns this?" he asked.

"That's mine," said Ott.

Flavia Torcelli had now picked her way over to the Dumpster. She stood back a little, but was watching, clearly fascinated.

"Madonna!" she said. "It's Mr. Ott."

Red sighed. "That's right. Doing a little follow-up on the security here, and I saw this guy acting suspicious."

Lukowski turned to Flavia. "You know him?"

"He's a bodyguard for Scott Duckworth," she said. "What's he doing here? It's where we throw our garbage."

Ott was struggling to get back into his jacket. "Bodyguard? Actually I am the Chief Executive Security Officer. Like I said, Mr. Duckworth, against my advice, has shown an interest in returning to this restaurant, despite an assassination attempt." He glanced over at Flavia. "Against all my professional advice."

"Oh really? Scott's coming back?" said Flavia with a big smile. "I was afraid he'd never come back to Alba."

Now the grizzled bum spoke up. "The food's excellent," he explained helpfully.

MacNab glanced at the Dumpster. "Is that why you were in there?"

"Well, yeah," said the bum. "I didn't mean any harm. I'm an urban scavenger. It's terrible what people throw away. 'Course now, people are supposed to recycle food scraps. But there's still sometimes some perfectly good stuff in there."

Flavia crossed her arms, frowned, and turned to Ott. "If you want to check this place out you should have come to me and told me what you are doing. Not climb into the Dumpster behind my restaurant. It's not dignified."

The grizzled bum seemed annoyed that no one was paying attention to him. "There's perfectly good stuff in there," he repeated.

"There's other places to get food," said MacNab. "You should stay out of Dumpsters. It's dangerous."

"Not all of the good stuff I find is food," said the bum. "Bet you'll never guess what else I found in there."

"What?" demanded Flavia. "What else did you find?"

"Never mind," said the bum craftily. "Can I go now?"

"Mind turning out your pockets?" said Lukowski.

The bum thought about it for a minute.

"It's a misdemeanor to go Dumpster diving," said MacNab.

The bum thought about it a little longer.

"Just turn 'em out, okay?" said Lukowski. "My latex gloves are in the car."

The bum started to do as he was told. Ott watched, transfixed. To his relief, the bum only produced a couple of bus transfers, some cigarette butts, a pencil, a can opener, and some string.

MacNab turned to Ott. "Okay, we've established why *he* was in there. What were *you* doing in there?" He narrowed his eyes. "You look kinda familiar. Haven't I had some dealings with you before?"

Ott smoothed down his comb-over. "Not that I recall. I told you. I'm checking security. And I'm glad I did because I've now ascertained that Dumpster could harbor someone with evil intent," said Ott triumphantly.

"Both you guys should stay the hell out of Dumpsters," said MacNab.

Lukowski turned to Flavia. "Thanks for showing us the area," he said. "We'll go back up now and question the valets."

Ott decided that there was no way he could risk going back in there. He'd have to hope that the Dumpster service would come and toss this whole load into the back of a truck soon and that the gun would end up in some landfill somewhere. Too bad. It was a really sweet weapon. But under the circumstances, Ott hoped it was gone forever.

CHAPTER TEN

//

IT WAS ABOUT FIFTEEN MINUTES after Lukowski and MacNab left the lower parking area at Alba that Tyler pulled his car into a slot there. He was making his way past the Dumpster area, when he noticed a skinny blond girl and a guy who seemed to be an elderly street drunk, with a horrible-looking white beard and a big overcoat that Tyler imagined he'd picked up at some mission somewhere.

Suddenly he heard her scream, "Give it to me!"

"No," said the old man. "I found it. It's mine."

The girl lunged at the old man. If it had been the other way around he supposed he'd have to come to her aid. But then he saw what they were struggling over. The old bum was holding a gun in his hand, high above his head, and she was scrabbling at his arm.

Without thinking, Tyler approached them. "Stop it. You'll kill someone!"

Both of them turned to look at him and he wondered what he had been thinking.

"I found it, fair and square," said the old man. To Tyler's relief, the old guy lowered his arm and examined the gun, a snub-nosed revolver, with a happy, toothless smile. The barrel was now pointing away from the girl and from Tyler.

"I was just trying to take it away from him before he kills someone," said the girl unconvincingly.

The old man laughed. "The cops tried to take it away from me, too, but this coat is top quality. It has an inside pocket."

He flapped it open to show a pocket in the stained silk lining, and then waved the gun in the girl's direction.

"Give it to me," she said.

"Ah, hell," said the old man. "You just want to sell it for some of that shit you're strung out on. It's worth something all right."

"Let's see it," said Tyler, in a friendly tone meant to convey he might be a buyer.

The old drunk handed it to him. The girl turned and said accusingly, "Who the fuck are you anyway?" to Tyler. "Why are you wearing that stupid jacket?"

"I'm in charge of this parking lot," said Tyler, stepping away and putting the gun in his jacket pocket. He didn't know enough about guns to know how to open it up and see if it was loaded. He strode purposefully away. The girl scampered back down the alley, and the old man said, "Hey. That's mine, I found it," but he didn't seem to be interested in taking any action to reclaim his possession.

Tyler would turn it over to Alba security, if there was such a thing, as soon as he could. He'd suggest they move that Dumpster closer to the kitchen, where maybe they could get a security camera pointed at it. If people just thought about it a little bit, everything could be better organized around here. Alba might seem slick with that Italian hostess and all, but in some ways it was creepier than Donna's.

MACNAB and Lukowski were in front of Alba. They were showing driver's license photos of both Smethursts to a valet named James Sorensen. Shift Lead Vic Gelashvili, sporting a swollen lip and a bruise on his cheekbone, stood by. James was drawing a blank.

"What kind of car are we talking about?" he asked.

"Audi S4, gray."

James perked up and handed back the photos. "Oh. Yeah. It had the XM satellite radio and the GPS was going with a big arrow pointed to here. There was dog hair and that kind of dog funk smell. The transmission was sticky."

A car pulled up and James grabbed a ticket from the box behind him and bounded toward the passenger door.

"Good evening. Welcome to Alba," he said with what Lukowski thought looked like a totally fake smile. A woman got out of the passenger side and James zipped around to the driver's side, where a fat man struggled to get out from behind the wheel. James grabbed the keys with a flourish, handed over half a ticket, and said, "Welcome to Ristorante Alba, sir." He got into the car and started the engine, but Lukowski yelled, "Hey! Come back here."

"I gotta park this car," said James nervously. "If they pile up here, it's a real problem. 'Cause people want to get out of the car right in front of the door. They get seriously annoyed."

Lukowski ignored this. "Yes, that sounds like the car. A gray Audi. Do you remember *anything* else?"

James scrunched his eyes closed to indicate he was trying hard to remember.

"I think there was maybe a Diet Coke can in the beverage holder."

"What about the *people?*" Lukowski said.

"I don't know," said James. "A man and a lady?" Detective Lukowski sighed. To this kid, all adults were the same.

"Do you remember *when* you parked the car?"

James said, "Well actually, I didn't park it. Like I said, it had a sticky trans—"

Vic Gelashvili spoke up. "I parked it for him," he said. "James has trouble with standard transmissions." James looked away, clearly humiliated, and Vic said, "I think I parked it around six."

MacNab rolled his eyes impatiently. "So do *you* remember these folks?" he flashed the Smethursts' pictures at Vic.

Vic shrugged. "No. Mostly I remember the bad transmission. James had contact with the customers."

"Did you go get it when they left?"

"No. Someone else must have got the car when they left."

"Any idea who?"

James and Vic looked at each other. "Maybe Tyler," said James.

Lukowski showed James the valet tag he'd gotten from the Smethursts' key chain. "So you can't tell from this when he left or anything?" Jessica at the Elite Valet office had already told him that, but experience had told him that people who did the real work often knew more about the details of an operation than their managers. These kids, however, especially James, seemed to grasp very little.

WHEN Tyler arrived at the valet station in front of Alba he was startled to see the two detectives he'd seen earlier at Jessica's office—the tall one with silver hair and the older, barrel-chested one in the orange jacket. They were talking to another valet Tyler knew was called James. The dark-eyed Vic hovered nearby.

The taller detective, the one with the silvery hair, turned toward Tyler. "I remember you," he said. "From over at the Elite Valet office." He handed Tyler a business card and said, "Seattle Police. We need to ask you guys a few questions. I'm Detective Lukowski, and this is Detective MacNab. Are you Tyler?"

Tyler was stunned. He'd assumed they were private detectives, working for the gray Audi guy's wife. But apparently they were actual cops. He felt himself gasp, and he hoped it wasn't audible. But apparently it was, because the other detective, MacNab, turned and gave him a sharp, kind of mean look.

Tyler nodded.

"Vic here says he parked this couple's car night before last. A gray Audi," said Lukowski. He showed Tyler the pictures of the Smethursts. "Did you deliver the car to him?"

"Yes, I did," said Tyler, who immediately felt himself blushing, probably because he felt weird about the three hundred bucks the guy had given him.

"Do you remember what time they left?" asked Lukowski.

"No, not really." Why was Tyler so rattled? It was something about the way the detective named MacNab was looking at him.

"Do you remember anything about them? Did they seem nervous or anything?" asked MacNab.

"The guy was complaining, to his wife," said Tyler. "He said she'd wrecked their dinner, and she said they had no choice. They had to leave early."

"What do you mean 'no choice'?" asked MacNab.

"Well, I just heard part of it while I was getting the keys off the board. She was talking to her husband and what sounded like a kid on her cell at the same time. She told her husband they had to leave because the kid's homework was really important."

Tyler felt he was babbling—overcompensating because he thought he'd come across as evasive in some way, thus getting the dirty looks the older guy was giving him. But he seemed unable to stop himself. "I'm sorry I don't remember when they left, but the guy said he'd only had time for their appetizer. But I bet if you talk to the hostess in there, she can figure out how long they were here based on that and when his reservation was for." Tyler now felt an urge to tell him all about the fact that the guy was a regular at the casino and had been concerned about his wife finding out, but he wasn't quite sure how to bring this up. Instead, Tyler supplied more detail about the transaction here at Alba. "I remember the guy saying something about a diorama. 'Can't the little brat make her own goddamn diorama?' and 'I did just fine doing my own damn homework.' And his wife was all stressed out."

"And what happened when you got their car back to them?" said Lukowski.

"Not much. They got in and drove off." Tyler had to stop babbling, but he was also overwhelmed with curiosity. "What happened?" he asked the detectives. "What did the guy do?" Maybe the gray Audi guy went home and punched out the kid or killed his wife. Or maybe it had something to do with the shooting. But how could that be?

Lukowski said, "These folks found a dead body in the trunk of their car. And they said the vehicle had been out of their hands for just about half an hour, when it was parked here."

"What?" said Tyler. "There was a body in the gray Audi's trunk?" Tyler started to tell the cops he'd seen the trunk partially open and had closed it. It might be important.

But before had a chance to bring this up, Lukowski said, "I

want you to take me down to the lot and show me where you picked up the car."

A VW Golf pulled up and Vic interrupted. "Tyler, take this car. I'll check and see if it's okay to take them back to the lot." He turned back to the cops. "I'll ask the restaurant manager if it's okay to show you the area."

"We're the police," said MacNab to Vic, stepping forward and getting in his face. "We're investigating a homicide. We outrank some guy holding a velvet rope." Now he turned to Tyler. "Any reason you didn't tell us that you delivered that car to them when we were talking to your boss up at the Elite Valet office? Earlier today. You were sitting right there. You heard us say it was a gray Audi."

"I don't know," stammered Tyler. "There's lots of gray Audis. I didn't know you were the police. I thought you were private detectives."

"Why did you think that?" said MacNab.

Tyler decided he'd better go into all that detail about the three-hundred-dollar tip.

Just then however, he was startled to see his mother pull up in the family PT Cruiser. "Hi sweetie," she said out the window. "Sorry to interrupt you, but I wondered if you found Daddy's slipper. The Ugg slippers I got him for Christmas? I know it sounds ridiculous but he said he left it here!"

The two detectives exchanged glances. Lukowski stepped forward.

"What's your full name, son?" he said. "Can I see some ID?"

Tyler reached into his back pocket for his wallet. As he did so, his jacket pocket gaped open.

Before he knew what had happened, Detective MacNab had pinned one of Tyler's arms behind his back, grabbed his face, and yanked his head back while Lukowski reached into his pocket and his mother screamed from the window of the PT Cruiser.

"I was just going to hand that over to you," said Tyler breathlessly. Lukowski had stepped backward and Tyler could see the snub-nosed revolver in his hand.

Chapter Eleven

///

D EBBIE MYERS, THE SEATTLE DETECTIVE who was
investigating the Duckworth shooting at Alba, sat across from
Scott Duckworth's personal assistant, Helene Applegate. Helene
was a small, fit woman in her mid-fifties with dyed auburn hair
in a short, chic cut and a sweet little face with arching eyebrows.

Helene thought Debbie, with her curly brown hair and pleasant smile looked like a nice, friendly person. Helene also loved
watching old "Law & Order" reruns—not the creepy newer ones
that had a lot of sex crimes—so she couldn't resist saying, "Wow!
What an interesting job you have! How did you become a detective?"

"Kind of a family thing," said Debbie. "My dad was a police
officer. But I bet people think you have a pretty interesting job,
too!" She sat in the guest chair opposite Helene's tidy desk in the
office area of the Duckworth compound, and pointed to a framed
picture of a couple of little boys on Helene's desk. "Cute kids!"

"My nephews," said Helene, beaming. "They're a lot bigger
now."

"So, can you think of anyone who would want to harm your
boss?" asked Debbie.

"Well, there are a lot of nuts out there," said Helene. "And
even though Scott tries hard to keep a low profile, it's not always
possible. For one thing, there's his charity work."

"The Duckworth Foundation?" said Debbie.

"That's right. Actually, his sister, Carla, really runs that."

"Is here anything controversial about that?" asked Debbie. "Any causes that might get someone worked up?"

"I doubt it," said Helene. "I mean, Scott feels strongly that we should go to Mars sooner rather than later. And he's interested in alternative human habitats. Like underwater."

What she didn't tell Debbie was that the things Scott really cared about were a small part of the foundation's work. Carla tried to focus more on the arts, so that she could hang out with a bunch of old-money people. Helene's personal opinion was that Carla, a divorcée, was shopping for a new husband, and felt that someone who already had a reasonable amount of money would be more suitable than some fortune hunter after the Duckworth billions.

"How about his business activities?" said Debbie.

Helene said perkily, "Well, he's always looking for new, interesting things to do. I think he's considering investing in Alba." Helene suspected this gourmet stuff was more social climbing by Carla. Scott loved peanut butter and jelly sandwiches and potato chips, stuff like that. Back in the day, she'd made many a PBJ lunch for her boss with a root beer float on the side and brought it to him on a tray at his desk. He'd loved it.

"Oh," said Debbie. "Is that why he was at Alba?"

"I guess so," said Helene. Suddenly her face crumpled a little. "I don't want him to ever go back there! I'm so worried about his security. He could be kidnapped or something! I don't want it to get around that he hangs out there."

"Yes. I already put in a call to Mr...." Debbie looked down at the notebook she held in her lap. "Ott."

Helene's lip curled a little. "Yes. Red Ott. He's in charge of Scott's security."

"Has Scott received any threats?" continued Debbie.

"All the time. I keep a complete file of kooky letters and emails. There's a woman in the U.K. who says she is Scott's twin separated at birth, and there is some weird *Da Vinci Code* kind of stuff, too. There are also a lot of marriage proposals." Helene lowered her voice. "Some of them include very inappropriate pictures of the women."

"Do you have copies of all this stuff?" said Debbie.

"Oh yes," said Helene. "Mr. Ott is not exactly computer-literate, and he goes over it as it comes in so I have to make hard copies. There's a whole box of the stuff."

"I'll want to take a look at that," said Debbie.

"I thought you would," said Helene. "But Mr. Ott carted it all out of here yesterday. Says he's conducting his own investigation." She picked up the phone and pressed a button. "Red, can you bring the nut file in here? Detective Myers wants to see it." She replaced the phone. "He's on his way."

"So was Scott a regular at Alba?" continued Debbie.

"I think he's been there about four or five times. Like I said, he mentioned he might want to invest in an Italian restaurant with authentic cuisine."

Red Ott arrived, carrying a cardboard banker's box. "To be honest," he said, "I think Scott might be more interested in that little Italian hostess they have there than in the food. He's determined to go back there, even though I don't recommend it. But you can kind of understand. She's a real looker."

Ott dumped the box on the desk, and turned to Debbie. "Very young and attractive women are interested in Mr. Duckworth," he said. "It's to be expected. And he's only human!" He chuckled.

How typical, thought Helene, of Red Ott to tell two women who were close to Scott's age that it was natural for him to be interested in twenty-something girls, even if it were true. Annoyed, Helene transferred her gaze to the office window and looked out at the Japanese garden Carla had had installed there. A young woman was carefully raking gravel, and a young man was scrupulously plucking the blossoms off a large rhododendron. Carla had explained that real Japanese gardens weren't supposed to have any actual flowers.

"Oh!" Helene said suddenly. "I just remembered. Another weird email arrived the night it all happened." Hearing from

Roger Benson after all those years had been strange, but she hadn't thought his message was nut-mail material.

She turned to her computer, tapped away until she found the message that had arrived in the inbox of the foundation, then hit Print. As it worked its way out of the printer, she felt a little embarrassed. Roger had actually mentioned her in the email.

"We can review those threatening messages together," said Ott importantly.

"Nope," said Debbie. "I'll just take them with me."

As Debbie skimmed Roger Benson's email she asked Helene, "Would you characterize this individual as a *disgruntled* ex-employee?"

"THE reason I had the gun," said Tyler, sipping at the cardboard-tasting coffee and trying to appear calm in the tiny interrogation room, "is because I took it away from some old drunk guy. I thought it was the right thing to do. He could have killed someone."

Finally! They were getting around to talking about the gun. Before that, Lukowski had asked him a bunch of pointless questions. Tyler had answered them in calm, measured tones. Yes, he'd managed to stay out of trouble since his conviction. He'd paid restitution and done some community service. He'd gone to college back East earlier. It was a small liberal arts college in New England. Yes, New England was nice but it was pretty cold. He didn't graduate because of financial issues. He was finishing up his undergraduate requirements at the University of Washington. He only needed a few more credits. He hadn't been working at Alba for long. In fact the day Scott Duckworth got shot at was his first shift. The detective sounded like a high school guidance counselor instead of a cop.

Lukowski leaned back in his chair. "But it was dangerous to take a loaded gun away from someone."

"I didn't know it was loaded," said Tyler.

"Did you get the old guy's name?"

"No. I was just concerned that he might kill someone. He was kind of weaving around. And there was this girl there with him.

Some pretty marginal people hang around that Dumpster. You guys should check it out. It's in the alley, right next to the lot where we park the cars."

Lukowski waved his hand dismissively. "We're aware of that Dumpster. I know the one you mean."

"I wasn't telling you your job or anything," said Tyler, thinking that perhaps he'd been less than tactful. It was hard to concentrate and answer these dumb questions when all he could think about was Mom and Dad and that slipper. He should have told the cops who were there the night of the Duckworth shooting the truth about the slipper when they asked him. He supposed if they went on to that topic he should just cave, and tell them he knew whose slipper it was but he had just been embarrassed that his dad had been bugging him at work in his slippers.

Lukowski now shook his head slowly while assuming a melancholy expression. Then he locked eyes with Tyler and tilted his head and said very gently, "But you understand what you did, don't you, Tyler? You put yourself in a really bad position."

"Yeah. But the gun didn't go off or anything. I mean maybe it wasn't strictly smart but…"

"I'm not talking about firearms safety," said Lukowski. "You put yourself in big legal trouble. Because you have a record. You're a felon."

"That old charge? That was just a stupid thing," said Tyler. "I mean, since that incident happened, malicious mischief has been reclassified as a misdemeanor."

"Well, it wasn't then. Which makes you a felon in possession of a firearm now. And there was the assault charge, too."

Lukowski looked as if he were sorry about that, but Tyler knew he wasn't sorry at all, he was just playing with him.

"The assault charge was dropped," Tyler said with dignity.

"Yeah, whatever. The fact remains you're still a felon in possession of a firearm."

"Technically," said Tyler. "For maybe two minutes."

Now the other detective, MacNab—Tyler knew their names now—came into the little room. He beckoned to Lukowski, who left, closing the door behind him. Tyler heard the door lock. Through the window, Tyler could see them talking together. MacNab was smiling and waving a piece of paper and now Lukowski was smiling, too, and gave MacNab a cheery high-five. Was this good or bad?

Lukowski returned, carrying the piece of paper. He sat opposite Tyler and seemed to be studying it thoroughly. Tyler sipped more coffee and tried not look rattled. Eventually, Lukowski looked up at him with a sad expression—quite a change from his high-fiving grin glimpsed through the window.

"You already admitted you picked up the gray Audi and returned it to the owners," Lukowski said. "So I can imagine that your fingerprints might be on the driver's door."

"And the passenger door," added Tyler. "To let in the wife."

"So I have a problem, Tyler. Why are they on the trunk?" Lukowski looked back down at the paper. "Looks like both hands, fingers splayed out. They even got a partial palm print on the right hand. So why were you slamming the trunk shut?"

"Because it was open," said Tyler.

"It was?" Lukowski looked confused. "Did you open it?"

"No! I happened to park a car right next to it—a Honda Civic. And when I got out, I was looking at the car and I noticed the trunk was slightly popped, and I thought I should close it."

"I see. Did you look inside the trunk?"

"Well, yeah, just enough to see there was a suitcase there. I thought it was unsafe to leave it open. So as a courtesy to the customer I closed the trunk. Besides, if anything disappears from the cars we park, it's a huge big deal. There are claim forms and stuff."

Lukowski didn't say anything so Tyler added, "I was just about to tell you this when you found the gun."

That whole time period between them finding the gun and then arresting him had been ugly. Not only had Mom been there crying, she'd been there when they ran the warrant check on him and found out he was a felon. Tyler hadn't mentioned that to her before.

She'd tried to argue with the police officers as they were pushing his head down and piling him into the backseat of the car, and finally Tyler had yelled, "Be quiet, Mom. I *am* a felon!" And at this point, Flavia Torcelli had clicked out onto the driveway and witnessed this whole horrible scene.

"Okay," said Lukowski. "So you closed the trunk because it was open. But why are your prints on the latch, too? Sounds like maybe you opened the trunk, too."

Tyler sighed. "I was concerned that there was something wrong with the latch. I checked it out to see if there was something stuck in there that would stop it from closing. Or a bent part or something."

Lukowski was silent.

"I mean, the guy was a regular customer!" said Tyler, alarmed to hear his voice rising. "I have to take care of my customers. If there'd been something wrong I could have alerted him to the fact."

"I'm confused, Tyler," said Lukowski. "You said it was your first day at Alba. How could he have been a regular customer?"

Now Tyler was embarrassed again. "I knew the car from Donna's. That's where I worked before. Elite Valet has a contract for both locations."

"Donna's? That casino down south?"

"That's right." Tyler decided that it was time to talk about the three-hundred-dollar tip. "The guy in the gray Audi came by Alba yesterday and asked me not to tell anyone he hangs out at Donna's after work. I thought maybe you were a private detective working for his wife."

Lukowski didn't look all that interested, but Tyler plunged on. "In fact, he gave me a three-hundred-dollar tip! Now I'm wondering if he was afraid he'd be tied in to the murder or something. Did you *ask* the gray Audi guy *why* he had a body in his car?" Suddenly Tyler realized he sounded ridiculous, and maybe even a little hysterical. They'd told him he could call a lawyer but he didn't think he really needed one. Maybe he did.

"You know what," he said, his voice now calm again, "I want to make a phone call. I get to make a phone call, right? I want to call my grandpa. His name is Gus Iversen."

Chapter Twelve

//

DEBBIE MYERS WAS STILL chatting with Helene in her office about Roger Benson's email. "So were you surprised that Mr. Benson wrote this stuff about you?" The cell phone in her pocket vibrated, and she looked at the phone and saw it was a Seattle police number. "Myers," she said, still scanning the printed-out email message.

"Hey, Debbie, it's MacNab, Homicide. Just wanted you to know. Today, my partner and I were down there at that Alba. We just took away a .38-caliber Smith and Wesson snub-nosed revolver from one of the valets there. Anyway, it looks like this valet's dad was there the night of the shooting, too. While we were there, we learned he left something really weird behind. Our guy's mom was there trying to retrieve it when we found the weapon on the kid."

"Was it a slipper?" said Debbie.

"That's right."

Debbie smiled. "Can you hold the kid?"

"No problem. He's a felon in possession of a firearm."

"Excellent," said Debbie.

"Lukowski's talking to him now. The kid's name is Benson. Tyler Benson."

Debbie scanned the email again. "If his dad is Roger Benson, I'm *really* interested."

Helene stared at her, slightly shocked. "Oh, Roger wouldn't hurt anyone," said Helene. "He might have been kind of a jerk, and kind of stupid, but he was really a sweet person. I always felt kind of sorry for him."

IN the back of the Everett auto body shop where Old Pasha had once worked, Dmytro Zelenko and Sergei Lagunov stood under a huge cherry tree that hadn't been pruned in decades and had achieved an enormous height—presumably a leftover from when the area was somebody's old farm.

But now, it was a weedy mud and gravel yard that looked like a mini–auto wrecking yard or an auto-parts hoarder's lair. Fenders, hoods, and doors were leaning against the fence, and there were also boxes of jumbled hardware—mirrors, trailer hitches—and odd bits and pieces like a rusted-out old burn barrel, some sheets of corrugated siding, and paint-spattered sawhorses.

The two men were watching another man loading up a collection of Cadillacs and SUVs onto a car carrier with two decks. While most of the 2000s Japanese cars that provided a steady supply of used parts were disassembled and distributed locally, the higher-end merchandise was regularly delivered from Seattle to Southern California in a straight shot down Interstate 5 on one of these car carriers.

"So you had this place long?" said Sergei politely.

"Almost thirty years," said Dmytro. "We used to be super busy here night and day. Stripping down those ten-year-old Camrys and Civics. Volodya and I started right out of trade school." He sighed. "I never thought we'd end up in the export business, or that we'd be working with these high-end cars."

"Sometimes when a business grows fast like that, it's not a good thing," said Sergei. "You lose control."

Dmytro nodded. "It was a lot easier back in the day. We just waited till someone brought us a car. Then we parted it out. Or, when we got really fancy, we'd leave the hulks out in the country somewhere, then hustle over to the auto auction to buy the frames and put it all back together again, nice and legal with a real bill of sale." He chuckled nostalgically. "Now I guess I'm a victim of my own success."

"You gotta realize that when you get a nice operation like this, you attract attention," said Sergei. "Hey, since I've been picking up cars for you, I've been curious about how it all works. So you're shipping these high-end cars down to Cali, probably getting them cloned. Hell, I bet the paper on them is so good they can even end up at dealers as fine previously owned vehicles. I'm impressed."

Dmytro waved a hand. "Actually, we got a buyer down there. Guy named Yuri. He handles all that stuff for us. They can't get enough cars down there. I'm happy to be just a wholesaler."

"Still, it's a good business," said Sergei. "You got the sourcing problem all fixed with those valets on the job. You got a good team going out picking them up. I'm proud to be part of it. But like I said, you could attract attention. And maybe you have." He changed his tone from one of fawning congratulations to grim seriousness. "I checked out the Gelashvili kid."

Dmytro looked alarmed. "What did you find out?"

"That guy in Tbilisi? Victor's uncle? He is one mean son of a bitch."

"Goddamn!" said Dmytro under his breath.

"This could be a real problem," said Sergei sympathetically. He let that sink in and then added, "And you got one other problem."

Sergei was delighted to see Dmytro kind of flinch into a hunched posture and look up at him with real fear in his eyes. "What's that?" he said in a small voice.

"Your cousin Volodya," said Sergei. "You may need to do something drastic about him."

TYLER was really embarrassed calling his grandpa. But he didn't trust his parents. For all he knew, they were in another interrogation room somewhere, talking about the slipper.

Gus Iversen was already agitated even before Tyler called to announce that he was being questioned by homicide detectives and that he needed a lawyer.

"What the hell is going on!" said Gus. "Your mother just called and the cops are over at your parents' house right now! She says they hauled you off in a cop car!"

"It's a long story," said Tyler.

"Well, for Christ's sake don't talk about it on the jailhouse phone!" said Gus. "I'll get my lawyer down there right away. Let's hope we can get you sprung before they haul your dad in there. Your mother says the cops think he took a potshot at some millionaire."

"I've always known your dad was kind of a screwball," Grandpa said matter-of-factly. "No common sense. Capable of pretty much anything." Gus Iversen had apparently forgotten about the need to be discreet on a jailhouse phone. "Listen, Tyler. Do you think they're going to arrest you?"

"I don't know," he said.

"If they do arrest you, what'd it be for?"

Tyler didn't want to say he'd be arrested for being a felon in possession of a firearm. He'd never told his grandfather that he actually was a felon, or about that stupid incident back on the night of his twenty-first birthday outside some dive bar in Ballard. The fact that the "weapon" in the case had been a gift from Gus made him feel even worse.

"I don't know, Grandpa," he said. "But I want you to send a lawyer. And don't worry. I can pay him." Tyler had managed to save quite a bit of his tip money. It would be too bad to spend it on a lawyer, but he might have to.

"It's a gal," said Grandpa. "She's a tough cookie. When I found out those tenants up in that little Crown Hill duplex were selling drugs, she put the squeeze on them and blasted them right out of there in no time flat. They didn't wait around to be evicted."

"That's good," said Tyler, beginning to feel a little impatient. Next thing he knew, Grandpa would be talking about a sagging porch at one of his other rentals. "Get her over here when you can, okay?"

"Okay," said Gus Iversen. "I'll hang up now and call her right

away. She's over at your parents' house trying to keep your dad
from saying anything really stupid."

DEBBIE Myers had gone directly from the Duckworth compound
to Ingrid and Roger Benson's large and carefully decorated turn-
of-the-twentieth-century, four-bedroom home on Queen Anne
Hill. She sat in one of two matching wing chairs flanking a large,
tiled fireplace in the Arts and Crafts style. Roger Benson sat in the
other wing chair.

Roger tried to look relaxed, but it wasn't easy, especially not
with Ingrid right there in the matching loveseat that faced the fireplace alongside that disheveled-looking lawyer her dad had sent
over. Veronica Kessler was an ample young woman with a cloud
of frizzy hair sporting a pair of horrible overalls and dirty sneakers. Gus was always meddling. Why did he want a lawyer there? It
would just make him look guilty.

"So you didn't notice that you'd dropped the slipper?" the
detective said. "Didn't it feel weird to drive home with one bare
foot?"

"I didn't actually drive home. My wife came and got me."

"How come?"

Roger looked pained. "I wasn't feeling well." His glance darted over to his wife, who was executing that annoying eye roll that
was becoming a perpetual tic. Detective Myers followed his gaze,
and seemed to take in Ingrid's scorn.

"Had you maybe had too much to drink?" asked Debbie in a
friendly tone.

Veronica picked at the untidy bun on top of her head. "I don't
see how that's relevant," she said. "The fact is, Ingrid went and
picked him up."

Debbie said, "Okay," then turned back to Roger. "Tell me
again why you were there in the first place."

Roger Benson looked more relaxed. "I thought it would be a
good opportunity to reconnect with an old business associate—
Scott Duckworth."

"Your old boss, right? And you knew he was going to be there
because your son told you."

"That's right. I thought Scott might be interested in a little business idea I had. It was kind of an impulsive thing."

"But before you left, you sent an email to Scott Duckworth's website, didn't you? Maybe that was kind of an impulsive thing, too."

"Yes," he said, stretching his arms and arching his back a little trying to look casual, but wondering if he actually looked vaguely simian. "Well, when Tyler mentioned that Scott was going to be there, it got me thinking. I felt kind of nostalgic. I Googled around on the Internet and I discovered a link."

"So you thought you'd say a few words about your old friend Helene, too," said the detective.

"Helene? Yes, I guess so."

Just then, Veronica Kessler's phone rang. She pulled it out of her overalls and murmured, "I have to take this," then went out into the hall.

"Hey, Gus," she said in a low voice. "It's okay. His story is pretty goofy. The most it looks like he's good for is drunk driving. But it's too late to Breathalyze him so they can't get him."

"Never mind him," said Gus. "Get down to police headquarters and see what you can do for my grandson."

IN the hall outside the glassed-in interrogation room where Tyler was still sitting by himself, trying not to look terrified, MacNab and Lukowski were having another conference.

"I just got a call from the kid's lawyer. She's on her way. She wants to know if we intend to arrest him."

"We'd be crazy not to," said Lukowski. "And we got him good. He's a felon and he's got a gun."

"Yeah," said MacNab. "But I just talked to the captain. The problem is the actual gun in question."

"What?" demanded Lukowski.

"It was stolen from the Seattle Police Department evidence locker about fifteen years ago. Apparently there was a big scandal—or almost a scandal—back in the day. I kinda remember all this. There was an internal investigation and there was some stuff definitely missing. And the only possibility was that a cop was helping himself to some stuff. They never actually nailed the guy—just eased him out of there. But frankly, the captain says he wants to see if we can work around this issue. After all, the only reason we actually picked him up is because of that gun. Maybe check it out and see if there's anything to this Dumpster story. The captain says we can always pick him up later. On something else that won't bring unwanted attention to the department. The captain said it's not a good time to bring this up, seeing as we're in the middle of this federal corruption investigation and all." The department had recently received some bad publicity, with the local press talking about "a culture of corruption that goes back decades."

Lukowski threw up his hands. "Check out his story? We're supposed to look for that old drunk?"

MacNab shrugged. "In a way, the kid's story does check out. I mean we saw the old drunk down there ourselves."

"So? There's a million old drunks hanging around Dumpsters."

"Yeah, but there's more," said MacNab. "The lab says the condition of the gun is consistent with its having been in a Dumpster behind an Italian restaurant."

"What the hell does that mean?"

"Apparently it has traces of a substance they think might be," he glanced down at the report, "Arborio rice."

"Arborio rice?"

"They make risotto out of it."

Chapter Thirteen

//

SUZZALLO LIBRARY ON THE University of Washington campus is a collegiate Gothic building built in the nineteen-twenties, and whenever he approached the entrance, Tyler always liked to look up at the statues that run along the top of the building, an eclectic collection that includes Moses and Dante, Louis Pasteur and Newton, Beethoven and Benjamin Franklin, Shakespeare and Adam Smith.

He loved the vast cathedral-style reading room, too, with its vaulted ceilings, stained glass windows, and oak bookcases and tables. It was a quiet place to study. He tried to concentrate on his structural analysis textbook, but then he started to think about those cops at Alba and how they had kind of sneered at him and acted like he was some kind of criminal. All he was trying to do was his job. If he could just park the damn cars and have enough time to study it would be fine. But no, he had to end up getting shot at, and then be treated like a thug!

Suddenly, he heard a strange sound above the tapping of computer keyboards. It was, he felt sure, a sob. Tyler turned to his side and saw that a young woman at the end of the table had buried her face in her hands. She looked like a million girls on campus in a gray hoodie and yoga pants, and she was clearly crying. Silently now, but he could tell by the way her shoulders moved that she was in tears.

What had happened to her? What was she doing crying in the reading room?

Then the girl seemed to pull herself together, straightened her spine, and pushed her hair back from her face. She blinked hard, and after wiping away a last tear, set a pair of severe black-rimmed glasses onto her face. He had the strange feeling that that he knew her but that he couldn't place her.

And then he realized that she was Flavia Torcelli, the stunning and snobby little hostess from Alba!

Her face was turned away from him now, and he wondered if he had only imagined that it was Flavia Torcelli. What would she be doing here? Without any makeup and wearing a gray hoodie? And glasses. Her hair wasn't in that big bubble thing on top of her head. It was just hanging straight down.

Maybe he was crazy. Maybe it wasn't Flavia Torcelli at all and he'd been so traumatized by the events at Alba that he was delusional. Now the mystery woman was collecting a bunch of books and papers and a laptop and an iPhone and was smashing them into a backpack.

Tyler found himself doing the same thing, but very quietly. And when she scraped her chair away from the table and rose, he was startled to realize he had every intention of following this girl to see if he was indeed delusional.

He lagged behind as she made her way out the west entrance into the light spring rain falling on the brick plaza known as Red Square. Through careful pacing and a longish stride, he managed to catch up with her just as she passed the building that housed the student cafeteria. He looked at her reflection in the window, and she looked at his. Now she turned around with her arms folded. She was glaring at him.

Tyler felt himself blushing, but he figured he could walk up and say hi to her. Why not? He knew her from work. Although her fierce expression was less than welcoming. "Excuse me," he began.

"Are you following me?" she demanded, blinking behind her glasses. The voice confirmed it. It was indeed Flavia.

"Well, I guess so," he said. She looked so different! Smarter and not so mean. She appeared not to recognize him. That figured. Probably all the valets looked alike in their black pants and white polo shirts.

He thrust his hands into his jacket pocket. "Um, I was in the library. I was sitting at your table."

"So?"

Suddenly inspired, he yanked his iPhone ear buds out of his pocket. "After you left I saw these on the floor under the chair where you'd been sitting. I thought you might have dropped them."

Her face softened a little but she still looked wary. She swung her backpack off her shoulder, and began to dig around inside it. "Here," she said, with a little bit of that imperiousness she sashayed around Alba with, and handed him a hairbrush. After that she handed him a pen, a notebook, and a paperback book, and continued rummaging.

Suddenly she produced identical ear buds and held them up. "They're not mine," she announced. "The ones you have."

He stood there stupidly for a moment, until she began to snatch back her belongings impatiently.

With those glasses she looked younger and sweeter and not so mean and snotty. Suddenly he blurted out, "You look so different with your glasses."

"Do you know me?" She was suddenly unsure of herself, and he decided that Flavia Torcelli in a confused and vulnerable state was kind of adorable.

"From Alba," he said. "I mean the restaurant, not the city."

"Oh." Suddenly she gave him her big phony hostess smile. "We hope you enjoyed your meal."

"I've never actually eaten there," he said.

Now she looked un-phony and confused again. Tyler felt himself reeling a little at her multiple personalities and the rapidity with which she flashed between the two.

Tyler assumed his own phony service persona, and said in an unctuous voice with a winning smile, "Welcome to *Ristorante Alba. Buona sera.*"

She still looked confused.

"Don't forget to leave the keys in the ignition," he continued, prompting her a little with beckoning hands.

"Oh my God! You're one of the valets!" She laughed nervously.

"What's so funny about that?" Tyler said.

"I don't know. What were you doing in the library?"

"Studying," said Tyler with dignity. "I'm an engineering student here. I work nights as a valet so I can pay off a big student loan I already got stuck with and finish my degree. College isn't free, like in Europe. Anyway, what were *you* doing in the library?"

"I go there to study. It's hard to study at home. I'm a student here, too."

"You are? What are you studying?"

"Marine biology." She looked as if she'd said too much. "But of course there is also the family business."

"The restaurant?"

"Of course." Suddenly her eyes grew wider. "Oh my God! You're the valet who was arrested!"

"It was all a mistake," said Tyler. "Look, I'm here now! I'm not in jail!"

She seemed uninterested in his personal story. "So much criminality here!" Tyler was alarmed at the rapidity with which she began to melt down. Her voice was getting louder and there appeared to be the return of tears in her eyes.

"I know. That shooting. Anyone would be traumatized."

"Ha! That shooting was nothing! Just part of it!" She looked at him with real terror, suddenly turned, and began to run away from him.

"Flavia. Wait!" said Tyler.

A large older woman walking a German shepherd was passing by, and she now stopped and scowled at Tyler. She clearly thought he was some creepy guy terrorizing women. He had thought of going after Flavia, and maybe suggesting she get some post-traumatic stress counseling or something. But it occurred to him this woman might sic her dog on him. Or worse yet, call the campus cops. That's all he needed today—another brush with the law.

He sighed and watched Flavia Torcelli bound away from him like a frightened gazelle. She moved so beautifully, he thought.

SINCE Vic worked nights, avoiding his parents was pretty easy. The Gelashvilis were always in bed when he got home, and in the morning when they left for work, he was asleep down in the remodeled basement of the sixties ranch house he'd grown up in.

So when he put his key into the lock at about 2:30 A.M., he was shocked to hear classical music coming from the living room. Cello and violin, of course. He hoped to avoid them and just slink downstairs, but then the music lurched to a stop.

"Victor!" said his father. "Is that you?"

"No, it's a burglar," he said.

"Victor, come here," said his mother in a voice he'd never heard from her before. Mad and sad instead of just sad. He was so startled he went into the living room. Dad was standing by the fireplace, his violin dangling at his side. Mom was seated behind her cello.

"We need to talk," said his mother.

"Right now?" said Vic innocently.

His father said, "We've been down in your room."

"What!" They hadn't been in his room in years.

"We found a lot of strange things. We want to know what you're up to. We've been waiting up for you."

"Can't we do this later?" he said. He turned to go into the kitchen where the basement door was. To his horror, they followed him.

"Dad looked at your laptop," said his mother.

Then she reached over and touched the bruise on his cheekbone. "Your lip, too. God, what happened?"

"What?" he said. "My laptop?"

"Come with me," said his father, shoving him toward the basement door and down the steps, his mother trailing behind.

"What is the matter with you!" Vic yelled at both of them. "What is this, the KGB?"

"What about the KGB?" shouted his father. "The first thing I noticed is, your screensaver is a portrait of Josef Stalin! What are you thinking!"

"Nobody messed with him," said Vic.

"He had oceans of blood on his hands," said his father. "He wrecked a whole country. You idolize that monster! A crude, sadistic peasant of the worst kind! Haven't we taught you anything?" Gennady Gelashvili was still shoving his son when they entered Vic's bedroom, his wife, Anna, taking up the rear.

"He was a Georgian," said Vic. "And he was one of the most powerful men on earth."

"A Georgian? So what?"

"But I'm a Georgian."

"Are you crazy? You *are* crazy! We have a Georgian name because of my grandfather, but you've never even been to Georgia! Neither have I! No one in our family has lived there for seventy-five years! What are you talking about! And look at this stuff on the walls!"

Gennady gestured toward a large *Scarface* poster with Al Pacino as Tony Montana in a white tuxedo dangling a gun. Next to it was a poster for the film *Eastern Promises*, showing a pair of sinister tattooed hands. "Gangsters! You are in love with gangsters!"

"Jesus, Dad," said Vic, a little whinily. "It's in our own family. I mean, didn't you tell me your cousin Ivan in Vladivostok was part of the mafia?"

"No! I told you I suspected he was involved in some black market business dealings back in the 1980s when everything was a little crazy. I don't know what he's up to! I haven't seen him in twenty years."

"That's not what cousin Gleb says," said Vic.

"Who is cousin Gleb?" demanded his father.

"Uncle Ivan's son," said Vic triumphantly. "I met him on the Internet. I think our family is pretty well connected, if you know what I mean. Don't deny it."

Gennady stared at his son. "Are you crazy?" he demanded once again.

"Ever since you dropped out of community college—" began his mother.

"It's gone beyond that, Annushka," Gennady snapped. He turned to his son. "What's all this GPS stuff on your computer? What are you tracking? Who are you tracking!" He went over to the corner of the room and pointed at some cardboard boxes that the tracking devices he and Chip used had come in. "This is something criminal, isn't it? Well, whatever you are involved in, it's not paying you very well, because you still live at home." He grabbed a big jar full of crumpled ones and fives from the dresser. "You're living on these tips from parking cars!"

"Not for long!" said Vic. "I'm about to move out."

"If you go back to school," said his mother, "we can help you with tuition. But this time you'll have to show us your grades. Not like before."

"You can't live here if you are involved in some dodgy business," said his father. "We came here to get away from all that. I gave up my position back home because all of a sudden the students were a bunch of mafia kids whose parents got them into university some dirty way. Now you're acting like you think that's glamorous! Scum! You want to be scum!"

"Fine," said Vic. "I'm leaving right now." With as much dignity he could muster, he gathered up his laptop. "I'll come get the rest of my stuff later." Then he grabbed his tip jar, turned it upside down, stuffed the bills into his pocket, and left the room.

"Where are you going at three in the morning?" shrieked his mother.

He didn't answer her and stormed out of the house, slamming the door behind him. He got into his Volkswagen Golf and drove straight to Acme Heated Storage off the freeway in another suburb, Woodinville.

He had calmed down by the time he put the key in the door of their storage unit. Thank God they'd gone for the heated option. They'd had to spend the extra money because it was the only space with a big enough door. Now he could curl up here and spend the night in comfort.

Once inside, Vic clicked on the flickering fluorescent lights and calmed down immediately. He walked among the whole collection, caressing the bodywork of all the cars he and Chip had gathered here. A Lamborghini, five Mercedes, a Ford F-40, a Maserati, a Jaguar, two Porsches, a Ferrari, and three Cadillacs.

Chapter Fourteen

"I CALLED YOU ALL HERE TODAY because there's a bunch of stuff going on that people aren't telling me," said Gus Iversen, sitting in his plaid recliner in front of the fireplace in his small Ballard home. The room was dominated by a large, old-fashioned boxy TV and a fireplace with a mantelpiece full of framed family photos. Above the mantel hung an oil painting of Grandpa's old boat, the *Ingrid Marie*.

In a smaller chair near Gus's throne-like recliner, sat his lawyer, Veronica Kessler, with a legal notepad on her knees. At her feet sat her elderly black Lab, Muffin, whom she had brought along apparently because she and the animal were inseparable.

"What do you mean, Dad?" said Ingrid Benson. "What kind of stuff aren't we telling you?"

"You're not telling me stuff that I think might cost me money later down the line," the old man said. "Legal bills. Rescuing you financially again. Plus I'm worried about Tyler, here." He turned to Veronica. "What did you find out?"

"Apparently, they could have held him because he was a felon in possession of a firearm," said Veronica, scratching behind Muffin's ears. "But they didn't. Beats me why. I would have thought they'd want to soften him up and see if he has anything to do with that criminal activity at his workplace. But for some reason or other, they let him go. Maybe it's straightforward." Veronica sounded doubtful on this point, as if nothing ever actually was straightforward. "Maybe they believed his story about taking that gun away from some old guy by the Dumpster."

"So tell me about that felony, Tyler," said Grandpa brusquely.

"Okay, it was my twenty-first birthday and a bunch of my friends took me out to the Viking Valhalla in Ballard."

"Oh yeah, I remember that place," said Gus. "What the heck happened?"

"So there was this girl—and there was this other guy and he was coming on to her and she didn't want him to...." Tyler sighed deeply. He had already gone over this evening in his mind many times. "Anyway, we ended up outside and he started giving me these little pushes and—"

Gus chuckled. "That's how it always starts. Those little two-handed pushes." He folded his hands into fists and made little pushes in the air, cocking up his chin in a threatening manner. "One time up at the Elbow Room in Dutch Harbor there was this big part-Eskimo guy just come off the halibut fishery—"

Ingrid Benson interrupted her father. "Tyler! You never told us a thing about this! Besides, we all celebrated your twenty-first birthday together! It was your spring break."

"That's right!" said her husband. "We took you out to dinner. I had monkfish drizzled with a tarragon vinaigrette!"

"That was the next night," said Tyler. "My friends took me to the Viking Valhalla right after midnight—like the first *minute* I turned twenty-one. I went out to dinner with you the next night. God, it was horrible! I just managed to make bail in time to meet you guys at the restaurant. I didn't even have time to take a shower!"

Veronica Kessler jumped in. "So they got you on assault and malicious mischief. Which means you must have both attacked the guy and wrecked something on purpose."

"Yeah, I hit him," said Tyler. "And I keyed his car." Tyler remembered the satisfaction he had taken drawing a clean line through the cherry red finish of the passenger-side door of the guy's Corvette.

"I can't believe you did that!" said Ingrid.

"Well, I didn't actually key it," said Tyler. "Because I didn't plan to drive that night. So I didn't even have any actual keys." He turned to his grandfather apologetically. "I used that Swiss Army knife you gave me for my twelfth birthday."

"Oh yeah," said Gus. "I remember that."

Gus turned to Roger. "Why are the cops interested in you? What the hell were you doing at the crime scene?"

"I was just trying to make contact with my old boss," said Roger. "I thought maybe he might be interested in investing in—"

"Not that stupid 'make your own dinner and take it home and eat it' business!" said Gus, flapping his blue-veined hand dismissively.

Roger produced an irritated sigh and Grandpa said, "I know. You don't like me bossing you around and asking you all this stuff, but as soon as Ingrid asked me for a loan, I got the right to boss you around and ask questions. And by the way, where's Samantha? I told you I wanted to talk to all of you."

"She's at the mall, shopping with her friends," said Roger. "She's on her way. They're dropping her off."

"Hah!" said Gus. "The only reason she should go to the mall is to get a *job* at the mall."

Roger ignored him and said to his wife, "I told you this was a bad idea. I feel like a deckhand on his fishing boat."

Gus Iversen laughed. Tyler thought it was because his dad would have made a terrible deckhand.

Now Gus turned to Tyler. "Tyler, your parents are broke," he said. "Flat broke. They want me to bail them out. You should know about it and so should your sister. You're both old enough."

Now Grandpa turned back to Dad. "If you hadn't blown all your money, you could be retired by now." Tyler had the feeling his grandfather had been waiting to say this for some time. "How much money did you get from that DuckSoft outfit, anyway? When they canned you?"

"Quite a bit," said Ingrid Benson.

Gus said, "I gotta have the whole picture if you want me to help you. How much money did you get?"

"Two point eight million," said Ingrid, shooting her husband a venomous look.

When Tyler had been in middle school, Dad had cashed in at DuckSoft and taken the whole family to Europe for a year. Mom had thought it would be culturally broadening. Then Dad had fallen in love with Italian food and decided that he would train as a master chef, and they stayed another year.

"Thank God I didn't invest in that business of yours," continued Gus. He turned to his daughter and said, "Why didn't you stop him?"

"Do you expect her to have tried to squelch my dream?" said his father indignantly. "I had a dream! A vision!"

Gus made a snorting noise. "You had a vision, all right. You're allowed to have those kind of dreams when you're young," he said. "That way, if they don't work out there's time to do something else. But not when you're middle-aged with a family. You should have invested that money in rental property, like I told you."

Ingrid said, "Look, Dad, I know we made some real mistakes. I admit that. But we need some help, just to get over this patch. We're behind on our house payments. We've been living on credit cards. And Samantha's tuition is coming up."

"Well, send her to public school," said Gus Iversen, sipping his coffee. "You went to public school, didn't you?"

"That's one area that's not negotiable," said Roger.

Tyler wondered if his dad had become completely delusional. He was hardly in a negotiating position of any kind.

"And if you can't afford to live there, then sell the house," said Gus.

"Well, I was thinking maybe if Tyler moved back in, he could pay some rent and maybe help us make the payments," said Roger.

"What!" said Tyler. "Are you out of your mind? I'm too busy paying off that hundred grand you stuck me with!"

"A hundred grand?" said Gus.

Tyler sighed. "When I went away to college, Dad gave me a bunch of paperwork to sign. It turned out I was borrowing every dime of my tuition and expenses for my first couple of years back in that expensive school. And then he got me to hand it over to him in cash. He said he wanted to pay my tuition on a credit card that gave him air miles.

"But in the end, he poured it into Ricotteria, before he paid the tuition. It was a mess. And I was stupid."

"Yeah, you were," said Gus. "But I guess you didn't realize your own father would screw you over."

"It was just a bridge loan," said Dad, biting his cuticle. "I wanted to add an open hearth to the concept."

"Geez," said Gus, shaking his head sadly.

"And I had trouble getting work visas for some of the peasant subject-matter experts," snapped Roger in a defensive tone. "That immigration lawyer didn't come cheap."

Ricotteria was the name of Roger's business—a place where people could come after work, make fabulous Italian meals from scratch under the supervision of real Italian cooks, and take it home to their families. It cost more than eating out, but the idea was it was better food because it was authentic.

"Look, Dad," said Tyler's mother, "if you don't want to help us with a loan—"

"You have to sell your place and cut your expenses so you can live on what Ingrid earns as an event planner," he said. "I can get you into one of my rentals cheap."

"But our *house*—" began Roger, "it's who we are."

"Well it's a lot nicer than mine, but mine is paid for," said Gus. "You can't afford it, so it isn't who you are at all."

Mom started crying, and Tyler thought he should go to her side and comfort her, but Roger was already heading toward her.

Just then, Samantha burst into the front hall, carrying some shopping bags. "Hi, everybody," she said, coming into the room, only to see her mother in tears, pushing her dad away. "Oh my God, what's the matter?" she said.

"Nothing serious," said Gus Iversen. "It's only money."

"That's right," said Veronica, looking completely unrattled by having sat in on the Bensons' tough-love therapy session. "I thought we were here to address criminal issues. Tyler and Roger, if the police want to talk to you again, don't talk to them. Call me. I think they could do some real harm with what they've got on the two of you. Squirrelly stuff like that, they're likely to get you in there and just chew on you until they think they have enough for an indictment."

"But we can't possibly be indicted for something we didn't do," said Roger.

Veronica rolled her eyes.

"GOD, it's good to be in the sun again," said Sergei Lagunov. "That weather in Seattle is so depressing. Wet, but worse, dark." He shuddered. He was sitting poolside with a sixty-seven-year-old man known as Yalta Yuri, who wore a tiny black Speedo bathing suit and had a fat torso covered in gray hair. Besides the Speedo, Yalta Yuri sported ominous-looking sunglasses and about ten thousand dollars' worth of white gold jewelry. He was splayed out on a lounger, while Sergei sat respectfully in a straight-backed cast iron lawn chair, wearing a dark suit.

"Yes, it is as lovely here in California as it is on the sun-kissed shores of the Crimea," said Yuri pleasantly. "But you are a Muscovite. You should be used to cold, dark places. Is there much snow there in Seattle?"

"No, just rain and darkness," said Sergei. "It's better now that it is springtime."

"I noticed you lost your tan. It makes your scar less noticeable," Yuri said kindly. "So tell me more about the situation there."

Sergei snapped his fingers. "It should be very easy. They are really pathetic. First of all, they act like hard-core professionals, but they're not. I think they picked up all their moves from the movies. The Zelenkos came to Seattle from Ukraine in 1989. They got here as asylum-seekers."

"Jews?"

"No. Some kind of crazy Protestants. They jump up and down and scream in church. They think everyone is going to hell. Very religious people."

Yuri nodded. "So the Zelenkos managed to convince the authorities they were Baptists?"

"That's what I thought at first. But then I met Dmytro's old mother, who's also Volodya's aunt. An old *babushka* with a big fat Bible under her arm on her way to some kind of a prayer meeting. So I figured they were *real* asylum-seekers. I asked around. Back in '89 a bunch of churches around Seattle sponsored them and got them out of Ukraine. Said the Communists were persecuting them because they wouldn't do their army service, weren't allowed to pray and all that.

"The Zelenko boys were just kids when they came here—in their teens. So I guess after they got here they decided they didn't care if they went to hell, and they got into the spare parts business. Breaking down stolen cars and selling the parts. Small-time stuff. But then they got into stealing the cars. Dmytro's the smarter one. He calls the shots."

"Not that smart," said Yuri. "Because they didn't know how to distribute the high-end cars they weren't chopping up, so they found me. Not that smart." He paused to take a sip of Diet Pepsi. "But they get some terrific stuff."

"They're in some other businesses, too."

"Such as?"

"They control a crummy little casino. Some old lady named Donna owns it and her son runs it for her. Cokehead named Hughie. A nice cash business, easy way to launder money. The son doesn't care, as long as he gets a little more money every month than his mother Donna would give him. He has an expensive habit."

"Sounds good," said Yuri.

"And then, through the valet company at the casino, they got into a nice restaurant. Very classy place. It started out as just a way to get high-end cars. One of the valets is a Russian and Volodya and I got him on the job. He scouts the merchandise, cuts some spare keys if he can, and he plants transmitters on the cars so the Zelenkos' team of car thieves can use GPS to find out where they are and go pick them up.

"The Italian restaurant was in financial trouble, so Dmytro gave them a loan. They're having trouble making the payments. He thinks he'll own the whole place soon. But he'll keep the owners on paper. Dmytro can't get a liquor license in Washington State because he has a record. Something to do with auto theft. He actually did a little time."

Yuri nodded. "Those guys shouldn't be running it without me. What do we have to do to make that happen?"

"Get something to squeeze them with." Sergei permitted himself a little smile. "Which I've done. I've got a gun Volodya used to kill some old guy in his chop-shop when he was drunk. He asked me to get rid of the body and the gun."

"Okay. You got the gun. What did you do with the body?"

"Volodya screwed that up," he said. "The cops have it."

"What a stupid son of a bitch," said Yuri. He was thoughtful for a moment. "Maybe that's okay. Now that the cops have the body, with the bullets in it, it makes the gun we have more valuable." Yuri rose, walked over to the side of the pool, and stuck in a foot. "By the way, who did this Volodya idiot kill?"

"Some old guy who worked in his shop named Pasha. Volodya said he was stealing parts from him."

"Pasha?" Yalta Yuri turned around, and made his hands into fists. "That's the guy that sent the Zelenkos to me in the first place! I knew him back in the day in the old country. We were together in prison in the seventies! Those sons of bitches killed that poor old man? They knew he was an old prison-mate of mine and they killed him! That kind of disrespect cannot go unpunished!"

He paused for a moment, and said in a quieter tone, "See that Pavel Ivanovich gets a proper funeral," he said. "In a real church, with a real priest. None of this Baptist shit. Make the Zelenkos do it. Tell them what will happen if they don't. That will be the very first message they get from me. They need to do what I want."

Sergei nodded.

"And then get them working too hard and rough for their taste so they get scared. Get them in even deeper than they are with Old Pasha getting killed."

"A couple of those valets have been stealing some of their own cars," said Sergei. "Volodya is pissed about it but Dmytro won't do anything."

"Okay. I'll send some guys up to deal with them. We take Dmytro along for the ride. Show him how we roll. And how to run a business properly. Teach those valets a lesson."

"One of them is in the hospital and the other one the Zelenkos think is a well-connected *vor* from back in the old country. That's why Dmytro doesn't want to mess with him."

"Is he?" said Yuri.

"I don't know," said Sergei. "Maybe."

Yuri waved a fat hand in the air, the sun glinting off a diamond ring. "Whatever. We just want to scare Dmytro. Really scare him. He'll be ready to pay us to take all this business off his hands."

Chapter Fifteen

///

AT AROUND TEN P.M. THE NEXT NIGHT, after the dinner rush at Alba was over, Tyler delivered a car to the front of the restaurant and noticed that Brian, who had been sent down from Donna's to deal with the post-shooting valet shortage at Alba, had vanished. Great, thought Tyler. He'd probably found a quiet car to sit in and work on his horrible screenplay. But instead, Brian bounded out of the restaurant. "Hey, Tyler. When you get a chance, grab an employee meal. They got some awesome food in there," he said. "Way better than Donna's, that's for sure."

Tyler had been looking forward to trying some of the food at Alba, but until now, he'd never been around when employee meals were served. Traditionally, employee meals were a casual affair. During slow periods, servers would be scrunched in odd corners of the kitchen scarfing up whatever hadn't moved briskly enough that night. If there was enough to go around, valets also got invited by the hostess. Tyler was actually kind of surprised that the standoffish Flavia even let the valets into her husband's kitchen.

She had her back to him when he came in, but even without her turning around, Tyler realized that the vulnerable, weepy college girl he'd met two days ago had been left back on campus. The heels were back on, the hair was pinned back up, and she had her hands on her hips in an aggressive stance and was yelling at her husband, the chef. Tyler knew that most Italians spoke some kind of regional dialect and that the one from Piedmont had a lot of French in it, just like the cuisine. But he could get the gist of it. She was telling him there was no point serving veal in America because the veal was too old and it wasn't milk-fed, and besides, Americans didn't like to eat baby animals.

Now the chef responded. "You cannot have *cucina Piemontese* without veal," he said. "Next time we just order less. What's the big deal?"

She clicked her tongue. "Can't you redo the recipe with pork? The pork around here tastes more like veal than pork anyway."

The chef threw a skillet into the sink. "I hear a lot of those fake Italian places use nothing but pork in what they call veal scaloppini. Is that the kind of place you want me to run?"

"I hate my life," she said. "I need more time to study and I hate restaurants. I want to do field work. Be out on a boat. I'm sorry Paolo, I want to help you, but I'm not even working for you, am I? Mafiosi. Shootings. Bodies. If I wanted this kind of life I would have gone to Calabria or Sicily. Not Seattle."

"Well, if you can get your boyfriend to bankroll this place, then you can be working for me again," said Paolo, frowning. "Or him, I guess."

"For God's sake, he's not my boyfriend! He's just awkward. I feel sorry for him."

"Sorry! Ha! He's one of the richest men in the whole world. You should feel sorry for me! For us! Anyway, stop yelling in front of the staff. It makes for *brutta figura.*"

Chef Paolo, clearly wanting to exhibit *bella figura* instead, immediately turned to Tyler and said with a dazzling smile, "What do you think? How do you like it?"

Before he had a chance to answer, Flavia, speaking Italian, started back in. "Stop worrying about them. They don't understand a thing!" she said.

Tyler smiled at the chef, and said in his careful schoolboy Italian but with a decent Florentine accent, "Your wife is absolutely right. The veal here isn't anywhere near as good as the veal there. But it's still fabulous."

Both Torcellis looked at him in horror. The chef, stating the obvious, said, "You speak Italian," and Tyler had a horrible sinking feeling.

Now Flavia turned to Tyler and spoke up in English. "I'm not his wife!" she said. "I'm his sister. My family made me come here and work the front end if I wanted to go to university!" And then she stamped her foot, pivoted 180 degrees on one impossibly high heel, and marched out of the kitchen.

DMYTRO Zelenko approached the receptionist's desk in the lobby of the King County Medical Examiner's office, a bland-looking lobby that could have been any county office, except this was the county morgue. His mother stood about a foot behind him, gazing passively at the young woman there. Dmytro said hello, and watched the receptionist take in his mother's steely bun, her mid-calf-length print housedress, nappy cardigan, thick cotton stockings, and black oxfords, and he knew no one would be surprised when he said, "This lady speaks no English. I would like to translate for her."

"Okay," said the cheerful young woman. "How can I help you guys?"

He turned to his mother and said in Ukrainian, "After we have finished here we can go out and get a coffee. Maybe some pastries. What kind would you like?"

"I'm not hungry," she replied. "I had a big lunch." Dmytro turned back to the receptionist.

"It's about the body they found. It was in the newspaper. There was a picture with it. The newspaper said they thought this person might be Russian. She thinks it might be a man who came to her church."

He turned back to his mother, and asked her what she had for lunch. After a length of time, during which his mother described some soup, he turned back to the receptionist. "He came to her church. And he spoke to her. He said he was ready to accept Jesus Christ as his Savior. So my mother wants to know if after the police have done all their investigation, she can arrange to have the body sent to a funeral home of her choice so the body can be prepared for a proper funeral. Her church would like to bury him properly."

The young woman rummaged on her desk and came up with a couple of sheets of copier paper stapled together. Dmytro saw that the top page was the artist's sketch of Old Pasha that had appeared in the newspaper. "Is this the deceased person? Can she identify the body?" She handed it to Dmytro's mother.

The old lady looked at the drawing in a puzzled way, then flipped to the second stapled page. Over her shoulder Dmytro saw that the second page was a blurry copy of a photograph. It was clearly the picture of Old Pasha as a slack-jawed, open-eyed corpse.

"They have called us here to see if we know this man," he said calmly to his mother. "He died, and they want me to identify the body. Can you wait here while I do that?"

His mother screamed.

Dmytro turned back to the girl. "She's too upset to identify the body. You shouldn't have shown an old woman the picture of a corpse!" Dmytro snatched the grisly paperwork and flung it at her. His mother began to wail, making an eerie keening sound.

"We'd like her to identify the body. It's still here."

"But I met him, too," improvised Dmytro. "Can I please do it? I don't want the poor lady to be upset."

"I'll call the detectives handling the case," said the girl. "They'll want to talk to you."

Dmytro grabbed his mother, hustled her out to the loading zone in front of the building, helped his mother into the backseat and got into the car himself. "Get out of here right now," he hissed to Sergei.

Sergei took off. "Did they say you could have the body?"

"No! They were calling the police! I have a record. I can't talk to them!"

"But your cousin doesn't have a record. Volodya can go with her and talk to the detectives."

"He's still in rehab," snapped Dmytro. The DUI lawyer had

said Volodya's defense would be greatly enhanced if he completed a stint in a residential treatment facility after an alcoholism counselor had determined he was a poor candidate for outpatient treatment. "And anyway, my mother won't identify the body!" he said. "It's ridiculous. She'll never lie. And they'd probably get an official translator!" He sighed heavily. "Can't you talk him out of this demand? The police will be suspicious immediately! They don't even know who he is, right now."

"Yuri Andreivich thinks that's so sad," said Sergei. "To die unknown without a proper burial. He is a hard man but has a soft heart."

"Well then, why doesn't *he* come up here and claim the body!" snapped Dmytro.

Sergei gave Dmytro a look of scorn mixed with pity. "Because he wants *you* to do it. Because he's mad about the way the poor old man died. And because he knows where the gun is that did the job. You have no choice. You need to atone, or he will be very angry."

Dmytro gave him a disgusted look. What a little traitor Sergei had turned out to be. He'd never *dreamed* Sergei worked for his customer Yuri down in California.

"Oh, and one other thing," added Sergei. "It's important to Yuri Andreivich that Pavel receive a *proper* burial. Not in that crummy Baptist church of yours. A real funeral with a real Russian priest."

Dmytro looked thoughtful. "That gives me an idea," he said. "There's a Russian church up on Capitol Hill. A few blocks off Broadway. Let's go there and see if the priest can come and get the guy. Let him just show up and get the body. I'll give him a generous donation for the church."

Twenty minutes later, looking out of the rear window at the onion-domed building, Dmytro's mother in the backseat grew agitated. "What are we doing here?" she cried. "This is not a real church! What is happening, Dmytro? I brought you up in a pure faith. Stay away from those evil priests! They baptize infants in there! And not full immersion! It is of Satan."

Sergei ignored her, and turned to Dmytro. "You better make this work. And after that, there's something else Yuri would like you to do."

AFTER listening to Flavia's rant at her brother, the chef, Tyler had gone home and thought long and hard about what he had heard. What had she been talking about the mafia for? It was hard to believe the Italian mafia had anything to do with Ristorante Alba. Seattle wasn't New Jersey, and Alba—the real one in Piedmont—wasn't Sicily. And anyway, in the movies, the mafia was into strip clubs, not five-star restaurants that got respectful mentions in the *New York Times* travel section.

But if there was some underworld connection, maybe that explained why someone had been shooting up the place. And why a dead guy was found there in the gray Audi's trunk. Tyler decided that it was important to let the police know about it, so they'd stop suspecting him and his dad.

He wasn't about to call those detectives himself, though. Grandpa's lawyer, Veronica Kessler, had made it pretty clear he wasn't supposed to talk to them about anything. And neither was his dad. Maybe Veronica could talk to the cops about it. Or tell him what to do. The next day, right before going to work, he left a message for her.

But when he got there he wondered if he should even have done that. Would Flavia get into trouble? Now that he knew she wasn't married, and that she was really more interested in marine biology than the restaurant business, he wondered if he really had any idea who she was at all. In fact, whatever her deal was, he realized he now felt sorry for her. Even though he still wondered if she was trying to get her gold-digging hooks into Scott Duckworth.

His thoughts were interrupted by the first flurry of lunch cars. When he got back to the front of the restaurant after parking his third car, he was startled to see Chip and Flavia standing there.

Flavia was shaking Chip's hand in a kind of formal way and said, "I'm glad you're better," then glanced at Tyler and gave him a frosty look.

"Just a scratch," said Chip.

"Mr. Duckworth asked me to give you this," she said, handing over an envelope. "He's sorry you were hurt."

Tyler couldn't resist asking her, "Does he think that bullet was meant for him?"

She shrugged elegantly, then turned and walked back to her post.

"Hey, glad you're okay, Chip," said Tyler.

Chip didn't reply. He was tearing open the envelope Flavia had given him. He pulled out a fifty-dollar bill and stared down at it with an expression that was both shocked and sad. Tyler thought Chip looked like an eight-year-old who didn't get the Christmas present he'd been counting on.

"That sucks," said Tyler. "Fifty bucks for taking a bullet for him."

"Not even a note!" said Chip indignantly. "Well, screw him. My ship's coming in soon, and I can blow off this whole valet thing."

DMYTRO'S heart was pounding with rage. How had it come to this? After an unfortunate encounter at the church, that had ended just as badly as the trip to the morgue, Sergei had driven to Dmytro's house to drop off his mother. He should have known that it wasn't a good idea to try and use her to get that body for Yuri's sentimental funeral! Dmytro had tried to calm her down while Sergei lounged insolently around in the living room of his own home helping himself to Dmytro's liquor and playing with Dmytro's dogs.

Dmytro was furious with the dogs. They seemed to like Sergei! What kind of loyalty was that? He had half a mind to put them both down.

Now, Dmytro was behind the wheel of his own car, driving to Alba with Sergei in the passenger seat flicking his cigarette out of the window and humming to himself as if he didn't have a care in the world.

Sergei had made it clear that he wanted Dmytro to drive, and

Dmytro had caved! Now he was the chauffeur and Sergei was the boss! All because of what Yuri had on Volodya and that gun!

Maybe he should just wash his hands of Volodya. Why not? Why should he give away a percentage of everything he had built just because of Volodya's stupidity? But he'd have to think hard about that. Even if he could bring himself to do it, Volodya could try to make a lot of trouble for him. He knew a lot about the business.

Maybe Dmytro could just retire. Hand over everything to Yalta Yuri, including Volodya, and just retire. Maybe open a little shop somewhere and just do a little legitimate body and fender work. He could afford to retire. All those laddered CDs at the credit union would still be there. Hell, he could even sell the house, get himself a nice condo. The market was looking better and he'd made a lot of improvements.

If only things had gone better at the church, Dmytro would have looked like someone who could handle things. Like someone not to be messed with. Dmytro told himself to try and think this through, and for now, just play along. And he'd suppress those defeatist thoughts about retiring. Why the hell should he just hand over everything he'd worked for to some guy from California!

"Listen, Sergei," he said, "I'll do what I can about this funeral business. But I can't believe you are being so reckless—jeopardizing my cousin and even me. And why did you tell me that it would be easy? Just a matter of asking to bury the body? Look, if Yuri wants me to take these kind of risks, maybe he can just buy me out of our new..." he paused "...partnership."

"Partnership is not really the right word," said Sergei. "But even if you don't feel you have confidence in Yuri's leadership, don't assume he would be willing to let you walk away from everything. He needs a good manager like you to run things. Think of it as a friendly takeover that's a win-win for everyone. No hard feelings at all." Sergei smiled ingratiatingly. "You know, if you take care of just a few things, Yuri Andreivich will feel more kindly about everything. It's your chance to show good will. There will be a nice cut for you. You will just operate under his roof. That's a good thing for you."

Dmytro sighed. "Okay, the funeral. And this new business arrangement. But you said he has other demands."

"That's right. First of all, if you think Vic and Chip are stealing from you, we need to do something about it right away."

"Okay, we get the restaurant to fire them. I can do that. I tell that little Italian girl to tell the valet company to get rid of them." Of course, that would put a huge crimp in his business, but if it was going to end up as Yuri's business, maybe that didn't matter.

"Yuri wants more than that," said Sergei. "He's sending up some of his guys to mess them up."

Dmytro bit his lip nervously. "But what about Vic's uncle, the *vor* from Tbilisi?"

"We'll be discreet," said Sergei. "Maybe Yuri can work things out with the *vor*," he added vaguely. "Or maybe you just mess up Chip. Vic will get the message. Anyway, Yuri will want you to work with the guys he's sending up and help him teach them a lesson. A test of your manhood. But if it is too much for you to discipline people who disrespect you, maybe you shouldn't be in this business."

Chapter Sixteen

TYLER GLANCED AT HIS PHONE and saw Veronica Kessler's name. This wasn't a call he wanted to take with other people around. "Hang on, Veronica," he said. As far as he knew, the banquet room would be empty now. The valets were always told ahead of time if a private function was scheduled there. He popped into the entryway. Flavia was hunched over the screen that showed which tables were reserved, and Tyler ducked into the little hallway that led past the rest rooms to the banquet room. It was all set up with lots of round tables and poufy napkins on the plates. Tyler positioned himself behind a big portable screen in three hinged panels, painted with baroque-looking flowers and birds, next to a long table with polished silver chafing dishes and serving pieces.

Veronica wanted to know if the police had been in touch.

"No. I haven't heard a thing," he said.

"Good," she said. "Let's keep it that way. Nothing good will come out of talking to them anymore."

"That's why I called," said Tyler. "I overheard something last night I thought they should know about."

"What's that?" said Veronica.

"Well, one of the owners here seemed to be saying that the mafia was somehow involved with the restaurant."

"With Alba?"

"That's right. Don't you think that might be relevant? Should I call the detectives?"

"No! They'll think you're some kind of nut job trying to find someone else to blame for that shooting. That's just the kind of stupid thing that scared suspects say. Hinting at some weird conspiracy. I don't want you talking to them. It's a miracle you're not a guest of the county right now." She paused, as if she were thinking, and then said, "I don't buy it anyway. It doesn't ring true. And that's what they'll think."

"Okay," said Tyler. Veronica was probably right.

Just then he heard Flavia's voice from the other side of the screen. "We can talk here," she said. He quickly ended his call and tried the door to the hallway so he could slip out, but it had apparently locked behind him. He stood as still as he could, and positioned himself so he could see a sliver of the room through one of the hinged gaps in the screen.

"Please sit down," said Flavia. Her voice sounded strained. There seemed to be two guys with her and they all sat down at one of the tables. He could see Flavia in profile, and bits of the elbows and backs of her two companions,

"We just wanted you to know that from now on, we won't be handling this business," said an older man in a Slavic accent. "From now on you'll be working with Sergei here."

"I don't understand," said Flavia. "We had an agreement, didn't we?"

A younger voice said, "And now I have an agreement with Mr. Zelenko. And I'm taking over this loan. Managing it for him."

"You can go ahead and make the payments the same way," said the older guy in a friendly way. "We'll make sure it gets to the right place."

Flavia nodded warily.

Now the younger man spoke up. "But we're going to have to make an adjustment. The interest rate is going to have to be raised."

"But we've almost paid it all off. In fact, I think I might be able to pay the whole amount very soon." Flavia tilted her chin up bravely.

"We'd like to continue to own a part of the restaurant," said the younger guy. "We've heard good things about it."

"But when the loan is paid off then my brother will own it again," she said. She turned away from the screen where Tyler was watching to one of the older men. "This was just to help us catch up—you know. We got behind on our payroll tax. And Labor and Industries. It was just growing pains. There is so much bookkeeping in this business."

The younger guy, apparently named Sergei, said, "You needed help. And this gentleman helped you. We think you should be grateful."

"But I don't understand," said Flavia.

Sergei continued. "And we think you have a terrific restaurant. We'd like to be a part of that and have an ownership position." He cleared his throat. "Unfortunately, Mr. Zelenko can't own a restaurant up front. Not if you want the restaurant to have a liquor license. He is a felon. So we have to do this quietly. Keep the government out of it."

"I need to talk to my brother," said Flavia. "This isn't a good time. It's the lunch rush."

Suddenly, Tyler saw Flavia tilting backward out of his frame of vision and the profile of one of the men came into view in the narrow space between the screen's panels. His face was leaning right into hers. There was a long scar down that face, a scar Tyler knew he'd seen before. He'd seen this guy at Donna's.

"We'd like to have lunch here right now," he said. "I trust you can get us a good table, seeing as we partly own this place." He reached out and grabbed her thin little wrist.

Tyler felt a huge surge of adrenaline and stepped around the screen. "Oh, sorry," he said in a loud voice. "I didn't mean to disturb you."

The guy with the scar released Flavia's wrist.

Tyler gestured toward the door. "I just came in because some lady says she might have left her phone in this room last night."

He sensed that his voice sounded too loud and phony and he
didn't know if they believed he could have entered so quietly. He
turned toward the door and yanked at the knob. "Oh, I guess this
locked after me. I'm really sorry." He turned back to face them
and spread out his arms in a too-wide apologetic gesture that suc-
ceeded in knocking the screen toward him. He grabbed it and
managed to set it upright again.

"That's okay," said Flavia calmly. "We're finished in here."
She turned to the two men and said, "I'll get you a very nice window table. It will take a minute to set it up. Perhaps you'd like to
wait in the bar."

The two men stared at Tyler and he stared back, then he
made his way past them to the customer entrance to the room. It
was definitely the guy with the scar he'd seen before at Donna's.
The older guy looked a lot like that drunk named Vlad or whatever it was who had kissed him at Donna's his last night there. He
paused for a moment just outside the doorway and outside of their
line of vision. Flavia, who sounded remarkably calm for someone
who had just been manhandled and threatened, was saying, "I
meant to ask you about the valet situation here."

Sergei said, "We want you to continue to use this company."

"Oh, I understand," she said. "But what about individual
valets?"

"You can get rid of anyone except Chip and Vic," said the
man who was called Zelenko.

So this was the mafia Flavia had been talking about. The Russian mafia. The same thugs who hung out at Donna's seemed to
be shaking down Alba. That's who Flavia was afraid of!

Back outside, a car was waiting. When Tyler got the car down
to the lower lot, it seemed the place was empty of people. But as
he locked the car and prepared to jog back up, he noticed Chip rising from behind another car. He'd seen Chip do that before—the
night that Duckworth got shot at. Tyler remembered wondering
if he was checking to see if he'd scraped the finish. Just what the
hell was Chip doing? Tyler hardly believed he could be checking
the undercarriage for rust. He pretended not to think there was
anything weird going on and waved at Chip.

Chip waved back and said, "I dropped some of my tips!"

Tyler made a mental note of just which car Chip had been lurking behind. It was a Lincoln. Tyler remembered it had been a red Mercedes that first time he'd seen him do this in the lot. Both nice cars that by rights should have been parked in the more secure lot near the entrance.

Why did Scarface want Vic and Chip on the payroll here? Why did those thugs even want Elite Valet here?

On his next trip down to the parking lot, Tyler parked a car as close as he could to the Lincoln where Chip had been. And then, looking carefully around to make sure he was unobserved, he examined the ground and crouched next to the car to inspect it. Then he ran his fingers along the undercarriage. He encountered a small object that didn't belong there, removed it from the car—it was attached by a magnet—examined it, replaced it, and took a picture of it with his phone. When he stood up again, he found himself looking straight at Vic who stood about ten yards away, staring at him. "Hey Vic," he said cheerfully. "I dropped my phone." He waved it in the air.

Vic just stared back at him.

"OKAY, there's good news and bad news," said Lukowski to MacNab, after listening to a voicemail message. The two men had just emerged from a diversity training session and were standing in the hallway of the Public Safety Building.

"A Russian guy and an old lady went over to the morgue to pick up tattoo guy's body, but when the clerk there told them they'd have to talk to us, they beat it."

MacNab frowned. "Did the clerk get a plate or anything?"

"Nope. I've also got a message from a Father Ushakov at St. Basil's—Russian church up on Capitol Hill. He says three people showed up at his church wanting him to bury the guy. There was some kind of a skirmish in the church or something. Either way, I'm guessing we're getting close to finding out who the hell our guy is. This priest says he'll be around at the church until two."

"Let's go to the church first," said MacNab, checking his watch. "We can grab a couple of burgers at Dick's on Broadway afterwards, then go talk to the morgue clerk." He sighed. "You know what really pisses me off? Those TV detectives always have one case to work on at a time. We got about six active cases right now. No wonder we never get to sit down and have a nice relaxed lunch."

At the church a pleasant blond lady with a slight accent led them to Father Ushakov's office, a cozy, book-lined room with icons and family photographs of a couple of teenagers in soccer uniforms, and an attractive wife laughing at the camera and holding up a newly caught salmon.

The priest himself was a middle-aged man with a neatly trimmed silver beard and light blue eyes. Lukowski had once been to a wedding at this church. He had never forgotten how tough it had been to stand up the whole time during the ceremony, with officiants in elaborate vestments wielding censers of incense.

He was surprised to see the priest, standing behind his desk to greet them, sporting Spandex bicycle gear. A bright yellow helmet served as a desk paperweight.

"Hello," he said, apparently noting Lukowski's slightly startled expression. "I was just about to ride home."

"We appreciate your calling," Lukowski said. "Tell us what happened."

"It was pretty weird," said the priest, indicating a pair of guest chairs and sitting down. Good. There were chairs in the office even if there weren't any pews in the church. "This gentleman appeared and asked me to conduct a funeral for somebody he didn't know. Apparently his picture had been in the paper—an unclaimed body. I knew what he was talking about because I'd seen the picture, too, asking for information, and saying the police thought he might have been from the former Soviet Union." The priest frowned. "What made you think that he came from there?"

"He had tattoos associated with the Russian mafia," said MacNab.

Father Ushakov sighed. "Oh dear," he said. "Well anyway, I happened to be in the church, waiting for a parishioner who wanted to come and make a confession. This middle-aged guy came up and said he wanted me to go down to the morgue and claim the body and bury him." He opened his desk drawer and took out a huge roll of bills held in place with a rubber band. "He gave me this contribution to the church." Father Ushakov smiled. "I already counted it. It's a thousand dollars. We've got to do some work on the roof of this church and these domes aren't exactly a standard repair job!"

"Did you tell him you'd claim the body?" asked Lukowski.

. "Of course not. I said I couldn't claim the body—the family had to go hire a funeral director who would handle all that. I didn't really know what to think. I told him that if he knew who the deceased person was, he should tell the police."

"What did he say to that?" asked MacNab.

"He said he had read about the situation and he wanted the guy to have a good Christian funeral service, because he was a fellow Russian."

"So this guy who showed up here was Russian?"

"I thought so at first. We were speaking English. He had a heavy accent, but his English was fine. Russian isn't my first language—my family came here way back in 1917, right after the Revolution."

"What do you mean you thought he was Russian at first? Did you change your mind?"

"Well, as I was walking him out of the office and into the church, an old lady came rushing in and I'm pretty sure she was speaking Ukrainian. I understood most of what she said. Apparently she was the mother of the gentleman who gave me the money. She said she didn't want him in an Orthodox church. She was some kind of Christian fundamentalist. There are a few Ukrainian Baptist congregations around here. She told him he would go straight to hell." Father Ushakov smirked a little, presumably amused by her bad theology

"Wow," said MacNab. "She said the deceased individual would go to hell?"

"No, she seemed to think her son, the guy who gave me the money, would go straight to hell."

"Your message said there were three individuals," said Lukowski.

"That's right. Suddenly, there was a tall, thin guy with a scar—a younger-looking man. He tried to get control of the old lady, and told her to get back in the car. From what I can tell, he *was* a Russian."

"He was speaking Russian to her—not Ukrainian?" asked MacNab.

"That's right. He was trying to calm her down. He spoke to her respectfully, but he was trying to get her out of here. I wanted him to because she was carrying on about the icons and I was afraid she might try to damage them. She was that agitated.

"Next thing I knew, the two men were kind of pushing each other. The older guy seemed to be trying to defend his mother. And the younger guy had her in kind of a bear hug and was muscling her to the door. It was very disturbing. I told them in Russian to leave the church and sort out their differences elsewhere. The old guy apologized and said he'd call me back. And they left. I followed them out the church steps and watched them get in their car and they took off."

"Did you get their license number?"

"No, I'm sorry I didn't. I'm not even sure what kind of car it was."

The detectives were silent for a moment while this all sunk in.

Father Ushakov spread his hands out in a helpless gesture. "I'm sorry I can't tell you who your victim is. Tattoos, you say?"

"Tattoos associated with the Russian mafia," said MacNab.

The priest sighed. "I'm not sure there's really any such thing," he said. "There are some bad actors from the former Soviet Empire around, all right. Even here in Seattle. A bunch of folks who grew up thinking it's okay to smash and grab, and sometimes they get together with other folks like them and run rackets and commit crimes."

He leaned back and closed his eyes as if preparing to give a little sermon. "Some recent immigrants brought some very bad habits with them. You have to understand that for almost a hundred years, Russians lived in a society where playing by the rules didn't work. You needed to bribe people to get your kid into college, or get an apartment." He shook his head sadly. "I have a nice lady in my congregation who told me when she came here and tried to bribe a cop who gave her a speeding ticket, he told her that's not how we operate here in America. She told me she felt so disrespected that he wouldn't take her gift."

"This body down in the morgue has a bullet in it," said MacNab. "We're not talking about bribing a traffic cop."

"Thanks, Father," said Lukowski. "If you hear from these folks again, we'd appreciate a call. In fact, if they call again, can you tell them you'll do the funeral? We'll get you the body."

"I don't know," said Father Ushakov. "I have no way of knowing if the deceased was in good standing with the church."

"Can't you give him the benefit of the doubt?" said Lukowski. "We don't know anything about this guy either, but we still need to find out who killed him. And the only clue we have is that someone wants him sent off properly."

Chapter Seventeen

//

IT WAS ABOUT TWO-THIRTY IN the afternoon when the two Slavs—Zelenko, the short squat one, and the menacing Sergei who had asked for a good table at Alba, not to mention a permanent piece of the ownership of the place, sauntered out to get into their car.

Tyler didn't want to deal with them, but it seemed they didn't want to deal with him either. When he asked them for their claim check, the older guy waved him away, and Vic dashed up to them. They immediately got into a huddle with him and seemed to be having a serious conversation.

Tyler was relieved when a Honda Accord pulled up and he was able to hastily press a claim ticket on the occupant, get behind the wheel, and pull away. Looking at the little confab in his rearview mirror, he was disconcerted to see Scarface point at the car he was in. Tyler didn't think he was talking about the chrome rims. They probably suspected he'd heard their whole shakedown routine from behind the screen in the banquet room. This was not good.

Tyler had spent the slow midafternoon part of his shift thinking about whether or not to tell Flavia he thought crooked valets were putting GPS devices on her customers' cars, presumably so they could be conveniently stolen. Maybe she even knew about it.

He wanted to reach out to her, but he didn't really know how. The last four encounters he'd had with Flavia—being handcuffed and arrested in her presence and yelling, "But I *am* a felon!" at his mom in front of the restaurant; appearing to stalk her on campus; eavesdropping on her conversation with the chef and then showing off his Italian like it was a big deal he spoke another language; and lurking behind that screen in the banquet room and then almost knocking it over—all these unfortunate encounters might have given her the impression he was unstable and creepy.

When he added all that to the fact that she had pointedly asked the thugs—within earshot of Tyler—if it was okay with them if she fired any of the valets, it looked like the odds were good his job security was shaky.

Tyler was pretty sure that Jessica, the Account Manager at Elite Valet, liked him, though. She'd find something for him at another Elite location. He just hoped to God it wasn't Donna's. Frankly, the less he saw of those scary Russians, the better. Maybe he should see if he could get on at the Harborview Hotel.

He now realized that the best thing to do would be to call Jessica as soon as possible. Tyler cheered up suddenly. If he told her about Chip and the GPS device, and showed her the picture he took with his phone, it would look like he only got fired by Flavia because he'd discovered what might be happening in the Alba lot.

JESSICA was sitting in her office on Lake City Way, trying to look enthusiastic. With her was Elite Valet's West Coast Regional Manager Chuck Green, visiting from regional headquarters in Fresno, California. Chuck, a bulky, fortyish man with gelled hair and wearing a gray suit with a pink tie and tasseled loafers, was in town to give Jessica her annual employee review.

"So if you're interested in some aggressive career development goals, Regional District Manager could be in your long-term future," he was saying. "Maybe not here, but some of our other less well-established locations. The Dakotas, for instance, and other rural Midwestern sites. Not a lot of restaurant and hotel action, but valet parking in big malls is a real growth area. Aging baby boomers and fat people hate to walk. And the demographics in the Midwest skew old and fat."

"Interesting," said Jessica.

"But let's begin by talking about the local Account Manager function, and how it aligns with Elite's overall vision and mission."

Her phone rang and Jessica looked down. "Oh, it's one of our—" She caught herself just in time and managed to say "service associates" instead of "valets."

"Put him on speaker," said Chuck in a pompous whisper. "I'd like to assess your managerial style. A coaching opportunity for me."

Jessica considered warning Tyler that he was on speaker, but Chuck's conspiratorial manner indicated he didn't want her to.

"Hey Jessica," said Tyler in an urgent, serious tone. "We may have a really bad situation down here at Alba. It looks like one of our guys might be putting GPS devices on customer cars. It's, like, a magnetic thing attached to the undercarriage."

"Why would they do that?" said Jessica.

"The only thing I can come up with is maybe to steal them later. They seem to be the high-end cars."

"Are you sure?"

"It's kind of circumstantial, but I found a device on one of the cars and I took a picture of it. Weird stuff is going on here. There seems to be some mafia thing happening."

Jessica glanced nervously over at Chuck Green. His bland face was now contorted into a mask of horror.

"Who would be doing something like that? Why would it be one of our associates?" asked Jessica.

"I saw Chip crouching underneath the car where I found the device. I think he was putting it on the car."

Jessica said, "Oh my God." Her were eyes wide and round. "Umm, I'll get back to you."

"Okay. And there's one more thing."

"Yes?" said Jessica warily.

"I have a feeling Alba might try to bounce me. I hate to dump all this crap on you. Hopefully you can handle it without those idiots from Corporate finding out about everything and screwing it all up for you with a lot of paperwork and stuff."

"I'll call you back," said Jessica hastily.

Jessica and Chuck stared at each other for a moment, then Chuck said, "This calls for immediate action. You and I are driving down to that location right away!"

"Um, right," said Jessica.

"That associate—what did you say his name was—Tyler? Is he some kind of a head case? Mafia? What's he talking about?"

"He's always been a good employee," said Jessica, allowing an element of doubt to creep into her voice, indicating subtly to Chuck that Tyler might have had a recent psychotic break of which she, Jessica, could not possibly have been aware.

"The last thing we want is his carrying on about this and getting local law enforcement involved!" said Chuck. "Or, even worse, the account! A primo account! Nobody must know about this until we conduct our own thorough investigation. And hopefully, not even then. Something like this could be very harmful to the Elite brand!" Chuck shoveled Jessica's employee self-assessment evaluation forms into his briefcase and clicked it shut.

"SO what have you got so far on Roger Benson?" said Lukowski. He and Debbie Myers were having coffee in the break room. "Are you taking him seriously as a suspect in your case?" Debbie had just told him that the ballistics lab had finally reported that the bullets in Scott Duckworth's car matched the gun that had been in Tyler Benson's pocket. And that their idea there had been two shooters was now confirmed.

"No witnesses put him at the scene then, but sounds like he was very agitated and possibly shitfaced drunk. He was fired from DuckSoft years ago and now he's in big financial trouble. His kid had to leave an expensive college back east. He might blame Scott for all that."

Lukowski looked thoughtful. "That could tie in the kid. Maybe Benson brainwashed the kid into thinking everything that happened to their family was Duckworth's fault. You know these spoiled brat kids. Feel entitled to everything."

"And the kid lied about the slipper that ties his dad to the scene," said Debbie.

"And presumably his kid tipped him off Duckworth was going to be there," said Lukowski. "And his kid later had the gun on his person—a gun that we now know fired bullets into Duckworth's vehicle."

"That's right," said Debbie. "Okay, so the gun was probably in the Dumpster, like the kid said. Coffee grounds and risotto, okay. But maybe the kid tossed it in there the night of the assault. Covering for his dad. Or himself. Could be a strong circumstantial case." Debbie sighed. "But Roger is all lawyered up. He's not co-operating at all. If I was his lawyer, I'd give him the same advice. The guy's a real fruitcake."

"If only we could have held the kid!" said Lukowski. "I'd still like to know why we can't."

"That property room scandal," said Debbie. "It was a pretty big deal."

Lukowski looked thoughtful. "If we could find out who took that revolver from the property locker in the first place, we might be able to establish a chain to the Bensons."

"I'll ask Dad," said Debbie. "He can't remember where he put his remote, but he remembers the old days pretty well. He knows where a lot of departmental bodies are buried."

Lukowski said, "But if this was a father-and-son deal, with two guns, we still don't know how, why, and when the bullets from the .22 got into the tattoo guy. Were Benson or his son taking out Russian gangsters, too?"

"The tattoo guy is an entirely different case," said Debbie. "But if the Bensons are good for the Duckworth shooting, I can still make it stick."

"Yeah," said Lukowski. "That's fine for you, Debbie. But the tattoo guy is *my* case."

Debbie said, "I think maybe you guys should lean on the kid. Okay, so maybe you can't pick him up. But you can at least lean on him. Why don't you drop in on him at work? He can't run away from you there, can he?"

She hitched her purse onto her shoulder. "I'm working on a way to lean on his dad."

AFTER his call to Jessica, Tyler felt worse, not better. He had expected her to be more interested in what he'd just discovered. Maybe even grateful. But she sounded lukewarm, if not actually cold. And then three customers in a row stiffed him on a tip. Maybe it was his demeanor, because he was so worried about everything.

He made a little vow to be positive and confident with everyone. When Vic came back to the booth, Tyler gave him a big friendly smile. "How's it going, Vic?" he said.

Vic scowled at him. "What were you doing under that car?" he demanded. "You can't be messing with customer's cars."

"I told you. I was looking for my phone under that car."

"Those customers told me you said you were looking for a phone in the banquet room, too," said Vic. "They thought you might have been trying to eavesdrop on their business conference." He narrowed his eyes in a menacing way that made Vic seem totally stupid, like a little kid trying to be creepy—and that was what set Tyler off.

Suddenly, he was furious. He hadn't been so mad since that night he turned twenty-one at the Viking Valhalla and keyed that Corvette. There was no way he was going to be afraid of Vic, even if he was all mobbed up. Vic was just too stupid. Surely his thug buddies didn't take him seriously.

"You know what?" he said, stepping toward Vic and lifting his chin in a belligerent way. "I kinda resent hearing any of this from you. As far as I can tell, you're one of the laziest, most useless valets I've ever worked with. Crappy attitude with the customers. So why are you all of sudden so interested in my job performance?"

"Maybe because I'm Shift Lead," said Vic, pushing him on the shoulder.

"Well, you were filling in for Chip and he's back. So if you've

got a problem, talk to him," said Tyler. "And don't touch me
again!"

Vic glowered and pushed Tyler's shoulder once more. "Don't
fuck with me," he said quietly. "Or my associates from Donna's."

"Associates!" said Tyler, laughing. "Your associates! That's
what people say in gangster movies!" He figured that laughing
at Vic might enrage him, and he wanted Vic to be enraged so he
would try to hit Tyler and Tyler could hit him back. "And didn't
you hear me? I told you not to touch me again." Tyler now pushed
Vic, using one hand on each shoulder, and managed to get him to
stumble back awkwardly and fall against the booth.

Just then a Ford Taurus pulled up. Tyler sprang to the passenger door and opened it, saying, "*Buona sera!* Welcome to *Ristorante
Alba.*" He was astonished to see that the passenger was his boss,
Jessica. From the alarmed expression on her face, he could see she
had just watched him push Vic into the valet booth.

Behind her was a second car. Vic was still lingering by the
booth, proving, Tyler thought, that he was indeed useless. Why
wasn't he trotting over to the second car?

Seeing as Jessica was part of Elite Valet, Tyler instinctively
went to open the doors for the paying customers in that second
car. He was startled to see that the occupants of this car were
detectives Lukowski and MacNab. "Up to your old tricks?" said
MacNab. "Assault, I mean?" He looked over at Vic. "You okay,
son?"

Chapter Eighteen

///

BEFORE VIC HAD A CHANCE TO ANSWER, the driver of the car Jessica had arrived in had let himself out of the car and was striding over to Tyler. He took in the suit and tasseled loafers and figured he was one of the Elite Valet executives. "Is this the associate we were talking about?" the man said to Jessica.

Tyler felt suddenly giddy, and as if he were operating in one of those dreams where everything keeps going wrong. "Associate!" he repeated. He had just laughed at Vic for calling those thugs associates, and now he was being called an associate. "Associate? Yes, I guess I am," he said vaguely. He wondered if he sounded as crazy as he felt.

"We need to talk," said the guy with the pink tie to Tyler. He nodded at Vic. "Can you take care of these gentlemen?" He indicated the two detectives.

"*We* need to talk to him first," said Lukowski, pointing at Tyler.

The guy in the pink tie said, "Our other associate will be glad to help you," in a firm tone. Tyler was horrified to hear himself snickering. The word "associate" was setting him off.

Everyone seemed to be staring at him, so he stopped laughing and looked down at the ground. Then MacNab pulled out a badge and stuck it into the face of the guy with the pink tie. "Seattle police," he said. "*We* need to talk to him."

"But I'm sure it's all a mistake," said the pink tie guy. "We'll be contacting you after our internal investigation. We'd hate to bother you—if you were contacted by this associate..." Tyler bit his lip. That stupid word again. The pink tie guy's confidence seemed to be ebbing. "Well...he wasn't authorized to call you."

"And you are...?" said MacNab.

"Chuck Green, Regional District Manager. Elite Valet," he said, presenting MacNab with a business card, smiling and holding out a hand, as if the detectives would be honored to meet him. MacNab stuffed the card in his pocket without reading it, then looked down at the outstretched hand and after a beat, removed his hand from his pocket and shook it.

"We need to talk to young Tyler here. Ongoing investigation. What do you mean, he wasn't authorized to call us? Since when does a citizen need permission from," he retrieved the business card and scanned it, "the regional district manager of a car parking company to call the police?"

Chuck Green's smile got smaller but didn't vanish entirely. "Well, apparently Tyler here thought there might be some unusual activity here and came to the conclusion that this might somehow indicate some activity of a potentially criminal nature related to possible car theft. Naturally, we'd like to check this out before the police get involved. We know how busy you are and—"

MacNab cut him off. "We're investigating a homicide."

Green looked taken aback, and glanced over at Tyler with horror. MacNab continued, "But if Tyler here knows about any other crimes, we'll be glad to talk to him about those, too. We'll be in touch if there's anything we need from you. I got your card."

Lukowski smiled at Chuck Green and said, "Am I getting this right? Are you saying this young man thinks there was some illegal activity going on? Car theft?"

"Um, that's right," said Chuck.

Tyler felt stupid. They were talking about him and he was standing right there. He started to say something, and reached for his phone to show them the picture he'd taken.

But then he heard Chuck Green say, in a simpering voice, "I

don't want to talk about any of this until I talk to our legal people." That reminded him of his own legal person, Veronica.

"Call me old-fashioned, but if you have knowledge of a crime, don't you think you should share it with the police," said MacNab. "As a matter of good citizenship?"

Tyler thought Chuck Green sounded like a spineless jerk talking about checking with the Elite Valet lawyers. But he also remembered what Grandpa's lawyer had told him. Don't talk to the cops. And after that grilling he'd undergone just a few days ago, he was determined to stick with the program.

MacNab turned around to Tyler. "What do *you* have to say about all this?"

"Um," he said, "my attorney says I can't talk to you about anything unless she's there. Want me to call her?"

"Did she represent you in that felony trial?" asked MacNab. "Too bad she couldn't get you off."

Chuck Green wheeled toward Jessica. "Did you hear that? He has a record! We are going to have to begin the termination process!"

"Oh for God's sake!" said Tyler. "If you want to fire me just go ahead and do it."

"There is a *process*," said Chuck. "But you better believe that process will be followed *to the fullest*."

Jessica bit a corner of her lip and looked at Tyler with an apologetic *Hey I'm sorry but there's nothing I can do about it* expression and a hopeless shrug. "Um, Tyler, we'll need to put you on suspension for a week until we sort this out."

Just then, Brian came out of the restaurant. "Hey, Tyler. Flavia wants to see you," he said.

"Great!" said Tyler. "She probably wants to fire me, too."

"Nobody's firing you yet," said Jessica. "You're just on suspension."

Before anyone could say anything more, Tyler turned away from his tormentors and headed toward the entrance.

MacNab started after Tyler but Lukowski put a hand on his arm and said, "Forget it. He won't talk without his lawyer. We'll call her and see if she has anything to say about his allegations, whatever they are."

To Tyler's surprise, Vic followed him. As soon as they were out of sight of the detectives and the representatives of Elite Valet management, Vic grabbed him by the upper arm and leaned in close to his ear. "If you talk to anyone here or the cops about something you might have found on a car, those guys from Donna's will kill you," he said. "You don't know what you are messing with. They will fucking kill you, I swear to God." And then, to Tyler's surprise and horror, he growled something at him in what sounded like Russian, and then switched back to English to hiss, "This is a fucking warning."

"Everybody here is crazy!" said Tyler. Vic slinked away and Tyler threw open the door to the cubbyhole office next to the kitchen.

Flavia sat behind a pile of papers and a laptop. She looked up at him and he saw she was wearing the glasses he'd seen her wearing on campus.

He repeated himself. "Everybody here is crazy!" he said to her.

"I know," she said. She pushed her wheeled chair away from the desk and he now saw she was wearing a fuzzy cardigan sweater over her power suit. She looked appealingly like a librarian who didn't know she was actually attractive.

"I suppose you called me in here to fire me," he said. "But forget it. You can't fire me because I already am being fired. By Elite Valet! Sorry to deprive you of the satisfaction!"

Flavia removed her glasses and stared up at him. "Elite Valet. Do the Russians also own them?"

"Russians? You mean those guys who were here just now? No way!"

"You're sure?"

Tyler thought about this. Would a company owned by gangsters with the thuggish manners of the little crew he'd just seen browbeating Flavia insist on all the bureaucratic paperwork he knew Jessica had to deal with? Or the mandatory on-line training an "associate" had to undergo in case a secret shopper had caught him out forgetting to smile or recite a stupid canned greeting? Not to mention the convoluted firing process that took weeks—the process Tyler was scheduled to begin immediately—all seemingly designed by HR specialists to avoid wrongful termination lawsuits? Surely *thugs* could figure out how to fire someone on the spot.

"Of course I'm sure!" he said. "It's a national company based in Pittsburgh."

Flavia looked doubtful.

"It takes them weeks to fire people," he said. "And if someone gets hurt on the job, they make my boss fill out tons of paperwork. They're afraid of people suing them."

That they were concerned about litigation seemed to cinch it for Flavia. "Ah!" she said. "I thought the Russians owned them."

"Why did you think that?"

"Because they made us use Elite Valet." She sighed. "I don't understand this country! Sometimes, everything is actually as it is supposed to appear to be."

She frowned in concentration, and Tyler, tired of standing in front of her desk in a servile way, decided if he was going to be fired he may as well be comfortable. He took a seat in the straight-backed guest chair and hooked one arm around the back of it in a gesture designed to make him look as if he felt he owned the place.

Flavia didn't seem to notice any of this body language. "Maybe your boss—this Jessica...somehow..." she said. She trailed off, turned to Tyler and raised her eyebrows in an interrogative manner. Was she suggesting Jessica was part of the Russian mafia—or on their payroll?

It seemed so ridiculous that Tyler actually laughed. "Jessica? She doesn't know anything about any Russians. She told me it was Hughie who arranged for Elite Valet to get your business."

"Hughie?" said Flavia. "Who is Hughie?"

"From Donna's Casino. Another Elite Valet account. He's Donna's son. You never heard of Hughie?"

"No. Is he Russian?"

"No, but he hangs out with them. In the bar at Donna's."

While it struck Tyler that Jessica was an extremely unlikely candidate to be part of a criminal conspiracy, Hughie might well fit the bill. He seemed stupid, and also seemed to be high a lot of the time. The Russians must have arranged for Hughie to set up the switch to Elite Valet.

Flavia said, "But why do you think I was going to fire you?"

"I thought you were mad I burst into the banquet room. And I heard you ask those Russians if you could fire anyone. And they said anyone but Chip or Vic."

"Essactly," said Flavia with a little flourish. Tyler loved it when she couldn't pronounce the letter x before a t. It was about the only mistake she ever made. "So maybe I did want to fire you, but now it is Chip and Vic I would like to fire. Because I hate those Russians and they want me to keep them. Now I don't want to fire you." She gave him the same big smile he'd seen her give Scott Duckworth just before someone had tried to kill him. "I want you here."

"Well, I'm on suspension for a week," he said.

Flavia waved her hand dismissively. "I'll tell Jessica I want you to work here anyway."

"Flavia," said Tyler, realizing he'd never actually called her by her name before. This gave him pause. He started again. "Flavia, I think you're in big trouble. I want to help you."

DEBBIE Myers was sitting in Helene Applegate's office at Duck-Soft. "Will you do it?" she asked.

Helene's eyes grew round. "Do you want me to wear a wire?" she asked.

"No, nothing like that! It's just that I think Roger Benson has a big crush on you and I'd like you to talk to him and maybe see if you think he might have had anything to do with the assault on Scott. I really need some insight into his thinking, and I bet the reason you've been so successful in your career here is because you have a good insight into people."

"I guess it looks bad that he was right there that night," said Helene.

Debbie pressed on. "And you told me no one but you and Red Ott knew Scott would be there. But Roger's son, Tyler, knew. And he must have told his dad."

"I don't know," said Helene. "It was weird that Roger sent that email on the same day. And I haven't really talked to him for twenty years or so; maybe he could have gone off the rails or something, and I never knew about it."

"It's clear he had a crush on you and still does. Did you ever have any feelings for him?" asked Debbie in the tone of a sensitive female friend.

"Oh, I don't know," said Helene. "He was kind of helpless. I felt sorry for him. I like to take care of helpless people."

"All helpless people, or just helpless men?" asked Debbie.

Helene thought for a second. "Helpless men," she said. "I think women don't need so much help."

"But Scott needs your help now," said Debbie. "Can you call Roger? Maybe have a little chat with him? He won't talk to us. Maybe you can find out what he was thinking. You may be the only one who can help Scott," she said. "I know he really counts on you. And your help. If you could get Roger Benson to tell you what he knows. And convince him to come in and make a statement or something…"

"I'll do it," said Helene, looking nervous but thrilled.

"Why don't you call him right now," said Debbie cheerfully.

ROGER was hunkered down in his office when the phone rang. He spent most of his time here these days when Ingrid was home. It wasn't enough that the police were trying to connect him to a homicidal assault! His own wife had turned on him, and that mean little butch lawyer his father-in-law, Gus, had dragged into his life wouldn't let him talk to the cops and clear his name. She wouldn't even let him try and get in touch with Scott.

"Hello," he said warily, wondering what fresh hell was about to be revealed.

"Hi Roger. It's Helene. Helene Applegate."

"Helene!" he shouted. "It's so good to hear your voice."

"Um, I was just wondering how things were going," she said. What a nice voice she had. That kind, sympathetic tone. Helene was really the only person he wanted to talk to right now.

"Could be a lot better," he said. "I can't believe it but the police have actually talked to me about what happened to Scott!"

"I know," she said. "I guess they have to talk to everyone."

"So I guess you showed them that email I sent."

"Well yes," said Helene. She sounded apologetic. He was so relieved that she sounded sorry. "They asked me if there'd been any disgruntled ex-employees. Oh, but I told them I couldn't imagine you had anything to do with it."

"You were always a truly decent person," he said solemnly. "When all that stuff went down years ago and they asked me to resign, you were the only person who showed any sympathy."

Suddenly the door to his office burst open and Tyler's sister, Samantha, said, "Mom wants you to drive me to the orthodontist because she has to hang around waiting for the downstairs bathroom sink to get fixed."

"Can't you drive yourself?"

"God, Dad, how could you forget? She just took me off the insurance because I didn't make honor roll! Remember?"

Roger swiveled around in his chair. She was glaring at him with her hands on her hips.

"I'm on the phone!" he barked, switching to more soothing tones to say, "Sorry, Helene. It's a zoo around here. I work at home these days."

"God, Dad," said Samantha.

"Oh, sorry to bother you," said Helene. "I just wondered how you were doing."

"You're not bothering me, Helene. Listen, is there any chance we could do lunch? It would be great to see you again. I guess you're kind of busy these days, but…"

"I think that would be nice," said Helene.

"We can have a real talk without all these stupid interruptions," he said.

"God, Dad," repeated Samantha.

He flapped his hand at her and said, "Helene, how about that little place where we used to eat lunch back in the day. Next to the old Duckworth offices. You know. Chez Marie."

"I think it's called something else now," said Helene.

"Whatever. Let's meet there," said Roger.

"Okay. How about tomorrow at noon?"

"Wow! That would be fantastic, Helene! I can't wait to see you. Noon tomorrow at what used to be Chez Marie! I can't wait to see you."

He put down the phone and turned in his chair to see that Samantha had gone to fetch the ultimate authority. Ingrid was now standing there dangling car keys at him. "Samantha. Orthodontist. Now."

"Can't you take her? I can wait for the plumber."

"The plumber is my dad. He's the only plumber we can afford. I think he'd rather deal with me, to be honest. At least I'll make him a cup of coffee and tell him we appreciate his help."

"Okay, whatever," said Roger, rising. Reading some magazines in a waiting room was preferable to having his father-in-law sneer at him because he didn't have the manly skills to make a faucet stop dripping.

"Hot lunch date tomorrow?" said Ingrid, slamming the keys into his hand. "I couldn't help but overhear."

"It's business," said Roger with dignity. "Despite everything that's happened. I'm still looking for fulfilling opportunities that will help us all get back on our feet."

Chapter Nineteen

V IC WAS STANDING IN THE DARK, behind a chain-link fence in a gravelly space dominated by a huge propeller, talking to the fish master of a 350-foot fishing trawler. The Russian vessel, in dry dock in Seattle for an electronics upgrade, blasting and repainting of the hull, and maintenance work on the deck gear, fish-processing plant, and engine room, loomed behind them.

"It's all there. Two grand," said Vic eagerly.

His companion flicked through the wad and began counting fifties, then encountered bills of a smaller denomination. "What are all these ones and fives?"

"My tip money," said Vic.

The man rolled his eyes. He stashed it all away in the pocket of his nylon windbreaker.

"So you're sure you'll be ready next week?"

"We better be," said his companion, a tall man. "We need to go fishing."

"You sure you got enough room?"

"I can get three thousand tons of pollock on here. I can easily get your stuff on."

"Everything's arranged from the Vladivostok end," said Vic. "We're all ready to go. And you don't need to worry about the rest of the money. It's all waiting for you as soon as you deliver the merchandise."

The fish master said, "Why should I worry? I'll have the merchandise. If anyone should be worried, it's you." He pocketed the roll of cash.

"I'm not worried," said Vic. "My cousin Gleb has it all arranged. He wouldn't screw me over!"

"You know your own family," said the other man. "But if he doesn't have the money, I'm not releasing those cars."

"You don't want to mess with Gleb," said Vic. "I told you all about him."

AFTER Vic went back to his car and drove away, Sergei Lagunov, who had been parked a few car-lengths away, waited a while, then turned on his own lights, glanced briefly at the smartphone that was tracking Vic, then pulled into traffic. He'd come back later and see what business Vic had aboard the trawler.

Vic seemed to be heading back to his parents' house over in suburban Bellevue. Sergei's surveillance of Vic hadn't provided any proof that he and Chip were actually stealing any of the cars they'd been fitting out with tracking devices provided by the Zelenkos for their own operation. And he wasn't any closer to finding out if Vic's family back in the old country were indeed high ranking *vory*, and if Vic's uncle Ivan and cousin Gleb were big players.

He'd check out the kid's home from the street, maybe get a feel for what his family situation actually was. When Sergei had Googled Vic's parents' names, all he could find out was that Gennady and Anna belonged to a community orchestra in Bellevue. The site had listed all the amateur musicians in the orchestra, who apparently performed for free in church basements. Doing something for free didn't sound like anything an elite criminal would be doing.

Sergei had also learned that Victor's father worked as a structural engineer—Sergei had found his picture on a company website citing an article he had written about adhesives used to repair aerospace composite materials.

Sergei pulled onto the gravel strip across the street where a sidewalk would have been if they hadn't been out in the suburbs, killed the lights, and lit a cigarette. In the dim light of the street lamp, he could see that the house itself was a sixties tract house with a neat little green lawn in front, a winding concrete path up to the porch, and a two-car garage.

Sergei, cigarette now dangling from his lips, took a pair of small binoculars out of the glove box, and examined the black mailbox on a post at the end of the path with the family name GELASHVILI stenciled clearly on it in white paint.

The only thing unusual about the scene was the sight of Vic's car, in the driveway. The trunk was open. Its interior light revealed a couple of suitcases and what appeared to be an empty aquarium tank filled with odds and ends -- some rolled-up posters, a can of tennis balls, and a hairbrush.

Suddenly, the front door opened. Sergei crushed out the lit cigarette to avoid being noticed, and watched the porch through the binoculars.

Three people emerged from the house. First came Vic himself, carrying two sturdy black trash bags and a tennis racket. He was followed by a middle-aged man, presumably his father, wearing an old-fashioned wool cardigan and baggy khakis, and a pair of felt house slippers. He appeared to be shouting at Vic. He was followed by a plump blond woman about the same age, presumably his wife, wearing a terry cloth bathrobe. Her arms were crossed against her ample bosom and she was sobbing.

Sergei cracked the window and leaned toward it. Despite the dull and respectable facade, things were apparently not tranquil in the Gelashvili home.

Dad was shouting in English. "What do you think you are planning to do with your life?"

Mom, in Russian, said, "How can we help you if you won't tell us what you are doing with your life!"

Now Dad turned to Mom and said in Russian, "He is living some crazy fantasy life. He is not right in the head."

Sergei smiled. This was all very interesting. Too interesting to observe from the curb. And what better time to interject himself into this drama than when the man was frustrated and angry and the woman sobbing. They would definitely be off their guard.

He slipped quietly out of the car, and made his way toward the front porch.

Now Vic was snapping back at his father in English. "It's not a fantasy. You're so in denial. Just ask cousin Gleb. You think you know so much!"

"Who the hell is cousin Gleb?" demanded his father. "Someone you met on the damn Internet!" He turned to his wife. "He's crazy."

"Cousin Gleb in Vladivostok!" said Victor.

Mom stopped sobbing and grabbed her husband's arm. "Didn't your cousin Ivan have a son named Gleb?"

"Gleb?" repeated Vic's father, putting a hand to his forehead.

"You remember," said his wife. "Your cousin Ivan's son." She turned to her son. "You need counseling. Your father is worried about you. His health plan will cover it."

"Leave me the fuck alone!" said Victor. He turned away from his parents and headed back to his car, dragging the trash bags along the concrete path, and then ran into Sergei coming up the path.

"Hey Victor!" said Sergei in a friendly way. Sergei, whose professional life was based on sensing fear in others, noted immediately that Vic looked petrified. Sergei pushed Vic aside and strode purposefully up to the parents. He was gratified to note that they, too, looked fearful—the woman pulling the two halves of her robe over her chest more securely, and the man stepping up next to his wife in a protective way, and eyeing Sergei nervously.

Sergei tilted his face just a bit to one side so the porch light would catch his scar. He'd hated it when he first got it, but had learned how to display that scar for maximum effect. He was rewarded by a solid flinch from both parents.

"You must be Vic's parents," he said in a pleasant tone. He stepped back next to Vic, who had satisfyingly frozen in his tracks, and was staring up at him in horror. Now, Sergei slipped his hand into his pocket, wrapped his fingers around the binoculars, and jabbed them into Vic's side through his jacket pocket. Vic stiffened, apparently convinced he had a gun stuck into his ribs.

"Hey, guy? Moving out? Need some help?"

After a long moment of silence, Vic's dad smiled nervously and said, "Is this a friend of yours?"

"We kind of work together," said Sergei. "At the valet company. I'm afraid I have some sad news."

"Oh?" said Vic.

He turned to Vic. "You remember Old Pasha?"

"Pasha?" stammered Vic.

"Hey, he died. And it's really important that you come to the funeral. Tomorrow. You and Chip." He paused while all three Gelashvilis stared at him. "We want a good turnout. Let me give you a hand." Sergei yanked the tennis racket from under Vic's arm and hustled him over to the trunk of his car. Obscured behind the trunk lid he leaned in close, pressed the binoculars deeper into Vic's rib cage, and said, "Things are different now. I'm in charge. And you and Chip need to be there at that funeral. Old Pasha got shot. We need you to show some respect. St. Basil's church. Noon. Bring Chip."

He emerged back up from behind the lid and waved at Vic's parents. "Sorry to bother you," he said cheerily. And in Russian, he added, "Poor Old Pasha. A tragic death." He turned to Vic. "Don't forget. Tomorrow. Noon. St. Basil's."

As he sauntered back to his car in silence, he congratulated himself. Yalta Yuri would be happy to have more mourners. And what better way to send a message to Vic and Chip. Meanwhile, he'd try and find out who the hell cousin Gleb was.

On the porch, Vic's mother turned to her husband. She still looked blotchy from crying, but her face was now businesslike. "You need to call your cousin Ivan in Vladivostok. Your mother probably has his number. We need to find out who the hell cousin Gleb is."

SVETLANA Gelashvili was standing at the sink doing dishes, an apron over her white uniform, when her cell phone rang. She tucked it between her ear and her shoulder, picked up her dishrag, and continued her task.

"No, Ivan isn't here," she said. "He's at work. I'm sorry, who did you say this was?"

"Gennady Gelashvili. His cousin in America. I'm sorry to bother you.... "

"Yes! I remember you," she said. "Is everything all right? Did someone in the family die?"

"No! No! It's, well," Gennady gave an embarrassed little chuckle, "to be honest, we've been having some trouble with our son. Victor. My wife is worried about him. We don't know what he's up to."

"Yes?" Svetlana could relate to this. But why was this long-lost cousin of Ivan's telling her this?

"My wife wanted me to see what he and Gleb might be up to on their computers."

"Gleb?"

"Apparently they are in touch."

"What! I didn't know that. Gleb is on his computer all day long. He plays this game called 'World of Warcraft.' He plays a Cyrillic version but I think he also plays in English. Is that how they got together? But they don't use real names. They're avatars. Like pretending to be a character. Are you worried that your son is spending too much time on-line?"

Gennady sounded apologetic. "I don't know what I'm worried about. He seems to be interested in the mafia or something. He said he and Gleb were emailing. Does Gleb still live at home?"

A young, skinny blond boy about five foot two inches tall came into the kitchen and looked in the fridge, then he came over to Svetlana and pulled her apron strings loose. She swirled around to face him and he laughed at her. Glaring, she slapped him across the face with her wet dishrag.

"Ow!" he shouted.

"What does Gleb do? Does he have a job?" asked Gennady.

"A job? Of course not! He's only thirteen years old," said Svetlana. She covered the phone to muffle it, and said, "Have you been emailing a cousin in America? Victor?"

Gleb gave her a little smirk. "I've just been kidding around with him. It's good for my English. Is that him on the phone? Does he want to talk to me?"

"No, it's his father, he's worried about him."

"Well, he should be," said Gleb, wandering back to the fridge. "That guy's crazy!"

His mother grabbed him by his bony shoulder. "Tell his dad about it," she said, lowering her voice to a fierce whisper and thrusting the phone at him. "And be nice to him! Who knows, he might be able to get you into an American university! You don't want to grow up to be some pathetic, grubby little hacker, do you?"

Chapter Twenty

INSIDE THE NAVE OF ST. BASIL'S, a small group dressed in black clustered around the coffin holding large candles while an altar boy swung a smoky censer. Detectives MacNab and Lukowski stood respectfully back a few feet, and while appearing solemn and holding their heads still, they peered through the clouds of incense, their eyes flicking across the faces of the mourners.

There was a burly guy in his late forties, with a round, jowly face who fit the description Father Ushakov had given them of the man who was paying for the funeral and the repairs to the church roof. Lukowski was delighted he'd actually called back to ask again about that funeral, and sent a guy who said he worked at a convenience store where Old Pasha bought a breakfast burrito every morning to identify the body.

He wore a black suit and had entered the church in the company of a handful of hard-looking men with a vaguely foreign appearance. One of them was a tall, thin guy in an expensive suit with a nasty scar on one side of his face. Besides the alarming scar, the fact that he was videotaping the ceremony on his phone made him stand out from the others.

There were also a few old ladies and a couple of teenaged kids. As they were the only ones crossing themselves at appropriate times and singing softly along with the haunting voices of the small choir, the detectives figured they must be the ringers from the congregation that Father Ushakov had said would be there to flesh out the skimpy crowd.

And then there were two young guys—a blond one and a dark one—whose all-black outfits were highlighted by a pink logo on the zipped-up nylon jackets that included the words ELITE VALET. One of them looked like the kid that Tyler Benson had been pushing around at their last visit to Alba's valet booth. Tyler, however, wasn't present.

The top half of the coffin lid was now opened, revealing white satin lining and the face and upper torso of the tattoo guy, whom the detectives by now knew was named Pavel Ivanovich Tarasov, and who the priest had learned from his bereaved friends, was a Russian immigrant with a green card who had worked in an auto body shop. His hands, folded together on his chest, held a crucifix. Now the bottom part of the coffin lid was opened, revealing a handsome white embroidered shroud.

Lukowski thought Pavel looked like he was tucked in bed. Those prison tattoos and the autopsy report describing his chewed-up liver, tarry lungs, and hardened arteries, and some unsightly scars that looked like they'd been made with a knife, had made it pretty clear the guy had had a hard life. Whether that was of his own making or not, Lukowski found himself saying a prayer for the poor old guy to rest in peace.

Now the priest was placing a small paper strip on the old man's forehead, and he removed the tall hat he wore and bent over to kiss the crucifix. Lukowski wondered how much longer the service would last. The uniformed officer who was taking pictures of all the license plates in the parking lot should be done by now.

On the other side of the coffin, Chip leaned over to Vic and said, "Hey that coffin opens up just like a forty–sixty split bench in a Ford Ranger."

Sergei Lagunov glared at both of them.

"Shut up," whispered Vic out of the side of his mouth. "Show some respect."

TYLER was on his phone in the valet booth in front of Alba. "I still think it's stupid for you or your dad to talk to the cops," Veronica Kessler said. "But I'll listen to what you and this gal have to say." She explained to Tyler that she didn't have an actual office per se, but that she was going to be over at his grandpa's tomorrow afternoon and they could all talk then.

Now, all Tyler had to do was convince Flavia to come with him. He turned to Brian, who was scribbling in his spiral-bound notebook. "Hey, I have to go inside to the office for a minute," he said. "I'll be right back. I'm not sure why it's just us. I wonder what happened to Vic and Chip."

"Vic and Chip said they had to go to a funeral," said Brian.

"Really?" said Tyler. "I wonder who died."

"Chip said it was some Russian guy or something. You know, I'm thinking my screenplay would actually work better with zombies. I think that vampire thing is so over—it's just like a chick thing now, you know. And I don't want just plain old zombies that just want to eat brains or whatever. It's more complex. Like a whole organization. With layers. Like some zombies are in charge of other zombies."

"A Russian guy?" Tyler had already figured that Vic was part of the Donna's Casino branch of the Russian mafia, but what was Chip going along with him for? "Did they say who he was?"

"I don't remember," said Brian. "But they were talking about some Russian guy earlier. He had a cool name. Capitan Zhukov. I think that would make a good name for one of my zombie masters."

"They're at some guy called Captain Zhukov's funeral?" repeated Tyler.

"I don't know. Chip told me they were going to a funeral for some Russian guy. But before that, when I first came on shift, I heard them talking about some guy named Capitan Zhukov. But, it wasn't, like, *Captain* Zhukov, it was, like, Cap-ee-*tawn* like a foreign language. He was leaving town or something. I don't know. Don't you think it's a cool name for a character? I'm thinking there's like a zombie initiation thing and—"

"Totally," said Tyler, cutting him off. "A totally cool name for a zombie master."

OUTSIDE the church, Gennady Gelashvili waited in his car. He was on the phone to his wife. "No, I didn't go inside, but his car's here." Vic had refused to respond to all the texts and voicemails they'd sent, and this was the only place they knew they might find him. That strange man with the scar had been very precise about the time and place. "I'll be sure and have a word with him when he comes out."

He looked down at the picture he'd printed up from the PDF that Ivan had sent him. It was a family snapshot with a smiling Ivan, wearing a leather jacket and holding a cigarette, his arm around his buxom wife, Svetlana, and standing in front, looking mischievous, little Gleb with a cowlicky blond haircut. He was thirteen, Ivan had said in the email, but small for his age. He looked about ten or eleven. Ivan explained that they had indulged his constant on-line fantasy role playing because he was so small for his age. They figured it was good for him to feel powerful and masterful in his pseudonymous on-line activities, and it seemed to make him happy.

Ivan had assured Gennady the boy was brilliant but not really motivated at school. In fact, Ivan had hopes of educating the boy at a university abroad. His English was coming along nicely, in part from spending so much time on the Internet. Could cousin Gennady give them some tips on how that could be arranged? He was sorry little Gleb had sent all those foolish emails, but he was just over-imaginative. It wouldn't happen again, and they had confiscated his computer for three weeks.

The doors to the church opened, and Gennady observed a group of men staggering down the steps with a coffin, while an altar boy in a lacy surplice and untied sneakers swung a censer. A priest and a small group of mourners followed the coffin and Gennady spotted his son and got out of the car. He felt like bounding toward him, but the solemnity of the occasion inhibited him. Instead he stood across the street and waved at Victor.

His son scowled and turned away. Next to him, the man with the scar followed Victor's gaze, muttered something to him, and strolled slowly across the street toward Gennady, pausing to light a cigarette. Victor took off in another direction with a youngish blond guy.

"Your son can't talk to you now," said the man with the scar. "We're going to the cemetery."

"I need to talk to my son," said Gennady, looking over the man's shoulder with a desperate feeling as his son strode away to his car.

"Now's not a good time," said the man.

"Look," said Gennady, "I want you to give him this. It's a picture of his cousin Gleb. See? Here's my cousin Ivan and Ivan's wife, Svetlana. She's a dentist. And there's Gleb. It's important. He's been emailing Gleb and Gleb's been pretending to be an adult. I just wanted him to know." He imagined he sounded slightly crazy.

The man took the picture and smiled. "Yeah, he's mentioned him," he said. "I'll make sure he gets this. And what does Ivan do?"

"He works for some company in Vladivostok that makes some kind of technical equipment," said Gennady, feeling a little more relaxed at this show of interest in the family. "I think he's a book-keeper."

"That's interesting," said the man with a little smile that dragged his scar upwards.

HELENE wasn't sure at first that the restaurant where she was meeting Roger was the one that used to be called Chez Marie. In the seventies and eighties it had been a cozy kind of place with red-checkered tablecloths. Chez Marie had served crêpes filled with savory, gloppy fillings like asparagus in Hollandaise sauce or bits of beef in Béarnaise sauce. Now, it looked like an abandoned industrial site with rusty-looking walls, stainless steel tables, and tall, uncomfortable stools. Helene put her purse down on the floor and climbed up on the stool, hooking the low heels of her pumps over a rung.

She looked at the menu, a strange selection of vaguely Asian dumplings and noodles with sides of puréed root vegetables and odd combinations of ingredients like jicama and pork bellies and kimchi and things with Spanish and Vietnamese names all together on the same plate. Well, Roger might like it. He'd always fancied himself a gourmet, sneering at Scott's love of peanut butter and jelly sandwiches and tuna casseroles.

Suddenly Roger appeared, and rushed over to her table. "Helene! It's so good to see you!" he said, standing in front of her tall stool with arms outstretched. She could barely make out his youthful self in the middle-aged face, but his voice was so familiar. It was funny how people aged. Their faces got kind of scrunched like apple dolls, and he had one of those wattle things under his chin just like she was developing. All her contemporaries looked like her parents these days—but he seemed to have held up fairly well.

He leaned over and gave her a huge hug, which alarmed her as she was afraid the wobbly stool might tip over, causing her to cling to him. Now he was planting a kiss on her cheek. "God, you look fabulous," he said, now holding her by the shoulders, staring into her face and tipping the stool backwards, in the manner of a middle-aged newspaper reader without reading glasses. "You always had such a sweet face!"

"Hello, Roger," she said, disentangling herself and patting her hair back into place as he repositioned her so the stool was now level. As he bounced youthfully over to the opposite stool and perched there, she noticed a woman about their age glaring at her over the menu at a table behind Roger. Maybe she found his effusiveness annoying. Something about the austere atmosphere of the place did make it seem like some kind of gloomy Zen temple to serenity—just like the bleak Japanese garden Carla had installed outside Helene's office window.

"But then you were always such a sweet person!" he said. "Always there for me."

"Well, I've been thinking about you lately," she said briskly. "After this business with Scott and all. I've been worried about you. That policewoman, Debbie Myers, has been asking a lot of questions about what you were doing at the restaurant that night." She paused and smiled self-consciously.

"It was kind of an impulsive thing," he said. "I was talking to my son and he said Scott was going to be there, and I kind of thought it would be great to see him again." He leaned over confidentially. "And, to be honest, I was hoping to talk to him. I had a business proposition for him."

"Oh, he gets lots of those," said Helene.

"Artisanal Italian take-out that you make yourself under expert supervision," said Roger solemnly. "Honest ingredients and authentic tools. Totally Tuscan décor. I started with just one location and planned to work it into an upscale franchise, but the startup costs were more than I planned for. But you can't cheap out on a concept like..." He paused and said dramatically, "Ricotteria."

"Well, I was hoping you could explain all that to Debbie," said Helene. "But she says you aren't co-operating with her. Don't you think you should explain to her? About this Ricotterie idea of yours."

He corrected her gently. "Ricotteria, actually. Ricotterie would be French."

"Okay, Rissoteria, then," she said.

He clicked his tongue in annoyance. "Ricotteria with a *c*. We thought of Rissoteria, but it wasn't as visually striking signage-wise. Anyway, to be honest, I've been advised by my attorney not to talk to the police," he said. "I mean, I didn't have anything to do with some nut taking a shot at Scott. But it's complicated. My kid works there as a valet. Just a little college job, and the police are leaning on him, too. I don't understand what's going on there, I really don't, but somehow they got it all mixed up with that email I sent, and they think I might be some nutty disgruntled ex-employee." Roger laughed. "Ridiculous, of course."

Just then a young woman with a crew-cut in a black apron over black pants and shirt came over and said, "Have you had time to look at the menu?"

"Give us a few minutes," said Roger. As she began to withdraw he added, "What kind of Pinot Grigio do you have by the glass? No, never mind." He beamed at Helene, and said, "How about some Champagne?"

"Oh, I don't think..." Helene didn't drink at lunch. Nobody did anymore. She was afraid she'd fall asleep at her desk. But Roger was now fiddling with the wine list. "Bring us a bottle of this! I haven't seen this pretty lady in twenty years or so!"

Helene managed to smile. This was probably okay. It might get Roger to be even more forthcoming.

Outside the restaurant, Debbie Myers pulled up, got out of her car, and peered into the restaurant through a large spiky plant in the window. He was there all right, beaming at Helene. This just might do the trick. She went back to her car and settled in to wait until they emerged.

In the car, her cell phone rang. It was her dad, back from his cruise right on schedule. "Hi, Daddy," she said. "Did you and Mom have a good time? I can't wait to hear all about it. But listen, first I want you to help me on a case. Remember that scandal back in the day? Thefts from the property room?"

Inside the restaurant, Roger and Helene clinked flutes, and Roger said, "I'm afraid that stock option money is all gone. We thought it would be a good thing to spend some of it taking the family to Italy for a year. It was great for the kids. Really helped them get well-rounded, you know. And while I was there, I realized the potential of artisanal do-it-yourself take-out." He leaned over the table. "Think Starbucks but it's food and you make it yourself."

"An interesting idea," said Helene doubtfully.

Roger bounced a little atop his stool. "You bet it is! But I was way ahead of the curve. I launched it too soon. Now is the time! That's why I need to talk to Scott. I was undercapitalized. And the public needed to be educated about the concept. I needed more promotion."

"Listen," said Helene, looking over the menu. "There's no way Scott will want to hear about it if it looks like you've been involved in that shooting. Carla won't let him. Red Ott won't let him. You have to clear yourself."

"Red Ott? That ex-cop security guard who worked for us?"

Out in the car, Debbie, still on the phone, was saying, "Red Ott! You're sure?"

"That was the word," said her father. "His uncle Ralph was the assistant chief at the time. They just kind of eased him out of there. No loss to the department, that's for sure! Maybe it was a good thing they kept a lid on it. Who needs a bunch of smart-ass reporters talking about crooked cops. It undermines respect."

Reluctantly, Helene ordered some pancakes with red cabbage and some kind of pickled fish. She'd liked those gloppy crêpes when this was Chez Marie. Her favorite had been melted Swiss cheese with ham. She took a sip of Champagne and leaned over the table. "If you agree to talk to Debbie, and get this all cleared up, I can put you on Scott's calendar."

"You'd do that for me?" he said. Suddenly he leaned across the table and kissed her. "I love you!" he said in a loud voice.

Helene pulled away and her tall stool tipped sideways. As it hovered slightly, and just before she toppled onto the floor, she saw the woman who had glared at them earlier throwing her napkin on the table and marching toward her.

"Ingrid!" said Roger. "What are you doing here?"

As the young woman with the crew cut and two other similarly ninja-clad members of the wait staff rushed to Helene's crumpled form, the woman said, "That's what I should be asking you! I heard you making this date yesterday! You can't even manage an affair properly!"

Helene, horrified, clambered to her feet, clutched her purse, and headed for the door. Tears were forming in her eyes. As she pushed open the door, one of the ninjas said, "Ma'am! Ma'am! Are you okay?"

"Yes, I'm fine," she said.

Out on the sidewalk, Debbie got out of her car and rushed toward Helene, who was addressing a knot of worried-looking young people in black in apologetic tones. "Don't worry, I'm not going to sue you or anything."

Just then, Roger and Ingrid Benson appeared on the sidewalk. Ingrid was saying, "You said you loved her!" She pointed at Helene.

Helene's head swiveled toward Ingrid. "Well, I don't love *him*," said Helene. "I just want *him* to talk to *her*." She pointed at Debbie Myers. "I love someone else," she said. "I'm worried about him. That's why I'm here." Now she burst into tears.

Debbie put her arm around her and said, "I know, honey. And I think you should tell him." Now she addressed Roger. "Can we talk?"

Chapter Twenty-One

DO YOU REALLY THINK WE CAN get rid of them?"
Flavia said. Tyler had arranged to meet her at the Jack in the
Box on University Way and now he was leading her to his car. His
valet instincts now fully ingrained, he opened her door first and
she slid past him. She was in her student uniform—yoga pants,
no makeup, hair down, and those sweet glasses. She even smelled
different. More like soap and less like the part of Nordstrom's near
the entrance where they sold cosmetics and perfume.

"If we can get Veronica to tell the police they are stealing cars,
I think we might be able to get the police to get rid of them for
you," said Tyler, closing the door with a professional thunk. As he
pulled into traffic, he realized it was weird driving her around, like
they were on a date or something.

"I'm scared," she said. "What if they find out?"

"They won't think *you* have anything to do with it," said Tyler.
"That's why we're having my grandfather's lawyer tell them."

"But you told me this lawyer didn't want you to talk to the
police about anything. Maybe she won't talk to them either."

"We can give it a try. If it doesn't work, maybe you should see
if Scott Duckworth can help you. Maybe he has some connections
that can get right to the police. Like that security guy he has."

"Ha! Red Ott! That moron!" said Flavia.

"Scott Duckworth must be an idiot to have a moron like that

156 // K. K. Beck

working for him," said Tyler, glad to be able to say something un-
kind about Duckworth. What a jerk! He could have saved Flavia
by now. What was wrong with him?

"Anyway," said Flavia, "what I really want is for Scott Duckworth to buy the business. Then he can deal with those Russians
and that loan. And my brother can just do what he wants, which
is to cook."

"Do you think he will buy the business?"

"I think he wants to. But his sister, Carla, won't let him."
Flavia narrowed her eyes. "She thinks it's just because he's at-
tracted to me."

"Well, I wouldn't be surprised," said Tyler, disgusted at the
thought of that old man touching the girl next to him. "A guy
like that, with all his money, I guess he could get anyone he wanted." Tyler didn't like the direction he seemed to be taking so he
changed his tone. "Anyway, I'm sorry you got so involved in your
brother's business," said Tyler. "It sounds like you're just like me.
You just want to go to school."

"It's my parents!" said Flavia. "They got me involved. They
have a restaurant in Alba. Very traditional. My father is the chef
and my mother does the front end. So when my brother ended up
here—after he fell in love with an American girl—my parents sent
me over here to keep an eye on things."

"To keep an eye on the business?"

Flavia nodded. "And on the American girl. They were worried
about his marrying a foreigner. They are very conventional. They
thought she was strange and that she dressed badly. And she was
terrible in the restaurant. She couldn't open wine bottles correctly,
or shave truffles over a dish with any style. She couldn't even walk
properly, they said. The restaurant business is theater. You are on
stage. They couldn't bear to have him run a restaurant with someone like that. She was not like Italian girls."

"What happened to her?" Tyler was starting to feel sorry for
the girl he imagined to be a typical hearty, uncoquettish Seattle girl
sporting Polar Fleece outfits and sneakers, and clomping around
in a kind of gender-neutral way.

Flavia shrugged. "She left him. She hated the business. Even if she could have done it well, she didn't want to stand around holding menus all day and smiling. I don't blame her! But she didn't understand. A family business—the whole family has to help. She ran off with her personal trainer and now she's studying to be a massage therapist."

"My father tried to start a business," said Tyler. "But he wasn't like your parents. He didn't know what he was doing—he just wanted to feel glamorous. He lost a fortune and stuck me with a huge bill for my college fees. I'm paying it off parking cars so I can go to graduate school without owing any more money."

"I love school," he added.

"Me, too," she said.

"Flavia, we both need to figure out how to do what we want—without our parents ruining everything."

THE fish master of the Russian trawler in dry dock looked at the picture Sergei showed him and laughed. "That's him? The criminal mastermind Gleb?" His voice echoed in the vast space. The two men were sitting in the cafeteria of the vessel. When the factory trawler was back at sea, the workers who dragged tons of pollock out of the Bering Sea and headed, gutted, and froze it in the factory inside the hull of the vessel would fill up this cafeteria, eating huge meals in around-the-clock shifts, but today, there were just the two of them, an ashtray, a bottle of vodka, and two glasses.

Sergei slipped the picture back in his pocket. "That Victor kid is pathetic," he said. "And if he does have all those cars he told you he had, they're mine."

The fish master shrugged. "I figured he was kind of off. But what did I have to lose? Anyway, just in case he was wasting my time, I told him I couldn't wait for Gleb to pay me off in Vladivostok. I told him I needed a deposit."

Sergei gave the man a big smile and clapped him on the back. "You know what," he said. "We'll let you keep that. No problem!"

"Thanks a lot," said the other man.

"You just need to let us know when the cars are arriving. I'll give you a number to call."

The fish master threw up his hands. "I don't need a number. I don't even want a number. I can tell you right now. It's all arranged. They're supposed to be loaded on right after the engineers from the company arrive from Vladivostok for the final inspection of the work we've had done here and right before we sail home. Early Tuesday morning. Around two in the morning."

"I'll be here with my guy and his rig. Leave the gate open," said Sergei.

"I was going to do that for Vic anyway," said the fish master.

IT wasn't until Tyler and Flavia rang the doorbell of Gus Iversen's house in Ballard that he suddenly wondered what Flavia would think of his grandfather's living room with its old-fashioned, well-worn decor, and of his grandpa's unkempt attorney, Veronica. But it was too late for all that.

Grandpa opened the door and Tyler introduced Flavia to Gus and Veronica, who was sitting there with her dog, Muffin. After Flavia had petted the dog and Grandpa had gone into the kitchen to bring them coffee, Flavia gravitated to the collection of family photos on the mantel. Pictures of Mom when she was a kid. A family portrait of Tyler with his parents and sister. And a horrible sixth-grade school picture of Tyler smiling with a mouth full of braces and a really bad bowl haircut.

Grandpa soon returned with the coffee in two mugs, one of which bore the legend WORLD'S BEST GRANDPA—a Christmas gift from Tyler when he was nine—and another that read YOU CAN ALWAYS TELL A NORWEGIAN BUT YOU CAN'T TELL HIM MUCH. Flavia gave him a dazzling smile and said, "A purse seiner!" Apparently she hadn't been looking at Tyler's horrible photo at all, but at the oil painting of the *Ingrid Marie*.

"Grandpa was a fisherman," said Tyler.

"When I retired and sold the boat, I had a guy paint that," said Gus, smiling proudly.

"Did you fish in Alaska?" said Flavia. "I'm trying to get on a research vessel that's going up there this summer."

"Not at first. We used to fish around here. But then back in 1974 the courts said the Indians could have half the salmon down here. Totally changed the fishery."

Tyler decided to cut him off before he got started on the injustice of the Boldt decision. "The reason we're here," he said, "is to talk about some stuff we'd like to tell the police. I think it might have something to do with that shooting. And also it might help Flavia."

Veronica turned to Flavia. "What's your interest in this matter?" she said.

"My brother owns the restaurant," she said.

Tyler added, "Flavia's brother got mixed up with some thugs who seem to be in the Russian mafia. A loan type of thing."

"Loan sharks!" said Gus. "You gotta stay away from loan sharks."

"Anyway," persisted Tyler, "I have reason to believe they're stealing cars out of the parking lot there." He explained about the device he'd found on the car. "And two of the valets seem to be mixed up with these thugs."

"These Russians, they also insist we use this valet company," said Flavia. "Tyler and I think it's so some crooked employees there can put these things on the cars.

"They're trying to take over our business," Flavia went on. "Maybe if the police investigate them, they'll stay away from us. But I don't want them to think I called the police. And I don't want the police to know my brother did business with them. Maybe that's illegal. I don't know."

Veronica Kessler looked thoughtful. "Okay. I can tell the police that my client—you, Tyler—has suspicions that there might be some criminal activity going on at Alba that involves Russians. The body they found in that Audi was apparently a Russian. That was in the paper. So I'm going to tell them that they should be pursuing that line of inquiry. But they might want to talk to you about what you saw. Tyler, whatever you do, don't talk to them without me."

"Okay. But you have to keep Flavia out of it."

"I'll try. But I'm representing you, not her," said Veronica jerking her thumb in Flavia's direction.

"I won't talk to them about anything if you mention Flavia or her brother," said Tyler, who was startled to discover he had just put a comforting hand on Flavia's knee. He withdrew it immediately.

"No problem. You'll just tell them about the device you found. So who are these bad guys we want to hang the crimes around the place on? Do they have names?"

"They're easy to find," said Tyler. "They hang out at the bar in Donna's Casino." Suddenly, Tyler remembered what Brian had said about the conversation he'd overheard between Chip and Vic. "I think the guy in charge might be named Captain Zhukov," he said. "But he might be dead. Chip and Vic went to some funeral."

"Captain Zhukov?" said Gus. "That sounds familiar. I swear I've heard that name."

"Okay, Tyler," said Veronica. "I'm going to call those detectives that gave you such a hard time. I'm going to tell them about your suspicions. But I don't like it."

"GET in the damn car!" Dmytro Zelenko was parked in front of a cedar-and-stone building surrounded by gravel paths and wide garden beds full of Japanese maples and low evergreens.

Leaning into the window of the car, his cousin Volodya, holding a small duffel bag, said, "Are you sure you don't want to come in and meet my counselor? And some of the people from my group?"

"Are you crazy!" said Dmytro. "Why would I want to meet them? A bunch of shrinks and drunks. Are you nuts?"

"They're not drunks anymore. They are in recovery," said Volodya, climbing into the front seat. "Like me."

"Yeah, okay," said Dmytro. He jammed his foot on the accelerator and squealed away. "This place gives me the creeps." He glanced over at his cousin. "You look good, though, Volodya. Not so puffy."

"I feel good, too," he answered, smiling, and gazing out the window at the bosky surroundings like a happy child on an outing.

"Well, you won't feel so good when I tell you what's happened while you were in there drying out," said Dmytro. "Sergei told me all about you shooting Old Pasha."

Volodya looked embarrassed.

"You can't just go around killing people!" said Dmytro. "Sergei thinks you might have shot up Alba when that billionaire was there, too!"

"But I didn't kill anyone that time," said Volodya. "I just was so mad at Vic and Chip. No one would even have known about Old Pasha if they hadn't messed up with the car he was in the trunk of."

"I don't know why I put up with you," said Dmytro.

Volodya sighed heavily. "I'm sorry about Old Pasha. That was booze shooting," he added philosophically.

"Yeah, but I doubt the cops will see it that way. What are they going to do, arrest a bottle of Stoli?"

"How will they ever know it was me?" said Volodya.

"Well, Sergei Lagunov—that car thief you hired—could give them the gun you used for both crimes," said Dmytro.

"Why would he do that?" said Volodya. "And how come he has the gun?" He wrinkled up his face in concentration. "A lot of stuff that happened before I got arrested, it's kind of a blur. Booze is very bad for your brain cells. They showed us a movie with a dead alcoholic's brain. It was full of watery pockets."

"You asshole! Right before you got busted for drunk driving, Sergei took it off of you and left the car you drove into the ditch!"

"Oh yeah! I do remember that. He kept saying, 'Give me the gun' after we heard the sirens."

"We gotta get it back," said Dmytro. "*You* gotta get it back. Sergei is using that gun to take over our business. He's threatened to rat you out and give it to the cops. They can match it to the bullets in the body. And he can probably convince them he got it from you. He's a protected witness. We know that because he already ratted out someone else back in New York."

"What are we going to do?" said Volodya.

"I'm not doing anything," said Dmytro. "You're going to get that gun back."

"You mean beat him up until he gives it back?"

"Nope. You can't do that. He's pretty well connected. You got to sneak that gun away. You can start by searching his apartment."

"What makes you think it's there?"

"It's a good place to start."

"I'm not sure I want to do that," said Volodya.

"It's the least you can do. I don't see why I should just turn over my business to that bastard Yuri just because you messed up." Dmytro sighed. And there was still the matter of Vic and his powerful uncle in Tbilisi to contend with. This wasn't the kind of thing he had signed on for years ago when he switched from his legitimate auto body work to making a little extra on the side by providing the marketplace with quality used parts.

VOLODYA finished looking very thoroughly through all the dresser drawers in the bedroom, making sure to put everything back carefully, just like Dmytro told him. The way they had planned it was that Volodya would make sure it didn't look like a burglary unless he actually found the gun. That way, Sergei wouldn't suspect they were searching his apartment. But if he did find it, then they'd make it look like a burglary, and hope that Sergei figured it was just your regular burglar, who, quite naturally, would steal a gun if it were there.

Volodya also investigated under the vast bed, and in between the mattress and the box springs, struggling to get it all put back together properly, taking care to smooth down the leopardskin-print bedspread perfectly with his latex-gloved hands. Dmytro had insisted on them, too.

He had already checked underneath the cushions of the black leather sofa and chairs in the living room. He had also searched the fridge and the freezer and the toilet tank and the closet in the bathroom.

He now turned his attention to the bedroom closet. Here he

discovered some expensive-looking narrow leather shoes with pointy toes in a neat row, some sneakers, an ironing board, a barbell and a collection of free weights, and a sports bag, as well as a tall wicker laundry hamper. He plowed through Sergei's dirty clothes—mostly black silk boxers and starched white shirts that smelled of cologne.

Volodya was about to investigate the shelf above his head, which seemed to hold some folded blankets, when he heard a key in the door. Horrified, Volodya stepped further back into the closet and slid the door shut. Now he heard Sergei's voice. Was he with someone else?

But then Volodya heard a pause and silence, followed by another burst of conversation. He must be on the phone.

Now, Sergei seemed to be coming into the bedroom. It was hard to tell with all this thick carpeting. But he must be right outside the closet, because now, Volodya could hear his voice perfectly. "Our Ukrainian friends are cooperating nicely," he said. "Dmytro is intelligent enough to understand his position. His stupid cousin is still in rehab as far as I know. To tell you the truth, I wouldn't put it past Dmytro to sell out the cousin. Thank goodness we have more leverage than that gun. Dmytro still doesn't realize the powerful *vor* Gleb is thirteen years old!"

Volodya heard Sergei laughing right outside the closet door. He squatted down and grabbed one of the dumbbells among the collection of weights, and rose just in time to be dazzled by the light from the now open closet door and the vision of Sergei with his phone in one hand, his tie undone, his eyes wide.

When Volodya brought the dumbbell down on Sergei's forehead, he put everything he had into it. Sergei collapsed instantly to the ground. As Volodya stepped over his crumpled form, he noted the way the skull was caved in, and the oozing blood from the wound and from Sergei's mouth.

As Volodya made his way toward the sliding glass balcony door off the bedroom that had served as his entrance, bloody dumbbell in hand, he heard a small, yappy sound coming from the phone. "Sergei! Can you hear me now?" the voice said.

Volodya crushed the phone with the dumbbell to make the little voice go away. And then he thought maybe he shouldn't leave
the phone here. The cops could find out who Sergei had been talking to. Maybe that would be a bad idea. Suddenly, it also occurred
to him the dumbbell should go, too.

He supposed Dmytro would want him to continue to look for
the gun. But it wasn't registered to Volodya. He'd bought it off
some kid who also sold him a car once. And without Sergei saying
Volodya had used it in a murder, who cared about the gun anymore anyway? Really, when you thought about it, Dmytro was
better served by having Sergei gone.

Chapter Twenty-Two

///

DETECTIVE DEBBIE MYERS AND Flavia Torcelli stood at the entrance to Alba, and Flavia gestured vaguely toward the front of the restaurant. "And the noise came from there," Flavia said.

"And where was Mr. Ott then?"

"It's so hard to remember," said Flavia. "It happened very quickly but it seemed to last forever. He was standing right behind Scott, and I was welcoming Scott. Shaking his hand, you know? And then suddenly we heard the shots. And Mr. Ott pushed Scott and he fell right on top of me!"

"And what was Mr. Ott doing then?" Debbie asked.

"How could I tell? I was completely smothered by Scott. He wouldn't get off of me!" She gave a little shudder and wiggled her fingers. Debbie smiled. Scott Duckworth may have had a crush on this girl, but it was clear the feeling wasn't mutual.

"Did Ott have anything in his hand?" asked Debbie. "A weapon?"

Flavia's eyes widened. "I don't think so!"

"Okay, then what happened? Can you walk me through it?"

Flavia led the way inside. "Then Mr. Ott kind of pulled Scott off of me and pushed us both into the kitchen. It's hard to remember essactly. But then he locked us in the kitchen! He wouldn't let me out!"

Flavia pushed a metal door that opened into a busy kitchen. There was a pleasant combination of the percussive sound made by employees chopping vegetables on a long table, and the sizzle from huge frying pans where others were sautéing mushrooms.

"Let's see," said Flavia, looking around the kitchen as if the surroundings would jog her memory. "Then he went away for a while and trapped me in here with Scott and the other security guy."

"Do you know where he went?" said Debbie.

"No. He was gone about, maybe fifteen minutes."

"And then he came back?" said Debbie.

"That's right," said Flavia. She stared over at the sink, and its sign reminding employees to wash their hands. "Then he did something strange," Flavia said. "I just remembered. He went over there and washed his hands. Really scrubbed them clean, you know? Why would he do that?"

"Good question," said Debbie. "Now I'd like you to take a look at this guy. Did you see him around here that evening?" Debbie handed over a picture of Roger Benson. "Does this guy look familiar?"

"No," said Flavia. "Well, maybe. I think I might have seen a photo of him but not him."

"His name is Roger Benson, and his son is a valet here," said Debbie.

"Oh." Flavia smiled. "I think I saw his picture at Tyler's grandfather's house. But I never saw him in person."

"Do you know Tyler Benson outside of work?" asked Debbie, astonished.

Flavia looked nervous. "Well, a little bit. We are both students at the university," she said.

Debbie acted as if this weren't interesting news. "Oh yeah? What else do you know about him?"

"Not very much," said Flavia, and then she added, "I have no reason to think he's not a really good person." And then she blushed.

"LOOKS like the guy was waiting for him inside the closet," said MacNab. The two detectives were in Sergei Lagunov's apartment standing over Sergei's corpse, now on a stretcher, as it was being zipped into a nylon body bag.

Lukowski shrugged. "Superficially, it's your classic burglary in progress. Guy comes home. Burglar hides in closet. Guy opens closet door. The victim's loosened tie and his position point that way. And the jimmied-from-the-outside patio door looks legit." Lukowski stepped over to the dresser, and pointed to a gold chain lying on top of it. "But the place looks totally undisturbed. And you'd think a burglar would have at least grabbed that on his way out."

"Seeing as our victim was one of the mourners at tattoo guy's funeral," said MacNab, "there might be a lot more to this story. Dave Chin is coming over to take a look." The two detectives had shared photos of Old Pasha's funeral with the Auto Theft department. Detective Chin had shown an interest because he'd been working on trying to get something on a suspected auto theft ring made up of Russians.

With the corpse now out of the way, MacNab began to check out the contents of the bedroom closet. He flipped through a series of suits. "Expensive stuff," he said. He reached up onto the top shelf, the one Volodya had been about to investigate, and pulled out what looked like an attaché case.

Through the open bedroom door, MacNab and Lukowski saw Detective Chin, a thin Asian man in his early forties, come into the apartment's entry hall. The technicians were preparing to remove the corpse, but Lukowski said, "Hey, show Dave our guy. See if he knows him."

The technician unzipped the bag just enough to reveal Sergei's face. "Doesn't look familiar," said Dave Chin. "But I guess he's not looking his best."

"He would have looked worse if the building manager hadn't come up here to bitch about his parking in a handicapped slot," said MacNab.

Chin said, "Oh, wait, I've seen him before. He's the scar guy from the funeral pictures."

"Did anyone else in those funeral shots look familiar?" said MacNab.

Chin nodded. "One of the older guys said he recognized one of them. A burly guy who did some time for auto theft back in the nineties. We checked him out: Dmytro Zelenko. He's been out of trouble since then. But I doubt he's mended his ways. Runs some kind of auto body shop that we don't have enough probable cause to really check out. But we're pretty interested. There's been a big spike in auto thefts, especially high-end stuff. We've figured there must be some organized enterprise pulling off these thefts." He glanced over at MacNab, who was now opening the attaché case on the floor. "What you got there?"

MacNab looked down at a collection of tools and electronic devices.

"I'm not sure," said MacNab.

"Wow," said Chin. "That's very interesting. We've got a combination of old-school and new-school stuff here. Slide hammer puller to break into the door locks and the cylinder lock. Test light. Screwdrivers, your basic slim jim. And we got the RFID microreaders to defeat ignition locks, and we got some tracking devices. And we got some electronic stuff I've never seen before. And here's some old-school spark plug fragments. These are a quiet but effective way to get safety glass to shatter. What else is in that closet?" asked Chin.

MacNab reached up and took down what appeared to be an oily rag. He carefully unwrapped it and the three men looked down at a handgun.

"Looks like a .22-caliber to me," said Lukowski happily. "If we're lucky, it's the one that killed tattoo guy and we can clear that case."

"Yeah," said MacNab. "But then we gotta find who killed the killer."

"Let's ask this Zelenko character," said Lukowski. "We gotta talk to him anyway, about tattoo guy."

HELENE Applegate was happy to see Debbie Myers. Helene kind of wanted Debbie to see her calm and in charge after that meltdown outside the restaurant. She liked Debbie. She seemed so understanding—like a real friend. And she'd been thinking hard about the advice Debbie had seemed to give her when they last met.

"Mr. Ott is running a little late," she explained. "How about a coffee?"

"Sounds good," said Debbie, settling into Helene's cozy office chair. Helene busied herself with a coffeepot and poured them each a cup.

"I'm kind of surprised you responded to Red Ott's request for a meeting," said Helene. "I know how busy you are." The email he'd asked her to send to Debbie had sounded arrogant to her—like a summons to an employee. He'd requested a meeting to "update Scott and myself" on the progress of the investigation, and to "share intelligence."

"I was interested in talking to Mr. Ott anyway," said Debbie. "Listen, Helene. Thanks for your help the other day. I was able to schedule an interview with Roger Benson. We'll be talking later this afternoon. So that's good."

Just then, Red Ott came into the room. "Good, you're here," he said patronizingly to Debbie, not apologizing for being late. "We'll meet in the conference room. Helene, can you come and take some minutes?"

When they were all ensconced in the conference room, Ott said pompously, "So what have you learned?"

"Well, Mr. Ott," said Debbie cheerfully, "we've learned that the nickel-plated Smith and Wesson snub-nosed revolver we found in the Dumpster was stolen from the police property room when you were still on the force. And some people say you were the chief suspect."

"That's ridiculous!" said Red Ott. He paused and cleared his throat. "And even if it were true, I'm pretty sure the statute of limitations has run out."

"And," said Debbie, "we've learned that some bullets from the gun were found in Scott's car. From the side of the car you were facing when the shooting began."

Helene gasped, but continued to take notes.

"And your point is?" said Ott. "I mean, that kid says he found the gun in the Dumpster."

"Yeah, and Flavia Torcelli says you were rummaging around in that Dumpster yourself two days after the shooting. I believe detectives Lukowski and MacNab will attest to that."

"I was making sure that the area was secure," said Ott, looking nervous now. "You can't prove that gun was ever in my possession."

"Maybe not," said Debbie. "But Miss Torcelli also said you washed your hands right after the bullets flew. Gave them a real good scrubbing. Why would you do that?"

Helene, now overcome, flung down her notebook. "Powder burns!" she exclaimed. "If he fired that gun he wanted to get rid of any powder burns. And he ditched the gun in the Dumpster, then went back to try and get it!" She rose, flung aside her notebook, and leaned over the table staring down at Ott. "Why did you shoot at Scott!"

Ott cringed, leaning away from her. "Okay, I might have returned fire when I saw Scott was in trouble. In fact, I did. The old training kicked in! And I was supposed to protect him."

"Thank God you missed him," said Debbie.

Just then, Scott came into the room with his sister. Carla had carefully arranged blond hair and wore an expensive black pantsuit and pearls.

"What's going on?" said Carla.

Helene ignored her and turned to Scott. She pointed at Ott. "He could have killed you! I knew he was no good." Now she turned to Carla. "Why didn't you listen to me when I said to fire him? Don't you care about your brother?"

"Gosh!" said Scott. "Helene, I've never seen you so riled up!"

"That's because she's in love with you!" his sister said, narrowing her eyes. "Isn't that true, Helene?"

"Yes, it's true and I don't care who knows it!" said Helene.

She fled from the room, while Carla folded her arms across her chest and glared at her retreating back.

"Mr. Ott, I'd like you to come downtown and make a voluntary statement," said Debbie.

THE two Zelenkos sat on white plastic lawn chairs underneath the cherry tree behind Dmytro's chop-shop. Despite the cluttered surroundings—auto parts, rusting junk, an oily puddle in the gravel—the scene was peaceful. The cherry tree was in bloom, and an intermittent breeze occasionally sent a flurry of pink petals to join the drift already settled on the gravel below. A robin, apparently building a nest there, flew back and forth with grass and bits of string and other junk from the site. Dmytro's two Rottweilers snoozed at their feet. Both men were drinking Diet Cokes.

After a moment of silence, while what Volodya had just told him sunk in, Dmytro said, "Jesus Christ, Volodya! I just told you to get the gun! Not kill the guy!"

"It was an accident," said Volodya. "I don't feel good about it either."

Dmytro had noticed that since coming back from rehab, Volodya seemed to be talking about his feelings all the time. "Okay, so tell me again what he was talking about on the phone. Before you crushed his skull."

"He said, 'The Ukrainians are cooperating.' He said I was still in rehab. But he was wrong about that." Volodya frowned.

Dmytro sighed. "I suppose you didn't check the phone to see who he was talking to?"

Volodya ignored him. "He said you were intelligent. And that I was stupid. That son of a bitch!"

"Is that why you hit him so hard?" asked Dmytro.

"Maybe it was," said Volodya thoughtfully. "That's interesting. Maybe I was angry. Maybe is self-esteem issue."

"Yeah, whatever," said Dmytro. "Anything else?"

"Oh, there's one thing he said I didn't understand. He said you still didn't know that some guy named Gleb was only thirteen years old. And then he laughed. Who the hell is Gleb?"

Dmytro grabbed his cousin's hand. "Are you sure?"

"Yeah. I'm sure."

"Okay, okay," said Dmytro. "So Vic was full of shit. And Sergei lied about it when I asked for his help. Maybe it's okay you took care of him." He leaned his head back thoughtfully and observed the robins flapping around near the top of the cherry tree.

Just then, the cousins were startled to see a troika of tough-looking men emerging from the shop's rear entrance, and approaching them at a good clip. One of them was a heavyset bald guy wearing a dark suit with an open silk shirt underneath it. Dmytro thought he looked like a retired weight lifter. A few feet behind him, one on each side of him, were a couple of guys in a collection of baggy nylon gear bristling with sports logos.

"Are you the Zelenkos?" said the guy in the suit.

Dmytro recognized the voice from their many phone conversations. "You must be Yalta Yuri," he said. "What brings you up here from California?"

"You must be Dmytro," said Yuri. "Which means this piece of shit is Volodya who killed my old pal, Pavel. Now I'm wondering what happened to Sergei," said Yuri.

"You guys wanna Diet Coke?" asked Volodya.

Dmytro and Yuri ignored him. Dmytro rose so they were both standing, and the two men stared at each other as one of the robins let out a melancholy low note.

"I was talking on the phone with him when it sounded like he got hurt," said Yuri.

"I was afraid that might happen," said Dmytro. "I think I know who might have done something like that."

"Oh really?" said Yuri. "And who might that be?"

"A kid. Named Victor Gelashvili. I think maybe he killed him."

"Who said Sergei was dead? I just said I thought he might have been hurt," said Yuri.

After a beat, Dmytro said, "Well, I figured that if he was just hurt, you would have found him. Talked to him. Learned what happened."

"So why do you think Victor Gelashvili wanted to kill Sergei?" said Yuri.

Volodya spoke up. "Sergei found out Vic was stealing from us."

Yuri waved his hand impatiently. "I know all about that. The cars. Kapitan Zhukov."

"Kapitan Zhukov?" said Volodya. "Who's he?"

"Come with us. We'll go there together tonight, after midnight. If Sergei's alive, he'll be there."

"What do we need to go with you for?" demanded Dmytro, suddenly red in the face. "I thought Sergei was working for me. Then he tells me I'm working for you. Now you accuse us of killing him! Why would I do that? So you can kill me? I don't even know what the guy was up to with this Kapitan Zhukov. Listen, you can have my damn business. I don't care. If you want it so much, just take it."

Yuri strode over to Dmytro and backhanded him across the face. Dmytro staggered backwards, into his cousin's arms. As soon as he did so, Yuri's two henchmen muscled their way up to both Zelenkos. One of them cuffed Volodya on the ear, and said, "Show some respect." Volodya dropped Dmytro into a greasy splotch in the dirt and gravel, and the second of Yuri's thugs kicked him while he was down, then slapped Volodya who was still standing, but tottering from side to side.

Yuri stepped toward him, and seemed about to give him the coup de grâce, when a voice speaking English said, "Is everything all right?"

The knot of men turned around and faced Lukowski and MacNab, as well as Dave Chin.

"Who are you?" demanded Yuri.

"Seattle police," said MacNab. "We're here to ask a few questions."

The Slavs stood up and brushed off their clothes. Yuri smiled. "We were just playing around," he said.

Volodya looked terrified. "What do you want to talk to us for?"

Lukowski spoke up. "We're investigating a homicide."

"I don't know anything about it!" said Volodya.

"Well, you attended the funeral of the victim," said Lukowski patiently.

Chin, meanwhile, was taking in the premises. "Nice little business you got here," he said. "Body and fender work, huh?"

Volodya's face relaxed and he produced a big smile. "You must mean Old Pasha's funeral. No, I wasn't there. I was in rehab."

"Are you Dmytro Zelenko?" asked Chin.

"No, he is," said Volodya. He pointed to Dmytro.

MacNab consulted the photograph taken outside St. Basil's. "Yeah, I guess you're right," he said, comparing the image to both cousins. "You guys look a lot alike."

"We're cousins," said Volodya helpfully.

"We're wondering what happened to Pavel," said Lukowski. "What do you know about him?"

Dmytro shrugged. "He was an employee. Very quiet. Kept to himself. Don't know anything about him at all, really."

Yuri spread out his hands to the detectives expansively. "I'm sorry I can't help you, officer. I just got into town today. Just visiting some old friends of my mother's from back in the old country."

Dave Chin stepped up to Yalta Yuri and said, "Mind telling us who you are? Got any identification? If that's your rental car parked out front, you must have a valid driver's license on you."

"I wasn't driving," he said. He nodded to one of his associates. "He was. But he doesn't have to show you nothing. This is America. You want to talk to me about anything, you talk to my lawyer in Santa Monica."

Now Yuri turned to the cousins and said in Russian, "I'll be back here at midnight." The cousins both looked obediently at their watches. "You're coming with us to Kapitan Zhukov. And if Sergei's not there…we'll see what happens next. Meanwhile, these guys got another job for you to do first." He nodded at his two henchmen. "We'll be in touch."

Chapter Twenty-Three

TYLER HAD BEEN ASTONISHED when Jessica called him and told him he was wanted back at Alba that night. "But I'm on suspension," he said.

"Not anymore. Because Flavia Torcelli called and insisted you be back there tonight."

"She did?" Tyler had said. He felt a rush of happiness. She wanted him there with her!

"Yeah. And the customer's always right. Get down in time for the dinner rush."

But when Tyler did arrive, and found an excuse to go inside where he ran into her at the reception desk, Flavia was all business, greeting him with her customary unsmiling nod. Smiles were strictly for the customers. "Good. I'm glad you're here," she said. "Vic and Chip will be leaving early."

"They are?" This was going to be awkward—being on shift with those two. Especially after Vic had threatened him at their last meeting.

"FUNNY how nothing happens, then everything happens all at once," said Lukowski. He and MacNab were in a small conference room at police headquarters with detectives Myers and Chin, and he was writing things down on a whiteboard with a pink marker.

"One. Ott admitted to Debbie he was the other shooter."

He printed out: 1. Ott fired at Duckworth assailant. "He panicked and fired at the retreating vehicle after Duckworth was shot at, with the snub-nosed .38-revolver that he probably stole out of the property room years ago. The bullets from that gun are definitely in the side of the Duckworth car he was facing. And the Italian gal is sure that Duckworth was already up by the door of the restaurant next to her and next to Ott when those shots were fired."

MacNab shook his head in disgust. "Can't we get him for something?"

Debbie rolled her eyes. "He was right about the statute of limitations on stealing that gun. But I'm going to talk to the prosecutor about nailing him for having an unregistered weapon, and for reckless endangerment."

"Good luck with that," said MacNab. "Think Duckworth wants the world to know he had a Keystone Kop as chief of security? He'll put the kibosh on that indictment for sure."

"Okay," said Lukowski, writing squeakily, 2. Gun from homicide and assault retrieved. "The gun that killed our tattoo guy and the gun that hit that valet are the same gun. And we got it. We found it in the apartment of a guy named Sergei."

"Have you found this Sergei yet?" asked Debbie.

"Yes, but he isn't talking," said MacNab. "Because someone bludgeoned him to death. He was standing right by the closet where the gun was. Maybe he was going for it while confronting someone. It doesn't quite fit with his body position. We may never know. It all seems to fit, seeing as the first victim appeared to be connected with Russian organized crime, and so did this Sergei, who didn't seem to have a real job and had a nice collection of high-tech auto theft tools."

"Okay. So maybe he's your guy when it comes to your homicide. But why in hell would he take a shot at Scott Duckworth?" said Debbie.

"That's where our little pal Tyler Benson comes into it," said Lukowski, beaming happily. "I just had a real interesting conversation with his lawyer."

"Did she tell you where he is?" asked Debbie.

"Nope. But she had a long drawn-out story about how the Russian mafia were using that restaurant, Alba, as a happy hunting ground for high-end cars."

Debbie looked thoughtful. "And Scott was thinking of buying Alba. Is that a motive for them to scare off Scott? Seems weird to me. There's still a lot that doesn't make sense."

"Okay, listen to this," said Lukowski. He turned to the whiteboard again and wrote, 3. Alba Valets working with Russians to tag cars? "According to the kid's lawyer, he says some of the valets there have been putting tracking devices on the cars, and maybe copying electronic key codes, so they could easily be found and stolen later. And the two valets he named happened to be the two who showed up to that Russian funeral."

MacNab said, "Gee, wonder why the kid decided to share this with us? Maybe because he's already trying to cut a deal?"

Lukowski handed around a sheet of paper. "Here's a picture he says he took with his phone. It's some kind of device that he says these other two were putting on the cars."

Dave Chin said, "It's similar to the stuff we found at Sergei Lagunov's apartment."

Debbie thought for a moment and said, "The only way Roger Benson could have known Scott Duckworth would be there at Alba is from the kid, Tyler. That's why I had trouble ruling him out."

"And we've had trouble ruling him out because his prints are all over the trunk of the car our dead guy was in," said MacNab.

"But you told me you think this Sergei did that guy," said Debbie.

"Maybe he had the kid deal with the body," said MacNab. "Accessory to murder. And he's trying to rat out the rest of the guys stealing cars to cut a deal."

"I want to talk to him, but I can't find him," said Debbie. "He never seems to be at his apartment. And his boss at the valet company says he's on suspension for this week, so we can't grab him at work. But that little Italian gal at Alba might know where he is. As far as I can tell, they're an item. She actually blushed when I mentioned his name. And apparently, she's already met his family."

"Action item number one," said Lukowski, adding a new line of text to his whiteboard. It read GET TYLER BENSON.

TYLER was tidying up the valet podium. He had just noticed that they were out of split rings, the little metal circles they used when customers took their ignition key off their own ring and handed it to the valet all by itself, when Flavia came up to him with a conspiratorial look.

"Listen," she said, lightly touching his shoulder, "the police just called me. Detective Lukowski. He wants to know if I know where you are."

"What did you tell him?"

"I said I didn't know," said Flavia. "I asked him if he had called Jessica at Elite Valet. Because if he did, then she would know that you were back at work, and that I was lying. And then I could have said that I didn't know where you were because you were parking a car."

Tyler did admire the way Flavia could think on her feet.

"So," continued Flavia, "he told me that he already spoke to Jessica yesterday, and Jessica said you were on suspension. So I think you're okay for now."

Tyler sighed. "I hate sneaking around like this. I just need to hear back from Veronica. I want to know if she had a chance to talk to the cops, and if she thinks it's okay for me to go ahead and talk to them. There's some stupid message on her voicemail about having to take Muffin to the vet."

Tyler's phone rang. "Maybe that's Veronica now," he said and looked down at it. "Oh. It's my grandpa."

"Your *nonno*? You better take it," said Flavia, exhibiting a nice family feeling that Tyler had always associated with Italians.

"Hey, Tyler," said Gus Iversen. "I just ran into an old pal of mine over at Mike's Chili Parlor. I knew his dad, who was a boilermaker back in the day. This guy works on marine engines. Regular old Ballard wharf rat. Anyway, let me get to the point here. He says he knows where we can find that Captain Zhukov you were talking about. I'm getting an address for you. Maybe you can go over there and check her out."

"Wow!" said Tyler. "Hang on." He turned to Flavia, and removed the phone from his ear, even though Grandpa was still talking. He heard the tinny sound of his voice from around his hip. "My grandpa says he knows where Captain Zhukov is. As soon as I go off shift, I'm going over there. Then, I can call the cops from there."

But just as he wasn't listening to Grandpa, Flavia wasn't listening to him. She was staring at a red VW sedan that was pulling up to the valet podium. "Look," she said. "It's Scott. He never said he was coming!" She patted her hair.

"I gotta go, Grandpa," said Tyler. "Call me back and leave the address on my phone if I don't pick up."

Scott Duckworth was a passenger in the VW. Instead of a commando-type driver, backed up by thuggish-looking bodyguards in the backseat, there was a middle-aged lady at the wheel. Tyler leapt to the driver's side. When women drove in, he opened the driver's side first. Even if the male passenger was Scott Duckworth.

The pleasant-looking lady accepted a claim check and climbed out of the car, and smiled while Tyler gave his customary greeting. Over the top of the car he could see Flavia smiling up at Scott. He suppressed the urge to say, "Hey Scott, why don't you buy this goddamn place and use your zillions to chase the Russian mafia out of here?"

Flavia was saying, "I'm so glad you came. What a surprise. No security?"

The lady who had driven in walked over to both of them and said, "Mr. Ott is no longer with us. Introduce me, Scott. This must be Flavia Torcelli."

"Hey Flavia," said Scott, "This is Helene Applegate. I wanted her to come and take a look at Alba. I told her I might be investing in this place."

"So nice to meet you," said Flavia, shaking Helene's hand

and pouring out all the charm on her instead of Scott. Perhaps, thought Tyler, she sensed, as he did, that this woman was a decision maker in the sale. Maybe she was some kind of foodie consultant, or something.

Scott confirmed part of Tyler's theory by saying, "I'm really interested in Helene's take." More dazzling smiles from Flavia to the older woman.

"I'm so sorry we don't have a reservation," said Helene, without sounding all that sorry.

Flavia tilted her head back, raised an arm in the air, and said, "Ha! Reservation?" as if the idea were ridiculous, which of course it was.

And then Scott Duckworth explained what Helene Applegate's role in the decision-making process was. "Helene and I are engaged," he said.

SOME hours later, in Woodinville, a suburb to the northeast of Seattle, Chip Lundquist and Victor Gelashvili entered their unit at the Acme Heated Storage facility. Chip said, "I'm almost sorry about saying good-bye to these awesome cars." The two of them gazed at their gleaming collection in silence for a moment.

"Well, you won't be sorry when we have an awesome balance in that Swiss bank account," said Vic.

"You really think this is gonna work?" asked Chip. "I mean, what if Gleb stiffs us? What could we do about it? Him being over in Russia and all."

"He's not going to stiff us," said Vic. "It's family, it's, like, an honor thing or whatever. He made that real clear. Besides, I already told him we're ready to start work on another shipment. So he won't even think about stiffing us."

"Another shipment? How do you know another Russian trawler will pull in here for repairs?"

Vic shrugged. "I don't. I just told Gleb that so he won't stiff us. Just a little measure of security. He'll want that next bunch of cars. He told me the demand for really good cars over there is insane."

"Right on," said Chip.

"Anyway, you gotta have faith. I mean, you won't get any-where in life with a defeatist attitude like that. It's happening. We're making it happen. Okay, let's get started. I'll take the Mase-rati. You take your car to get us back here for the next one."

"No fair," said Chip. "I wanna take the Maserati."

"Forget it," said Vic. Chip looked hurt so he said, "Okay, you can take the Lamborghini on our last run. But no speeding. This is going to take a long time, but if we get stopped, we're screwed. And cars like these are prime bait to a motorcycle cop."

IT was almost midnight, and there were just two cars left in the lot. Tyler went inside with the cash box to Flavia's office so she could lock it up along with the restaurant receipts. She was sitting at her desk counting bills under her breath in Italian.

She looked up at him and smiled. "Isn't it sweet?" said Flavia. "Scott Duckworth marrying that nice lady. So sweet those two old people finding each other!" She beamed, and Tyler felt bad that he'd ever assumed Flavia was a gold digger. Just because someone was attractive enough to be a trophy wife to a billionaire didn't mean she wanted to be one.

"Ah!" she said now. "But what were you trying to tell me when they pulled up? Something your *nonno* told you?" Now she was bundling the bills up with rubber bands.

"He has an address for this mysterious Captain Zhukov," said Tyler. "I was thinking of driving out there. Maybe it's their mafia clubhouse or something. Maybe we could tell the police about it."

"When are you going?" Flavia said, looking excited. "Will you take me with you?"

"I was thinking of right now," said Tyler. "Are you sure you want to come?"

"Of course I want to come. We're just driving by to take a look, right? What could possibly happen? I want to come with you! I'll tell my brother you're giving me a ride home tonight. And I'll go chase that last party out of the bar. You've been busy without Vic and Chip," she said. "Did you get anything to eat?"

"No, but I'm okay," he said.

"I'll make you something. Maybe a sandwich? We have a lot of antipasto stuff left over tonight."

Tyler went back outside, and to save time went and pulled the last two cars up to the stand, as well as his own. Within a few minutes, two young guys in business suits came out of the bar. One of them was weaving and looking pale. Tyler looked sharply at the other guy. He seemed sober enough and had his ticket and a ten-dollar bill all ready.

Tyler pointed to the two cars. "Which one is yours?" he said to the sober guy.

"The Outback. The other one is my buddy's."

The drunk guy's knees sagged a little and his head was lolling. He gazed over at his own car. "That's mine. I think," he said.

Tyler ignored him, and turned to the first man. "Your buddy shouldn't be driving. Are you going to give him a ride home? He can leave his car here." Tyler didn't add that Elite Valet wouldn't be responsible for the car. He just wanted these two out of here so he and Flavia could go check out that address.

"Okay," said the first man, not sounding too enthusiastic about this errand. When he opened the passenger door, the drunk guy collapsed onto Tyler's chest.

Tyler sighed and began to push him back off, but suddenly, the drunk guy began heaving. A second later, Tyler felt warm vomit all over his chest.

"Goddammit!" he said.

Just then Flavia came outside wearing her office cardigan over her suit and carrying her purse. She let out a little shriek, then said, "I'll go back and get you a bar towel. *Poverino!*"

The drunk guy said, "Hey man, I'm really sorry," and collapsed into the car. Tyler kicked the door shut.

"Jesus, Ryan," said the driver, throwing the car into gear and taking off.

Tyler peeled off his jacket and his shirt. He heard the click of Flavia's heels as she returned, and snatched the towel out of her hand and scrubbed his chest with it. "Have you got a plastic bag or something for my stuff?" he said.

"Sure," she said and went back into the restaurant and he put on his spare shirt and a uniform jacket that was hanging on a hook inside the booth. Chip kept it there in case anything happened to his uniform while he was working. He always looked perfectly turned out, and had explained to Tyler that a perfect appearance paid off in tips.

He popped the trunk of his own car, ready to throw his clothes in there as soon as Flavia returned with the plastic bag.

A second later, he felt a tap on the shoulder. Surprised, he turned around. He hadn't heard her heels clicking back. But it wasn't Flavia at all. It was some guy in an Oakland A's shirt. Another guy wearing something with a Nike swoosh on it lurked behind him.

Before he knew what was happening, he was pushed into the trunk. Then he heard the raspy sound of duct tape being ripped off a roll. And a short, sharp female scream he could only assume was coming from Flavia.

CHAPTER TWENTY-FOUR

//

FOUR MEN STOOD OUTSIDE Dmytro Zelenko's house in the dark next to the massive door of his triple garage—Yalta Yuri, his two henchmen, and Dmytro himself. The view from the street was obscured by dense shrubbery. In the driveway were two parked cars—Tyler's, and the dark van with tinted windows that had followed it back from Alba.

Dmytro was listening to Yuri, and looking worried. "Okay," said Yuri, "now it's your job to step up and explain to him how he can't be ripping us off. You gotta show me you can run this business properly."

"What about Vic?" said Dmytro.

Yuri shrugged. "He wasn't there. But it's okay. Just scare this guy and he'll scare Vic." He chuckled. "I make it easier for you."

"So what do you want me to say?" said Dmytro.

"At first, you say nothing. Just maybe that you're disappointed. Then you're going to have to get physical. Silent and physical. After that, he'll tell you what he's been up to and apologize. I guarantee it."

"I'll start with the dogs," said Dmytro.

"Oh, we had to take the Italian girl, too," said Yuri.

"What!"

Yuri shrugged. "She was there while we were pushing him into his car. But no worries. We already control her. She won't make any trouble. She makes trouble, her brother's business is gone and she knows it. Maybe it's good to let her know who she's dealing with."

TYLER and Flavia were on the other side of the garage door and could hear the men talking, but couldn't make out what they were saying. They had been hustled inside this garage from the car after Tyler had endured a long, bumpy ride with his wrists duct-taped together, making it impossible for him to work the safety latch on the inside of the trunk or reach his phone. Flavia had been yanked out of the backseat.

In the few seconds when they had stood in the driveway, restrained by the two thugs, Tyler had ascertained they were in some dark suburb, and not far from the street. Another man, an older guy, had taken his phone, and asked Flavia for hers. She had handed it over from the purse hanging on her shoulder. Right after that, they'd been pushed deep into the garage, and the garage door had slid down.

"Where are we?" she said in a tiny voice.

"Did you see anything from the window?" he said.

"They made me lie down in the backseat."

Tyler looked around. "We're in somebody's garage." The lights were off but he could still see. There was a workbench with some tools on it, garden furniture, and a lawn mower. "Can you get this tape off my wrists?"

Flavia started silently picking at the tape. Tyler continued looking around. At the back of the garage, opposite the main door, was a regular door that looked like it led to a garden. And that's where the dim light was coming from. There must be some kind of exterior porch light there. The door had a large pane of glass in it and some crisscrossed molding. Tyler looked over at the tools on the workbench. He saw an electric drill there and some hand tools, including a couple of hammers and a light-weight sledge-hammer.

"They didn't prepare this place to be some kind of a prison," he whispered.

"They even gave me back my purse!" she said, hopefully, arranging it so the strap crossed her chest, the way Italian women often carry purses.

Tyler pointed to the workbench. "We can use those tools to get out of here through that door, even if it's locked." He wondered if the drill was charged up. It could be a pretty effective weapon. If they could get out that door to the garden, maybe he'd take it with him.

"This place isn't far from the road," said Flavia.

"So if we get out of here we'll probably be near other houses," said Tyler. "I can bust out that door and get help."

"No! I'm coming, too," said Flavia. "Don't leave me alone here!"

She yanked off the last of the tape. "Are they just trying to scare us? Who are they?"

"Did they talk in the car?"

"Yes, but in Russian. And they made one phone call but that wasn't in English either."

"There were three of them?"

"That's right. One sat in the back with me."

Suddenly, the garage door began opening. Flavia and Tyler stared at it. After it had risen about two feet, they saw two Rottweilers and a pair of human legs. A second later, the opening was about three feet taller. Now they were looking at a portly guy who was holding on to two leashes. Tyler grabbed Flavia and pulled her into a dark corner of the garage.

"I guess you wonder why I brought you here," said Dmytro.

"Mr. Zelenko?" said Flavia.

"I got no beef with you," he said strolling purposefully toward them. "I got a beef with him." He leaned over to the dogs and started whispering to them. Then he went over and grabbed Tyler and pulled him into the light. Suddenly, he looked astonished. "Shit!" he said, dropping the leashes and running back out. In another second, the door was being pulled back down.

The dogs began to growl. Tyler picked up Flavia and carried her to the workbench, where he sat her down. "Stay up there!"

he said, grabbing the drill, while she scrambled into an upright position.

He pointed the drill at the more aggressive of the two dogs, and depressed the button. One of the dogs bared his teeth.

Meanwhile, Flavia was rummaging in her purse, and soon was frantically opening a Styrofoam clamshell box. It contained the snack she'd made for Tyler with tonight's antipasti. Tyler could smell salami. She handed him a long, crusty roll. He dropped the drill and divided the roll in two. Each side was full of salami and cheese.

The dogs stopped growling and trotted over, still dangling their leashes. Soon, they were bolting their treats, wagging their tails and licking Tyler's hand.

From outside the garage door, they heard Dmytro Zelenko's voice. "You assholes!" he was shouting. "I swear to you that's not Chip!"

"They think I'm Chip?" said Tyler.

Flavia was scrambling off the workbench. She pointed at his jacket. Tyler looked down. Even upside down, the laminated nametag pinned to the Elite Valet jacket he'd snagged from the booth right before he was jumped clearly read CHIP.

"Listen, Flavia," said Tyler. "They're confused. They're arguing. This might be a good time to go out the back door!" He ran over to the door with its cottagey window. The dogs had finished bolting their sandwiches and came over and groveled at his feet. He ignored them and rattled the round doorknob. It seemed to be locked.

He went back to the workbench and grabbed the sledgehammer he had spotted earlier. And then, from outside, after hearing a bunch of Russian men screaming at each other, he heard a new voice. A woman's voice.

The garage door was being raised again, with a groaning sound. Tyler and Flavia froze and stared at the door.

An old lady with a witchlike mane of gray hair stood there. She wore an old-fashioned pale blue flannel nightgown, and she was screaming in a Slavic language and gesturing wildly. From behind her they heard the voice of Dmytro Zelenko yell in English, "Fuck you. Now my mom is upset! Are you guys crazy!"

"Listen," said Tyler, "I'm not Chip."

The old lady stopped yelling.

"You have an issue with Chip, I don't care," Tyler went on. "We can just forget about this. I guess you guys just made an honest mistake."

The old lady started yelling again and pointed at the dogs, then at the sledgehammer in Tyler's hand. Then she flapped her hands at Tyler and Flavia. Tyler set the sledgehammer back down on the workbench. Now the old lady turned to her son and began berating him, ending with a sharp smack across his face. Yalta Yuri and his henchman flinched sympathetically.

"Okay," said Tyler. "I guess we'll just walk over to the car now and be on our way. Come on, Flavia."

Dmytro Zelenko was now stroking his mother's arm and speaking to her in soothing tones.

Flavia surprised Tyler by beginning to walk calmly out of the garage. Tyler walked out with her.

Dmytro turned to look at them. "Hurry up, just go!" he said.

"Are the keys in it?" asked Tyler, pointing to his car. The guy in the Oakland A's shirt nodded.

Dmytro turned to Yalta Yuri. "Okay, it's the wrong guy so let's just forget about it. My mom is really upset."

The old lady had now begun to sob.

"Yeah, whatever," said Yuri.

"Can we please have our phones back?" said Flavia.

A few minutes later, after they had driven away and managed to find the entrance to the freeway, Flavia said, "I knew he'd let us go as soon as I saw that he was afraid of his mother."

"Okay, now I'm calling Veronica," said Tyler. "She can call the cops and tell them exactly where they can find these guys."

"But it's two in the morning!" said Flavia.

"Well, I can at least leave a message on her phone if she doesn't pick up."

Surprisingly, Veronica answered. Tyler gabbled on for a

while about being abducted, and asked her if they should call the police.

"Listen," said Veronica. "I can't deal with this. I'm very upset right now. Muffin is really sick."

"I have an address for the guys that abducted us," said Tyler.

"The address will still be there tomorrow," said Veronica. "We'll regroup in the morning when the detectives will be available. I don't want to explain all this to a 9-1-1 operator. And I don't want to get up and go with you to make sure you don't screw up when you talk to the cops. Muffin can't be left alone."

"Okay," said Tyler.

"But don't go home. Either of you. This whole thing sounds very weird. I don't want those guys to track you down again. Why don't you guys spend the night at your grandfather's house in Ballard?"

When Tyler explained all this to Flavia, she said, "Can we go by that address for Captain Zhukov on the way there? It's close to your grandfather's house, right?"

DETECTIVE Dave Chin elbowed his dozing partner. The two men were parked in the shadows in a nondescript van in an alley behind the Zelenkos' body shop.

"Hey," said Chin. "I told you it was a good idea to keep an eye on this place. I had a clear sense these guys all had some unfinished business. Even though they were speaking Russian, when that guy from Santa Monica barked at the Zelenkos, both of them looked at their watches. I figured they had some kind of appointment, and knowing the kind of guys these are, I figured it might be under cover of darkness."

His partner rubbed his eyes. "What's happening? Is Volodya Zelenko still in there?"

"Uh-huh. And those three clowns from Cali who were there earlier today just dropped by. And they got the other Zelenko with them. Dmytro. Volodya must have been waiting for them. I seriously doubt he just happens to be in there beating out a door panel at this hour."

The detectives fell silent and now observed five men—the two Zelenkos and the three visitors who'd been there earlier in the day—heading out to a large black Cadillac Escalade SUV behind the shop. There was the sound of crunching gravel in the alley and car doors slamming.

Detective Chin started the engine. "Get on the radio, will you? I don't know what these guys are up to, but if there's any reason to stop any of them, I'd like to have some uniformed backup."

CAPTAIN Zhukov's address was at the end of a short gravel street that dead-ended at the water's edge in Ballard, tucked behind an upscale gym, all chrome and glass, that catered to the affluent young singles who had been moving into the neighborhood. The newcomers lived in the massive condominiums that had replaced a lot of the old blue-collar businesses and little wood-frame houses where Ballard fishermen and carpenters had lived a hundred years ago.

Tyler hadn't known what to expect, but there had to be some mistake. There wasn't anything here. He pulled over and killed the engine and the lights. In front of them was a dusty collection of the kinds of plants that spring up in neglected corners of Seattle—horsetails, Scotch broom, and Himalayan blackberry—and then a chain-link fence with some morning glory working its way upward. And there was a big gate in the fence with a thick chain wrapped around it a few times.

At the entrance to the fenced-in area was a small building made of concrete blocks. Faded painted letters in pale green read Swanson Dry Dock Company.

Behind the fence, across an expanse of asphalt, loomed a giant ship, painted white with touches of rust here and there. It was many stories high, with metal steps like old-fashioned fire escapes zigzagging up the multiple decks.

"That's a factory ship," said Flavia. "They go fishing up in Alaska and gut and process and freeze the fish on board."

"Maybe someone named Zhukov is the captain of this trawler," said Tyler. "But it seems kind of weird for a sea captain to be moonlighting as a mafia chieftain. Maybe Grandpa got the address wrong. Or I maybe I entered it wrong in my map search." He took out his phone and started searching again.

"Wait," said Flavia. "Can you read those Russian letters? Look!" She pointed to the side of the vessel, where the vessel's name was painted in Cyrillic letters. Капитан Жуков.

Tyler changed his search to one for an application that converted phrases in the Roman alphabet to Cyrillic. He found one and entered "Captain Zhukov," then held up the phone to compare the results to the side of the ship. It was a near match. Tyler figured the Russian word for captain was slightly different. But the Zhukov part was identical.

"Wow! *Captain Zhukov* is a ship, not a person," he said. Come to think of it, Grandpa had said "go check *her* out" when he'd called.

Just then they heard another car pulling up alongside them.

"Duck," said Tyler, sliding down in his seat and putting his hand on Flavia's shoulder and pushing her down. Cautiously, he peeked out the window into the dark. The car had stopped right next to his. It was a Toyota.

Someone got out of the car. A man with a lit cigarette. Tyler lowered his head quickly as he walked right next to Flavia's window and flicked the cigarette at it. Tyler could see her scrunched down, her arms wrapped around her knees. She was staring up at him with wide eyes.

The man unwrapped the chain on the gate. Strangely, there wasn't a padlock on it. And whoever this was now opening the gate appeared to be wearing an Elite Valet windbreaker.

Chapter Twenty-Five

//

IN THE BLACK CADILLAC SUV, parked at a right angle to the little cul-de-sac, in the parking lot of the Malibu Fitness Center, Yalta Yuri and one of his henchman sat in the front seat. Wedged in the backseat, between the two large Zelenkos, was his other associate.

From this position, they had a good view of the gate area from the side. "Okay," said Yuri. "That makes fourteen. So we wait for the last one. Maybe the second guy comes in his own car and they go back together and get the last one. Or maybe, if they're smart, the other guy comes in the last one to be loaded. Because if they're smart they'll have one of their own vehicles parked around here somewhere to leave in."

"Okay. Let's go and get them now," said Volodya.

"Hey, we gotta wait till the last car comes back," said Yuri.

"But if that's the second-to-last one, we can deal with Cheep first and take care of Veek afterwards when he gets here. Is more efficient," said Volodya.

Dmytro reached across the man between him and his cousin and punched Volodya on the arm. "Shut up!" he said. "Let Yuri organize the work however he wants." Now Dmytro leaned forward and addressed Yuri in the front seat. "We're just gonna beat them up, right? Just scare them?"

"That's right," said Yuri. "Because they cannot ever think

they can fuck with us. It's disgusting how you let them get away with this shit!"

"Well, it's working out okay for you, because you're getting all the cars," said Dmytro mildly. "Not that I care if you get the cars, of course. But I'm not sure why my cousin and I even need to be here."

"Because you need to learn how to run things properly," snapped Yuri.

THE surveillance van with Detective Chin and his partner was parked further away from Yuri's vehicle, a little higher up in an alley, but it was also positioned to be able to view the main gate of Swanson Dry Dock, and with the aid of binoculars, to read the plate numbers as the cars waited to be driven into the dry-dock compound.

"Geez," said Thompson. "That one's stolen, too." He had just called in the number of the Mercedes Vic had delivered. "That makes fourteen! How much do you think it all amounts to? I'm really stoked. Think it's a five-million-dollar bust? I'd definitely call that grand theft auto."

"Resale value depends on where the cars are ending up," said Chin. "And judging from the writing on that ship, they're going to Russia. They can probably get a heck of a lot more for them there."

"Are you sure we shouldn't send one of those backup cars to tail those valet kids and find out where their stash of cars is?" said his partner.

"Why bother? They're delivering them to us like clockwork. I don't want to spook them."

"So when do we move?" said Thompson. "I mean, we can round up these guys any time."

"Yeah, the delivery boys. But I still want to know what our Russian friends are up to. It's like they've got these kids under surveillance. They're not helping or anything. Why do they need to be here? I want to see if they are going to participate somehow. And who knows how many Ivans are on that boat?"

"It would be nice to go over and ask those guys in the SUV some questions."

Chin sighed. "It's not against the law to sit in a car. They're all lawyered up already. I would kind of like to see them take an active role."

"That would make seven arrests in all. Nice night's work."

"Thank God we've got backup squirreled away in the gym parking garage," said Chin.

WHEN Victor Gelashvili pulled in to the dead-end street in the fifteenth car, a Lamborghini, he started to feel a little giddy. It was almost over. He felt a strong urge to laugh. He told himself to calm down, not to let down his guard until they were both back at Chip's apartment.

Ahead, he saw Chip's car, and then he saw that Chip was waiting for him just by the gate, still holding the chain that they had wrapped around it to make it seem locked. But then Vic had the strange sensation that something was different about the little cul-de-sac.

He looked to the right, and then to the left. There was a car here that hadn't been there before. And, it was a car that looked familiar. As a valet, Vic had developed a photographic memory for vehicles, and Vic knew he'd seen this older Volvo before. He also knew, before he remembered whose car it was, that he associated it with someone who really irritated him. Suddenly, he remembered. It was that damn Tyler Benson, the one who'd tried to push him around at Alba. What the hell was *his* clunky old Volvo doing here?

Enraged, Vic set the hand brake, and flew out of the Lamborghini to take a look at Tyler's car. Maybe he should do something to it to teach Tyler a lesson. Pull the distributor cap or something.

But when he went over to the car and glanced inside, he couldn't believe it. There were two people crouching down in the front seat!

"Hey Chip," he yelled, "come over here right away!" He ran over to the driver's side. Sure enough, it was Tyler Benson.

Chip, carrying his chain, ambled over.

Inside the car, Tyler was horrified to see a face peering into the car. He pulled himself up on the seat—there was no point hiding anymore—and he was prepared to pull out right away, but the Lamborghini, its engine still running, was blocking his exit. He'd have to take a chance that there was some way to leave the area further up the short street—other than the waters of Lake Union. Maybe he could get into that parking garage that seemed to be attached to the Malibu Fitness Center from here, then find another exit out into the street.

"Stay down," he said to Flavia, but she was sitting back up on the seat. "What's going on?" she demanded.

"Oh, shit," said Tyler. He had just spotted Chip coming toward them with a heavy length of chain. "It's Vic and Chip."

"ALL right!" said Yuri from his vantage point. "It's Vic and Chip. Let's go get them."

"Yeah, but Chip is carrying a chain," said Dmytro.

"Well, go take it away from him and then we'll take care of them both," said Yuri. He got out of the car and began striding forward in a purposeful manner. The others piled out after him, his two thugs flanking him, the Zelenkos following behind.

Meanwhile, Vic had started to yell. The men weren't sure what he was saying, but it seemed odd. Who was he yelling at? Yuri stopped. The others all stopped, too.

Back in the cul-de sac, Vic was yelling at Tyler through the driver's-side window. "Get out of the car now!"

Tyler had now decided he'd have to reverse out of the cul-de-sac, and if he floored it and went really close to a shed on the left, he might be able to squeeze past the Lamborghini. But before he had a chance to do that, Chip had swung the chain into his windshield. The windshield remained intact, but made a horrible, loud sound. Flavia let out a scream.

Yuri and his party had now begun to proceed cautiously forward. But at the sound of a woman's scream, they stopped again.

Now Chip had moved to the driver's side of the car. He bent down and looked at Tyler. Then he yelled to Vic, "Give me a goddamn ninja rock!"

"Listen," said Tyler to Flavia in Italian. "Get into that other car behind us and take off—the engine is running. Get in there and get out of here! I'll follow you." He hoped he could. He knew that a ninja rock was what thieves called a ceramic spark plug when it was used to shatter tempered auto glass, and it wasn't just an urban legend that it worked.

"Che?" said Flavia.

"Get into the other car!" He reached across her and opened the door. *"Subito!"*

He gave her a push, and she rolled out onto the ground, and he was vaguely aware of her scurrying toward the idling Lamborghini when he heard the spark plug hit the driver's-side window. Suddenly, it looked like a spiderweb and a second later, Vic and Chip were punching it out.

Vic's and Chip's faces now filled the entire window opening, framed by broken glass. "What the fuck are you doing here? Is that Flavia? What's she doing here?"

"It's a long story," said Tyler. "But we were just leaving." Why wasn't Flavia gone yet? "Go, go, go," he screamed.

"I don't know how to drive!" she yelled from the other car. "Aren't you coming? You said you'd follow me."

"Damn," thought Tyler. He'd meant he'd follow in his car.

Vic was now kicking in the door panel on the driver's side. "You're fucking everything up!" he said.

Chip's hand was now inside the car, fumbling for the button to unlock the door.

Tyler started to clamber over the gearshift to get to the passenger side and get out to the Lamborghini. He didn't think he had a chance, but he couldn't leave Flavia there alone.

Suddenly, he saw a group of men loom up behind Vic and Chip. Terrified, he assumed all of these guys were going to join the two valets and pile on him, but to his amazement, the new arrivals punched Vic and pushed Chip.

As Tyler scrambled toward Flavia, who was sitting in the passenger seat of the Lamborghini, one of the thugs grabbed the chain from Chip and started swinging it. Now the two valets started screaming and hit the ground. Volodya pushed past his cousin Dmytro and started kicking them in the ribs, and the man with the chain joined him.

Yuri stood behind them all, overseeing the operation, and noticed Tyler moving from his car to the Lamborghini. "There's another one! In the same jacket!" He thumped Dmytro on the back.

Tyler now slid behind the wheel and threw the Lamborghini into reverse. With Flavia's passenger door still open, he started backing out fast. The engine protested, and he released the emergency brake, an operation which caused them to careen from side to side. She managed to pull the door closed at the end of the cul-de-sac. He turned onto a curved street that presumably led to Leary Way, the main road out of the area, yanked the car into first, and headed right. He wasn't sure where these back streets that seemed to snake among various industrial sites led, but he didn't care.

"He's getting away," said Yuri. "Come on. We'll get him, too. Get in this car."

Dmytro dutifully crawled inside the open passenger door of Tyler's Volvo and opened the driver's door. Yuri clambered in behind the wheel.

Flavia was now sitting up, clutching the headrest and staring out the back window. "Those guys are following us! In your car!"

DETECTIVE Chin was on the radio yelling at his backup patrol cars. "All hell is busting loose! Get down there and seal off the cul-de-sac! But don't turn on your sirens and lights. Thompson and I are going down there on foot on the water side. At least two guys in valet jackets, and a bunch of other guys—I think five. I want 'em all. When you're in place we'll move."

Tyler had just realized that the winding alley he took had now dead-ended in a large gate with a sign on it that said MARINE ENGINE REBUILD. QUALITY WORK SINCE 1954. DOGS ON PATROL.

"Damn," he said, spinning around 180 degrees to get back out and clipping a Dumpster and a pile of bricks. Even in his adrenaline-laced state, the old valet instincts kicked in, and for a nanosecond he worried about how majorly pissed off the owner of this Lamborghini would be when he got his car back. He was driving halfway on what appeared to be some kind of sidewalk with a curb. "Put on your seat belt!" he yelled.

Now Flavia was looking out the front window. She was speaking Italian way too fast for Tyler to understand her, but it was clear what had agitated her. Tyler's car was headed right toward them. He floored the Lamborghini and managed to pass it on the left. "Oh my God!" she said, now in English, fumbling with the seat belt.

"This Lamborghini is way faster than my Volvo," said Tyler.

He tore back down the little lane. Flavia was now reporting from the rear window again. "They're turning around!"

Tyler got the Lamborghini to the end of the lane and headed back to where he had emerged from the cul-de-sac, then made a sharp right toward what he hoped was a short spur to Leary Way.

"Can they see us?" he yelled. "Can they see which way we turned?"

"Not yet," said Flavia.

But he knew they would in a few seconds. So when he saw the parking garage entrance of the Malibu Fitness Center, he turned into it and executed a quick series of corkscrew turns. Damn! The car handled them beautifully. But at this rate of speed there were some amazing squeals coming from the tires. "Maybe we can hide here," he said, pulling his phone out of Chip's spare Elite Valet jacket. "And maybe we should call 9-1-1." He was pretty sure whoever was following them would fly right past the entrance. But did he really want to call the cops? What would he tell them? That Vic and Chip messed up his car window?

"WHERE the hell did they go?" demanded Yuri as he emerged onto Leary Way.

Dmytro said, "Maybe it's better this way. Maybe we should get out of here."

As Tyler executed his final turn up onto the parking garage roof, he was amazed to see a police cruiser heading straight toward him. And there was one more right behind it.

He threw the Lamborghini into reverse, and corkscrewed back down almost as fast as he'd come up, his head over his shoulder. Flavia stared straight ahead, making eye contact with the two policemen in the patrol car. The front bumpers of each car seemed about ten inches apart and both of them were hurtling in circles toward the street.

"Jesus!" said the cop at the wheel. "He's got a female passenger."

"Whoever he is, he sure knows how to drive fast backward," said his partner. He grabbed the radio. "Got some kind of exotic Italian car right in front of us. Male driver, female passenger. Want us to proceed to the cul-de-sac or follow this vehicle?"

"You get over to the cul-de-sac, and the other car should stop the Lamborghini," said Chin. He and Thompson had now run on foot to the yawning chain-link gate of Swanson Dry Dock and unholstered their guns. They crept up behind the group of men. There seemed to be three assailants who had now dragged the two guys in matching windbreakers to their feet and were backhanding them across their faces. Chin drew his gun, while Thompson looked up at the looming trawler. "There could be more of them in there. Wanna wait for backup?"

"HE'S gone," said Dmytro to Yuri, the wind from the broken window ruffling his hair. "We can never catch a Lamborghini in this car. Let's go back." He tugged plaintively at Yuri's sleeve.

"Goddammit!" said Yuri, executing a U-turn and heading back to the trawler. "You people fucked this up real good!"

Tyler had now pulled onto Leary Way from the parking garage and headed in the same direction he assumed his pursuers had taken, away from the cul-de-sac. One police car was behind him. The other went in the opposite direction.

"The police are right behind us!" shrieked Flavia.

"I know, but I want to lead them to those guys in my car. I don't want them to get away. In this car, I can definitely catch up to them. We can explain later." Behind them they now heard sirens.

"Wait! There's your car," Flavia screamed as Tyler's Volvo shot past them in the other direction.

Tyler made a sharp U-turn and headed back after his own car. The patrol car executed the same turn, but not so tightly, and followed Tyler and Flavia in the Lamborghini, with the Volvo ahead of it. "I've almost got him!" said Tyler.

As the trio of cars tightened into a closer formation, right at the head of the cul-de-sac, a twenty-foot auto hauler with California plates crossed their path, headed toward the *Kapitan Zhukov* to take on a load of high-end stolen cars for delivery to California. It was empty and loose and jangly, and because it was very long and the entrance to the cul-de-sac was narrow and at a sharp angle, it had slowed down considerably, so that it was practically stationary.

The driver of the car hauler noticed three cars coming toward him from his lofty cab and jammed on the gas to get out of the way. The front of the carrier hit a darkened patrol car blocking the cul-de-sac, and fishtailed slightly to the left on impact, but the driver had just managed to avoid getting hit from the side by the elderly Volvo carrying Yuri and Dmytro. Instead, the Volvo crashed into a second car carrier that had been following the first one.

Close behind it, Tyler took in the sight of the two car carriers, one tangled up with the police car, the other with his own car. He managed to pull the Lamborghini slightly to the right so it bounced off his Volvo and ended up crashing into the tail end of the second empty carrier.

Just then, the police cruiser that had been pursuing the Lamborghini plowed into the back of the Volvo, then ricocheted into the side of the Lamborghini.

In a matter of seconds, the night was filled with the sounds of engines, squealing tires and brakes, a total of six crunching collisions of metal on metal, at least one car alarm, and two police sirens.

Suddenly, there was silence. Smoke rose from the collection of overheated and mangled vehicles. Tyler helped Flavia out of the passenger side past the airbag—the door on his side was caved in. They stood there, hand in hand, as police officers got out of both patrol cars looking dazed. The drivers of the car carriers were hanging out of their cabs looking at the four cars that were now entangled with parts of their vehicles.

"Are you okay?" Tyler said to Flavia.

She nodded.

Tyler looked over at his car. Yuri was getting out of the driver's seat. Blood trickled down his face. He looked shaky until he saw Dymtro emerge from the other side of the car, then he started yelling at him in Russian, and pounding on the roof of the car.

"I can't believe it," said Tyler. "My car got hit three times. And the windshield is messed up, too."

Flavia turned to him and put her hand on his chest. "I didn't know Americans could drive that fast!" she said.

Chapter Twenty-Six

THE MEETING AT THE PROSECUTORS' office had just broken up. Detectives MacNab and Lukowski from Homicide were out in the hall talking to Debbie Myers from Crimes Against Persons and Dave Chin from Auto Theft.

"So did I get this right? Everybody flipped?" said MacNab. "Chip and Vic ratted each other out? The Zelenkos ratted out this California dude—Yalta Yuri?"

"And so did the car carrier drivers," said Dave Chin.

"What about the Russian guy on the trawler?" said Debbie Myers.

"He ratted out Vic. But he said he was coerced by some Russian mafia guys back in the old country. And then he skipped back to Russia," said Chin. "We're not sure if somehow the trawler got out of port with him aboard, or if he just flew commercial. Alaska Airlines can get you to Vladivostok. And the guy who killed your tattoo guy and shot at Scott is dead."

"That's right," said Lukowski. "Sergei Lagunov. The Zelenkos said he killed Old Pasha and he was shooting at Chip, not Scott Duckworth, for trying to muscle in on Yalta Yuri's car smuggling deal. Hard to dispute, since we found the weapon used in both shootings at Sergei Lagunov's apartment."

"So who killed Sergei Lagunov?" said Debbie.

"For a while it looked like Dmytro Zelenko was ready to rat

out his cousin Volodya on that one," answered Lukowski. "But he couldn't come up with any reason why Volodya would have killed Sergei. And the most we could get out of Volodya was that he didn't do it, but if he did, it would have been self-defense. Then they both stopped talking."

He shrugged. "So we ended up not charging anyone for either the murder of the old guy or the drive-by shooting because the killer is dead. And we don't really have a lead on why anyone would kill him, other than that he was a general scumbag."

The detectives were silent for a moment.

MacNab said, "Too bad we couldn't get that annoying Tyler Benson on anything. Maybe reckless endangerment. He could have killed someone with those driving stunts of his."

Chin looked thoughtful. "Yeah, but without him, we wouldn't have been able to nail Vic and Chip and those goons from California. Anyway, the prosecutor wasn't interested in him. Looks like Auto Theft was the big winner here."

Debbie Myers added, "I hear the extortion unit is checking into the Zelenkos' leaning on that Italian restaurant."

Lukowski shrugged again. "Well, we got a lot of paperwork to do. But when it's done, we will have cleared up a couple of cases. And Duckworth's pals at City Hall won't be all over us. Let's go get a beer." Then he paused. "Wait a minute. What's happening to Red Ott?"

"Oh," said Debbie. "They're getting him on an unlicensed firearm thing. He could have wiggled out, but he was such a jerk about everything they decided to nail him. His uncle died years ago. I guess he finally ran out of any goodwill from the department."

She frowned. "Maybe we cleared a few cases, but I think we might be missing something."

HELENE Applegate and Scott Duckworth sat next to each other on the sofa in her office. "I went ahead and cut that reward check to Roger's son, Tyler," said Helene.

"Okay," said Scott, pecking away at an iPhone.

"And as far as Roger's desire to have you bankroll that Riga-toniria thing, I hope you agree it's not a winner. I mean, the customer does all the work and then the food would probably all spill in the car on the way home and get cold. I feel sorry for him and all, but you can't cave in to everybody that wants a piece of you. It's not like Alba. That's a good investment. They have a proven track record. And the food is so wonderful! Flavia and her brother are nice young people and they deserve a break."

"Fine with me," said Scott. He gestured toward the window. "What's going on out there?" A team of landscapers was at work, removing large amounts of gravel in wheelbarrows.

"Oh, I thought I told you about that," said Helene. "That Japanese garden was so depressing. We're doing a kind of Mediterranean patio. Pots of geraniums. It will really cheer me up."

"That's good," said Scott. "I really want you to be happy."

"Oh, I am," said Helene.

"OKAY," said Tyler, sitting in the passenger seat next to Flavia. "You're doing great. You can change lanes now. So signal." She'd had her learner's permit for a month.

From the backseat Gus Iversen said, "Tyler, I'm really looking forward to this. It's pretty exciting to have an in with the owner of a fancy restaurant like this. And we've got so much to celebrate. You graduated. You paid off your student loan. The cops aren't after you, and Veronica got that felony off your record."

Tyler said, "And Flavia's doing great, too. Okay, see the red light? Prepare to stop. Think you can make it all the way? Are you ready for downtown? We don't have to take the freeway."

"I never take the freeway," said Grandpa. "What's the point? Surface streets are good enough for me. Why's everyone in such a rush?"

Fifteen minutes later, when they arrived at the valet area in front of Alba, Tyler said, "Okay. Now all you have to do is pull up, but leave the keys in the car."

Behind the valet podium, Brian put down his pen and the notebook with his zombie screenplay in it and opened both Tyler and Grandpa's doors, and Carlos, another valet who had been promoted to Alba from Donna's, opened Flavia's door.

"Hey, I think I did everything right," said Flavia, unfastening her seat belt and looking at Tyler with a dazzling smile of triumph. While Gus poked his cane out of the car and got out of the backseat, Tyler leaned over, removed Flavia's glasses, tossed them into the beverage holder, and kissed her.

"Yes, you did everything right. Just don't forget to tip the valet on the way out."

About the Author

K. K. BECK is the author of many mysteries and the creator of two series sleuths (besides Lukowski & MacNab): Iris Cooper, a 1920s coed, and Jane da Silva, a down-on-her-luck lounge singer. Under her full name, Kathrine Beck, she wrote the biography *Opal*. Her short stories have been nominated for the Edgar, Agatha, Anthony, and Macavity awards. She is the mother of three grown children and lives in her hometown, Seattle.

More Traditional Mysteries from Perseverance Press
For the New Golden Age

K.K. Beck
Tipping the Valet
ISBN 978-1-56474-563-7

Albert A. Bell, Jr.
PLINY THE YOUNGER SERIES
Death in the Ashes
ISBN 978-1-56474-532-3

The Eyes of Aurora
ISBN 978-1-56474-549-1

Taffy Cannon
ROXANNE PRESCOTT SERIES
Guns and Roses
Agatha and Macavity awards nominee, Best Novel
ISBN 978-1-880284-34-6

Blood Matters
ISBN 978-1-880284-86-5

Open Season on Lawyers
ISBN 978-1-880284-51-3

Paradise Lost
ISBN 978-1-880284-80-3

Laura Crum
GAIL MCCARTHY SERIES
Moonblind
ISBN 978-1-880284-90-2

Chasing Cans
ISBN 978-1-880284-94-0

Going, Gone
ISBN 978-1-880284-98-8

Barnstorming
ISBN 978-1-56474-508-8

Jeanne M. Dams
HILDA JOHANSSON SERIES
Crimson Snow
ISBN 978-1-880284-79-7

Indigo Christmas
ISBN 978-1-880284-95-7

Murder in Burnt Orange
ISBN 978-1-56474-503-3

Janet Dawson
JERI HOWARD SERIES
Bit Player
Golden Nugget Award nominee
ISBN 978-1-56474-494-4

Cold Trail
ISBN 978-1-56474-555-2

What You Wish For
ISBN 978-1-56474-518-7

TRAIN SERIES
Death Rides the Zephyr
ISBN 978-1-56474-530-9

Death Deals a Hand (forthcoming)
ISBN 978-1-56474-569-9

Kathy Lynn Emerson
LADY APPLETON SERIES
Face Down Below the Banqueting House
ISBN 978-1-880284-71-1

Face Down Beside St. Anne's Well
ISBN 978-1-880284-82-7

Face Down O'er the Border
ISBN 978-1-880284-91-9

Sara Hoskinson Frommer
JOAN SPENCER SERIES
Her Brother's Keeper
ISBN 978-1-56474-525-5

Hal Glatzer
KATY GREEN SERIES
Too Dead To Swing
ISBN 978-1-880284-53-7

A Fugue in Hell's Kitchen
ISBN 978-1-880284-70-4

The Last Full Measure
ISBN 978-1-880284-84-1

Margaret Grace
MINIATURE SERIES
Mix-up in Miniature
ISBN 978-1-56474-510-1

Madness in Miniature
ISBN 978-1-56474-543-9

Manhattan in Miniature
ISBN 978-1-56474-562-0

Matrimony in Miniature (forthcoming)
ISBN 978-1-56474-575-0

Tony Hays
Shakespeare No More
ISBN 978-1-56474-566-8

Wendy Hornsby
MAGGIE MACGOWEN SERIES
In the Guise of Mercy
ISBN 978-1-56474-482-1

The Paramour's Daughter
ISBN 978-1-56474-496-8

The Hanging
ISBN 978-1-56474-526-2

The Color of Light
ISBN 978-1-56474-542-2

Disturbing the Dark (forthcoming)
ISBN 978-1-56474-576-7

Janet LaPierre
PORT SILVA SERIES
Baby Mine
ISBN 978-1-880284-32-2

Keepers
Shamus Award nominee, Best Paperback Original
ISBN 978-1-880284-44-5

Death Duties
ISBN 978-1-880284-74-2

Family Business
ISBN 978-1-880284-85-8

Run a Crooked Mile
ISBN 978-1-880284-88-9

Hailey Lind
ART LOVER'S SERIES
Arsenic and Old Paint
ISBN 978-1-56474-490-6

Lev Raphael
NICK HOFFMAN SERIES
Tropic of Murder
ISBN 978-1-880284-68-1

Hot Rocks
ISBN 978-1-880284-83-4

Lora Roberts
BRIDGET MONTROSE SERIES
Another Fine Mess
ISBN 978-1-880284-54-4

SHERLOCK HOLMES SERIES
The Affair of the Incognito Tenant
ISBN 978-1-880284-67-4

Rebecca Rothenberg
BOTANICAL SERIES
The Tumbleweed Murders
(completed by Taffy Cannon)
ISBN 978-1-880284-43-8

Sheila Simonson
LATOUCHE COUNTY SERIES
Buffalo Bill's Defunct
WILLA Award, Best Softcover Fiction
ISBN 978-1-880284-96-4

An Old Chaos
ISBN 978-1-880284-99-5

Beyond Confusion
ISBN 978-1-56474-519-4

Lea Wait
SHADOWS ANTIQUES SERIES
Shadows of a Down East Summer
ISBN 978-1-56474-497-5

Shadows on a Cape Cod Wedding
ISBN 1-978-56474-531-6

Shadows on a Maine Christmas
ISBN 978-1-56474-531-6

Shadows on a Morning in Maine
  (forthcoming)
ISBN 978-1-56474-577-4

Eric Wright
JOE BARLEY SERIES
The Kidnapping of Rosie Dawn
Barry Award, Best Paperback Original. Edgar, Ellis, and Anthony awards nominee
ISBN 978-1-880284-40-7

Nancy Means Wright
MARY WOLLSTONECRAFT SERIES
Midnight Fires
ISBN 978-1-56474-488-3

The Nightmare
ISBN 978-1-56474-509-5

REFERENCE/MYSTERY WRITING

Kathy Lynn Emerson
How To Write Killer Historical Mysteries: The Art and Adventure of Sleuthing Through the Past
Agatha Award, Best Nonfiction. Anthony and Macavity awards nominee
ISBN 978-1-880284-92-6

Carolyn Wheat
How To Write Killer Fiction: The Funhouse of Mystery & the Roller Coaster of Suspense
ISBN 978-1-880284-62-9

Available from your local bookstore or from Perseverance Press/John Daniel & Company (800) 662–8351 or www.danielpublishing.com/perseverance